THE EVOLVED ONES

# ACCEPTANCE

BOOK THREE

NATASHA OLIVER



Marshall Cavendish Editions

Published by Marshall Cavendish Editions
An imprint of Marshall Cavendish International

A member of the
Times Publishing Group



Other Marshall Cavendish Offices:
Marshall Cavendish Corporation, 800 Westchester Ave, Suite N-641, Rye Brook, NY 10573, USA • Marshall Cavendish International (Thailand) Co Ltd, 253 Asoke, 16th Floor, Sukhumvit 21 Road, Klongtoey Nua, Wattana, Bangkok 10110, Thailand • Marshall Cavendish (Malaysia) Sdn Bhd, Times Subang, Lot 46, Subang Hi-Tech Industrial Park, Batu Tiga, 40000 Shah Alam, Selangor Darul Ehsan, Malaysia

Printed in Singapore

Cover design by Kelley Lim

*To the woman who's got kids* and *a dream.*

*To the middle-aged woman brave enough*
*to try something new.*

*To the woman who has failed*
*but refuses to bow out.*

# CHAPTER ONE

## AmLife

August 7th, 9:30pm EST

"They have the *money*, Cliff! It's not easy funding *your* research all over the world," Harry said. "Stop worrying, your name will be included."

*Included?* Is that what Harry thought? He was upset about inclusion? "I have risked my life—" Tusk squeezed the arms of his chair as he regained his composure.

They were dining at a popular establishment among the DC elite. An outburst was not necessarily out of the ordinary, but Harry had said he was trying to keep a relatively low profile tonight – not exactly an easy accomplishment when you're dining with one of the country's most well-known senators.

"Listen, they have facilities everywhere. Pick a country and they'll even open an office there for you. The point is, there's no need for us to pay off the local authorities or manage the costs of rundown facilities on our own anymore. It's a win-win, Cliff."

It wasn't about the money. It was about trust! If Harry

thought politicians were cut-throat, wait until he was on a team of scientists working towards a common goal. History only ever had the space to remember one person's name.

"No more hiding or running from Katherine and her team. This will give us legitimacy, Cliff. Think about it."

Tusk didn't trust Dr Mallory Fined, the newly emerged leading scientist on evolved abilities – and his former assistant's aunt. He had gone to graduate school with Mallory, and while most of his classmates were taking on six-figure debts to follow their passions, Mallory wore designer outfits to class. Her backpacks were more expensive than the books she placed in them. But she was intelligent, and no one could take that from her. As much as Tusk and the others *wanted* her to be there because of her money or her family connections, the truth was, she was there because she deserved it, and that wound up Tusk even more.

Dr Fined went on to become the founder of a small biotech company that focused on genetic manipulation to reverse the effects of terminal diseases. Her company recently announced it was five years away from uncovering the genetic markers that activated evolved abilities. It was, of course, hyperbole, but the public didn't know that. The public couldn't understand that each human was different. They didn't want to hear there wasn't an easily identifiable and replicable pattern to evolved abilities, or that scientists were at least a decade from finding a "trend" that could then hopefully be extrapolated to the general population (or at least the evolved population).

Dr Fined had old money, plus new money from her biotech firm, and these combined to create an attractive façade. Tusk had worked with her kind before. She would come in, take over his research, use it to advance her own, and then take all the credit. Oh, sure, his name would be "included", but only as a footnote a research student *might* mention somewhere in a thesis.

"I don't trust her, Harry," Tusk said. "And neither should you!"

"You don't trust anyone."

"And neither should you. Have you asked her why all the secrets? Why didn't Leona just tell us in the beginning who her aunt was? That she was the head of AmLife? They're after my research, Harry."

Harry sat back as the sommelier approached and refilled his glass. Tusk rolled his eyes and waited. He expected Harry to fire back some banal defense for the Fineds; instead, he spun his wine glass around by its stem while it still sat on the table.

"Harry—"

"How long have we been doing this, Cliff?" Harry finally looked at him. "Aren't you tired of the running? The cat and mouse chase?"

"It's about the science—"

"It's about the ego, Cliff. You and I both know that. But we're getting old now. Too old to be living on the edge like you've been doing. Barely escaping Katherine's noose." Harry lifted his glass to his nose and inhaled before putting it back on the table. "I want legitimacy, Cliff. And I know you do, too. We've worked hard enough, and for long enough, hell, we deserve it. I've started the process to close the remaining facilities that Katherine hasn't found."

Tusk ground his teeth to stop from launching across the table.

"I've made it so that you can finally step out into the light, Cliff. No more hiding in the shadows. No more facilities with unstable power supplies and local authorities we have to bribe."

Tusk's thoughts were circling too fast for him to focus on just one.

"You are the lead scientist on Project Tomorrow. You. Not Fined or anyone else on her team. They all answer to you."

Yes, that was how things worked on paper, but sooner or later, he would be enveloped into *her* fold. He would have to use *her* systems and *her* scientists, *her* lab equipment and *her* engineers to build it, which meant all his designs, his research, his planning and findings would ultimately belong to AmLife.

"Harry," Tusk began, but then Harry held up his left hand.

"Hear me, out, Cliff. I'm chair of the Science, Space, and Technology Committee. The subcommittee is submitting a proposal to us tomorrow afternoon that the National Science Foundation award AmLife a 75-million-dollar grant. Seventy-five million! That will secure their position as the company the country – no – the *world* looks to for understanding evolved abilities. There's no stopping that train, but you ... You are the congressionally appointed scientist with oversight. You approve the spending of that money, you approve the team members, you approve which of Fined's projects get pursued and to what extent."

Tusk sat back in his chair, completely unaware he had been leaning forward. His hand was shaking so much he would've spilled his wine if his glass had been filled any higher, but his thoughts were circling too fast for him to notice.

"What's the catch?" It was the only question that really mattered, Tusk realized, and when Harry shrugged and gave him that politician smile, Tusk knew this arrangement had come at a high cost.

"The research and findings belong to AmLife."

Tusk shook his head and then pushed his chair back. He was done. He would happily go back to a life on the run if it meant he got to keep his work. Harry had always been his financial backer, but he would find others. Any number of the organizations he had sold subjects to would support him, not to mention the few governments that had already approached him. He would find a way.

"Sit down!" Harry whispered sharply. "We don't have a choice."

"What do you mean 'we don't have a choice'?"

"I mean, you've been gallivanting all around the world … *Taking* what you want, *eliminating* what doesn't work for you." Harry chuffed. "I can only help you so much. Katherine's on our asses, Cliff. And it's only a matter of time before she actually gets her hands on you, which means she'll finally have the proof she needs against both of us, and I can't have that." He sat back and lifted his glass like he was going to take a sip, but once again just inhaled it before putting the glass back down. "I've got people on Katherine, I've got one of her associates somewhere no one can find her, but Cliff, for you, this is the best there is, and trust me, it's pretty damn good. You start with a clean slate. Clean … you know what I'm saying here?"

In the pursuit of science, Tusk had broken a few laws. *A lot* of laws. "It was necessary, and you know that."

Harry chuckled, and this time he did take a sip of his wine. "Even a jury of your peers won't see it that way."

Harry was right. But this deal *didn't* feel right.

"I need to know if you're alright with this because if not, I've got about twelve hours to find a new congressionally appointed scientist."

"This is not how I envisioned our dinner unfolding," Tusk said.

"That's the thing, Cliff – things evolve."

~

## Change of plans

August 7th, 10:30pm CST (-1 EST)

Rox watched the black and white images on the screen from the surveillance drone overhead. It was a simple, 2D image of white dots moving inside a transposed digital copy of the floor plan of the house it was flying over. Its purpose was only to show how many living heat signatures were inside. Right now, it showed three dots. There should have been four.

Rox looked over at Danny where he crouched beside her underneath the canopy of red oak trees that marked the perimeter at the back of the property. He didn't move, didn't flinch, didn't have an itch to scratch or a shiver to make him shudder. The only thing in motion were his eyes, and she could swear when he was in deep concentration, his left ear twitched, but just the top.

The night was clear with only a few clouds slowly making their way across the sky. The moon was less than half, but the stars were visible this far out from Houston's city center. They were deep inside middle-class territory. Each house was a replica of the next: two-car garages, basketball hoops set up in the driveways, and front lawns perfectly manicured to look like the cover of a home and garden magazine.

Rox reached out with her ability, and the first thing her mind catalogued was the heartbeat next to her, and then the smaller animals taking refuge in the treetops above. She pushed farther, into the backyard and past the sprinklers on a timer. She pulled back when she reached the walls of the house. Its electricity scratched along the base of her neck as it sought to merge with her energy. She exhaled a slow and steady breath before pushing through the discomfort into the back door. She came across the two white dots that were moving in a back-and-forth pattern. The third dot was stationary on the second story. Asleep?

"We've got a problem," she whispered to Danny. "We're missing one."

His gaze pivoted to her as he extended his hand, silently asking her to pass him the drone's monitor so he could have a look. It was his first sign of movement since they wound through the copse of towering red oaks bordering the back of the houses in this neighborhood. Rox would hate to come across him in the dark of night. It was not his army fatigue-like attire; it was the solidness of his physique and the granite features of his face that displayed no emotion other than a stern determination.

She had worked with Danny long enough to know he played by his own rule book. He considered working with Halo a low-risk gig, but he had said often enough that it was the low-risk assignments that got good soldiers killed.

Technically, she was the field lead, and the next decision was hers to make, but Danny signed on with them for a single purpose: to shape Rox into field-lead material. So, while he wouldn't tell her what to do, she knew he had an opinion about their next course of action.

Four hours ago, Halo had couriered a package to the family residing in the house the drone circled. The package had been signed for, and someone from the family had opened it and used the mobile phone inside to call the only number listed in its address book. The conversation had been brief, but the extraction was confirmed for four: Tessa Andersen, dental hygienist in her mid-forties; her husband, Glen Andersen, residential property manager only a few years older; Tessa's eldest son from a previous relationship, Christopher Andersen, aged seventeen; and Tessa and Glen's only son together, Tommy Andersen, aged ten.

"Your call," Danny said.

He had drilled into her that the safety of her team was almost always paramount. When she asked what could be worth more than the lives of those who trusted her, his answer was swift and succinct. The mission.

This was a simple extraction. There was nothing in the Andersens' background that pointed to them being anything more than the unfortunate victims of an EO hate crime. But where was that fourth dot?

Rox glanced over at Danny. He was watching her with that same intense look he had on his face whenever she caught him staring at her. It was as if he were trying to read her thoughts, figure out some secret she had no idea she held.

"I don't think it's a trap," she said.

In addition to the background check that Walter ran, Meita had Tessa and Glen Andersen followed for a month and their financials analyzed by an investigative auditor she kept on retainer. They would've never green-lighted this mission if they had not been confident this family needed help.

"What evidence you got it's not a trap?" Danny asked.

He was testing her.

"Doesn't feel like one. Too unsophisticated."

"Unsophisticated plans are the best ones. Got anything else besides your gut?"

Danny taught her that nothing would ever be more valuable than her instincts and to always trust them. They were telling her right now that the family in that house needed Halo's help. She had been that family. Or something close enough to it to know that bad things happened to EOs who didn't know how to protect themselves. The Andersens relied on the local police for protection, but sadly the local police were too afraid of the exaggerated news reports about EOs to offer any meaningful assistance.

"Stop making it personal," Danny said and took a step closer. "They aren't you."

For a moment she forgot to breathe, then she remembered Danny wasn't evolved. He couldn't read her thoughts, but the intensity of his stare was just as unnerving.

"We don't know what they are," she said as she broke eye contact with him.

"Your call."

It was. She didn't have the time to write out a list of pros and cons, so she took his advice and followed her instincts. "Pops, can you review the drone footage for this place?" She used the field name that Danny had given Walter three years back when they infiltrated Wonderland together to rescue her.

"I've already scanned the footage for the last two hours; nothing seen coming or going," Walter replied.

Rox stretched her jaw to ease the discomfort that ran through her ear canal whenever she used her earpiece.

"What're you thinking?" Danny asked her.

Ruby. She was thinking about the time when Ruby snuck out to meet with her boyfriend to discuss where they were going on their first date. It had been the worst possible time for an after-dark rendezvous, and as a result, she and her little brother, MJ, were kidnapped. The memory of the journey it took to reach them in Luang Prabang still gave Rox nightmares.

"Can you also check to see if the older son has a girlfriend?" she said.

There was a moment of silence. "And how is that relevant?" Walter responded.

"We're missing a dot," Rox said.

"Oh."

Danny slowly nodded as he realized what she was thinking.

"I'll have to get back to you because I've got to read through the file," Walter said.

"Fine. Also, set a timer," Rox said.

"For?" Walter asked.

"Fifteen minutes to find out why we're short one white dot."

"Right. I don't hear from you by then, I'm sending Po," Walter replied.

The first time Rox met Po was in a fight. He had snuck up behind her and jammed a needle into her neck. In his defense, she *was* trespassing on private property and, despite being shot with two tranquilizer darts, was still quite mobile and dexterous. In *her* defense, however, a military-grade armed response, complete with helicopter and wolf, seemed like overkill at the time.

Po's real name was Curtis, and he was parked two blocks away in a sleek, new silver minivan that blended into their surroundings. He was their support if anything went wrong. Curtis was a former police detective whose wife went missing ten years ago. They never found her body or any clues leading to her disappearance. It was a cold case, and if Halo hadn't taken him in, he wouldn't have survived. He owed Sam his life, but now that Sam was gone, he stayed with Halo just to piss off Walter.

"Follow my lead," she said to Danny.

She walked to the edge of the trees where she crouched

and crept along in the shadows until they were against the fence separating the Andersen house from its neighbors. Someone had discovered that the Andersen family was evolved, or at least had an evolved member because the wife had been abducted on her way home from the grocery store five months ago. She had been blindfolded and pushed into a nondescript van. She had been too scared to remember the route or anything about her kidnappers except the anti-EO hatred they spat at her. Her escape had been the result of either dumb luck or "kidnapper incompetence" the police report concluded. Tessa had been the one to reach out to Halo.

Rox remained in a crouched position as she hugged the Andersens' side of the fence until they were parallel to the back door. She stepped out onto the grass without hesitation and walked up to the house like she was the homeowner. Danny positioned himself off to the side, but with a clear line of sight in case things went sideways.

Rox knocked.

This was the moment of truth for the Andersen family. Were they really going to leave their worldly possessions behind? Adopt new identities with lesser skills and a smaller bank account? It was one thing to ask for an extraction, but quite another to actually take it.

Walter's only rule for extractions: you can lead a horse to water, but you can't make it drink.

Rox waited for the Andersen family to respond.

A timid voice replied. "Hot dog?"

"With mustard," Rox said.

A few seconds went by before the locks disengaged and the door opened.

"Are you Halo?" It was the husband, Glen, who opened the door, but it was his wife, Tessa, who spoke. She stood in the hallway leading from the kitchen to the rest of the house.

"Yes, may we come in?" Rox said and reached out with her energy once more for the missing fourth dot.

An awkward silence fell after Danny followed her inside. Danny was a third-generation military brat. He had dedicated his life to his country, working in special ops, and finally on unclassified assignments that had no visible chain of command, just phone calls, drop sites, and clandestine meetings. He joined Halo eight months ago after an assignment ended his career. He had been lucky to make it out alive, but he was broken, struggling to find a reason to get up in the morning, so Meita recruited him.

Danny entered the kitchen at six-foot-one, but it was his girth that was impressive. It was clear he took care of his body, and just by looking at him, you knew where you stood. Rox had been training with him, and one thing remained certain, she would never best him without the use of her ability, and even then, she found him hard to take down.

"This is my partner," Rox said, and then she smiled. "He's here in case we run into any problems."

Glen was visibly shaken as he put his arm around his wife. Then the sounds of feet rapidly descending the staircase drew their attention, and Tessa spun around to stop her youngest son, Tommy, from rushing in.

"Is that them?" Tommy tried to peer around his mother.

"How do we know we can trust you?" Glen asked.

Rox inhaled and nodded like it was a good question. Trusting strangers was always difficult and often ill-advised, but sometimes, strangers were your only option.

"You don't know if you can trust us," she said. "But, we're here to help, and any time you change your mind, you let us know and we go away. But we won't *ever* come back."

She hated that last sentence, but it was necessary. This was the only shot the Andersens had at receiving Halo's help.

Tessa wiped a tear from her face and tightened her grip on Tommy's forearm. It was an odd place to hold on to a child, but it was also secure, making it harder for him to wriggle free. Rox understood her action.

"Go upstairs and get Chris," Tessa said to her husband.

"No." It was a single word, but Danny's tone stopped all movement.

"There are only three of you in this house," Rox said. "But the extraction is for four. Why is that?"

Tessa looked at her husband and then back at Rox. "What do you mean?"

"You, your husband, and your two sons."

Tessa nodded. "C-Chris, my eldest is upstairs. In his room."

"No, he's not." Rox said.

Tessa's energy ebbed off her in fitful waves as her fear reached new levels. Her face broadcasted her thoughts as if she were speaking them. She wanted nothing more than to turn around and race up the stairs to check on her eldest son, but Danny had said "no".

"Tessa," Rox said softly. "I know you're scared. But I'm going to be honest with you here. If you want our help, you've got to do exactly as I say. If anyone leaves this room, my partner and I turn around and *we* leave." Rox held Tessa's stare like they were the only two present. "Nod if you understand me."

It took a few seconds, but Tessa nodded.

"I can assure you that Chris is nowhere to be found in the house. Now, do you know where he is?"

Tessa burst into tears, and it was Glen who answered. "We left him in his room a couple of hours ago."

"How do you know he's not in his room?" Tessa asked.

Tommy tugged on her arm. "Maybe he went to say goodbye to Jenny."

"Now we have a problem," Danny said between tight lips.

There was a tense moment of silence while Rox ran through the possible outcomes if they remained to help and weighed them against what would happen to this family if Halo chose to abandon them.

"I hate risk," Danny said as if he were reading her thoughts.

He was ready to turn and walk away from them, but there was something about the way Tessa held on to her youngest that resonated with Rox.

"Who's Jenny?" Rox asked.

Danny glanced at her. "Our brief said two parents, one male, one female, and two boys."

"Please, he's young and it's his first girlfriend and he ..." Glen said, "... he didn't want to leave her, but he's only seventeen—"

"Where is he?" Danny asked.

Tessa and Glen looked at each other, and it became apparent they didn't know.

"We could call him," Tommy offered.

Tessa's hands were shaking when she reached into her back pocket and pulled out her mobile phone. She pressed his number and put the call on speaker. It rang once, and then one of the latest hit songs blasted from upstairs.

Danny swore.

What teenager went anywhere without his phone?

"Update," Walter's voice broke through on her earpiece, and Rox stretched her jaw. "According to Meita's files, the hormonal teenager has a girlfriend as of a few months ago. She didn't note anything about the severity of the relationship, but they're teenagers so it could be over in the next hour or they could be on their way to elope."

Danny stilled and his lips thinned as he looked between the parents. Then his gaze stopped on the boy. The top of Danny's left ear twitched. He, too, didn't want to abandon this family. He didn't need to be an EO to sympathize with their plight. He had been part of the rescue team which had saved Rox and Miles from Wonderland. He had witnessed what they did to her kind.

Tessa inhaled as if she were about to say something, but Danny held up his hand.

"We'll be departing from the mission's critical time path in three minutes," he said.

The critical time path, as Danny liked to refer to it, was the time set for each phase of a mission to complete. Once they crossed the threshold into the Andersens' kitchen, his mental timer had started. He allowed five minutes of ice breaking, the "emotional chit-chat" that helped to put a family at relative ease. Another five minutes to exit through the back door and cross the yard. Fifteen or so to hike through the woods at the back of the neighborhood until they reached the rendezvous point where Curtis would meet them with transportation. Danny would remain behind to make sure they weren't being followed and dispose of all the Andersens' electronic equipment. Curtis and Rox would drive them to the airfield where Josh was waiting for them. Josh was the only one who knew the Andersens' final destination.

Very few assignments ever ran precisely to schedule, but each member was always accounted for, and Rox sensed what spooked Danny most was the missing teen. Danny felt responsible for her safety, and while he had no abilities of his own, he took his role seriously. Rox was beginning to sense that the Andersen family was losing the quiet debate Danny was having on their behalf.

"Do you know where she lives?" Rox asked Tessa.

"What do we care?" It was Danny's tone that made the question so abrupt.

Rox had to buy the Andersen family more time. She might be the lead, but Danny had reserved the authority to abort any mission at any point if he felt things were deteriorating beyond salvation.

"Pen and paper?" Rox asked Tessa.

Tessa dragged her youngest son with her as she went over to the drawer. She yanked it open, and Danny lifted his gun and pointed it at her head.

"What are we doing, Paladin?" he asked.

Rox hated her field name, and Danny knew it.

"And that's time, ladies and gentlemen," Walter said into their earpieces. "Do I send in Po?"

Danny and Rox both answered simultaneously, each saying the opposite.

Tessa began to cry again. Tommy wrapped his arms around his mother's waist and buried his face in her shirt. Glen shifted his weight from one foot to the next as if he couldn't decide whether to go to his wife or stay where he was.

For a brief second, Rox closed her eyes. She couldn't tell if someone was lying, but she could pick up on fitful waves of energy when someone was frightened or bold waves when they were angry.

Tessa was petrified, and it didn't take Josh's mind-reading ability to know she was torn. Tessa grabbed her son's arms and roughly untangled them from around her. She pushed him towards her husband, who immediately stepped in front of the boy.

"Glen," Tessa said without looking away from the barrel of Danny's weapon. "Take Tommy and the two of you go with them."

"What?" Glen shouted. "No. I'm not leaving you."

"Mommy?" Tommy said.

"Go with Daddy, baby," Tessa said. Her attention still held by Danny. "These people will keep you safe." She looked at Rox. "Isn't that right?"

There are some experiences that must be lived to be understood. Motherhood was one of them. Rox knew exactly what Tessa was thinking. There was no scenario where she would leave her son, Chris, behind. Especially, if she knew Tommy was going to be okay.

"That's not the arrangement—" Danny began.

"Sending Po in three, two—"

"We've got this, Pops," Rox said. "Have Po stand down. There's been a slight hiccup. The eldest son, he pulled a Ruby."

Walter groaned. "Young people and their first love." Then he chuckled. "How you wanna play it?"

Danny's teeth grinding was audible in the silence. "Yes, Paladin, how do you want to proceed?"

Rox knew from his tone they would have a conversation when this was over. She cleared her throat. "Lead will take the father and youngest to Po, who'll take them to the extraction point."

"And me?" Tessa asked, aware they were speaking to someone not in the room.

Rox looked at the mother of two and offered her a small smile of hope. "We're going to find your son."

~

## Boundaries

August 7th, 11:00pm CST (-1 EST)

Rox slid Chris' fitted baseball cap over her braided curls and pulled the brim down so it acted as a visor against anyone looking at her. It was tight because of her hair, but it would have to do.

"Sorry about the mess," Tessa said softly as they slid into her car.

Rox looked around the sedan. It was relatively new, not more than a few years old, but it was clean. It even had one of those air fresheners stuck in the air vent that made the car smell like artificial lemons.

"Not the car," Tessa said with a nervous smile. "I mean the garage."

The garage looked like one of the sheds at Halo: messy, but functional. That thought sobered Rox. There were people depending on her to come back home and to keep them safe. She was taking a risk by deviating from the original plan.

"Tessa?" Meita had taught Rox that if she wanted people to take her seriously, she had to behave seriously. "If you try anything that threatens my safety or the safety of my team, I will kill you."

Tessa's grip on the steering wheel tightened, and Rox followed Tessa's gaze back to where her husband and son stood in the doorway between the kitchen and the garage. Danny was behind them, his weapon out but not raised.

"I just want to find my son," Tessa said as fresh tears dripped in her lap.

Rox waited until Tessa finished blowing her nose with a tissue that had been sitting in the cupholder separating their two seats. "Are you sure you want to do this?"

Tessa looked confused. "What? Go get my son?"

"Leave those two?"

Tessa's sob was audible, but she nodded. "I could never live with them knowing—"

"Eight-nine minutes," Danny's voice cut through Rox's earpiece. "I suggest you save the girl talk."

If Rox didn't arrive at the airfield with Tessa *and* Chris within ninety minutes, then no one was getting on that plane. The risk would be too great to Halo because, eventually, Glen would try to contact his wife.

"Be careful," Danny said as the garage door rolled open. "And we'll discuss this when you get back."

Danny's "discussions" were more lectures that took place in the training room while he threw her down on the mat. Repeatedly.

Tessa's car was dark gray with shiny bits that looked like glitter. It was a hybrid and the only sound it made was when its tires rolled across the loose gravel. The car's safety feature sounded once and Rox remembered to secure her seatbelt. She slid her seat back until she was parallel with the passenger's doorframe, effectively blocking her from the view of those in passing cars.

Hopefully, anyone looking out their window at this hour would assume that Tessa was on a midnight run for ice cream, or perhaps she was taking Chris to the emergency room. These types of things happened with kids, but Meita had warned them this neighborhood was invested in its safety with an active watch group. Unfamiliar cars, unknown joggers, loud parties, anything that could be perceived as a catalyst for trouble would be reported, and the police had a rapid response time given this community paid higher taxes. Rox would have between three to seven minutes before she saw flashing lights.

Tessa had an unnatural grip on the steering wheel that made her driving jerky. She accelerated and then tapped the breaks to adjust her speed as she eased up to a stop sign. She looked left, then right, then left and right again before she remembered to signal, then looked once more before she started a slow left turn onto an empty thoroughfare.

They rode for a few minutes in silence while Tessa struggled to keep the car steady between the dotted lines. The police would pull her over for suspected drunk driving at this rate.

"How long have you lived here?" Rox asked, trying to distract Tessa from her own thoughts.

"A little over five years." Tessa slowed a bit early for the red light, and by the time the car reached the crossing, the light had switched to green.

"Where were you before?"

"Seattle," Tessa said.

They passed a strip mall with the usual fast food restaurants and chain coffee shops. All of them were closed at this hour, and for a moment, Rox got lost in the expansiveness of the US, Texas in particular. There was so much space. Everywhere. It reminded her of Crossroads, but so much had happened since then. Everything she had thought she knew and believed at that time had changed.

Tessa turned off the main road onto a side street that led to an adjacent neighborhood. The difference between this area and Tessa's was immediately apparent. While Tessa spoke about her life and her separation from Chris' father, Rox took in the change in the houses. Gone were the brick and stone frontages, and in their place were faded or rusted sidings. A few homes had shutters missing from their windows, and the well-manicured lawns of Tessa's street were replaced with metal fences running the entire perimeter of the properties.

While it had been just a twelve-minute drive, it was obvious that Jenny's family didn't have the same earning power as Chris'.

Tessa switched off the ignition and was about to open her door when Rox reached out to stop her. "We don't go in the house. We're just here to collect your son. There's no need to explain anything more than that."

"What if they ask who you are? Chris won't know you."

"I'm your friend from dental college. I'm in town because I'm looking for a job, and your practice is thinking of hiring me."

Tessa nodded, and they got out of the car, both closing their doors quietly. The gate to Jenny's property scratched along the path when it was opened, so Rox lifted it as she pushed it wide. She looked for something to keep it propped open and found a cinder block near the base of the house's front steps. She told Tessa to wait as she positioned it against the gate to keep it open.

The lawn had been recently cut, but the grass was dry and brittle from the Texas heat. Rox doubted they had a sprinkler system like the Andersens, which meant their grass would have to wait for the weather to change.

The front steps were painted the same pale blue as the house, and just like the house, the paint was showing age. The porch ran the entire length of the front and looked more spacious than any of the homes in the Andersen neighborhood, but it lacked the luster, the feelings of security and white-collared neighbors. This was also middle class, just a few rungs down.

Rox positioned herself behind and to the side of Tessa as she rang the doorbell. It was late, or early, depending on how one categorized time, but the door swung open with a frantic woman staring back at them far too soon for her to have been in bed.

An orange filter slid over Rox's eyes as she took hold of Tessa's life energy.

"It's not her," the woman shouted to someone inside the home before she looked back at them. "Have you seen her? My Jenny. She's missing."

This was not good.

"I'm looking for Chris, my son," Tessa said. "I think they're dating."

"Hank," the woman shouted again as she re-cinched the belt on her purple house robe. "She's run off with Chris."

Hank was a man of average height and build, but he came thundering down the stairs like a man who had just discovered his daughter had a boyfriend.

Rox took a step back and reached out with her abilities.

There was no one else in the house except Hank and his wife, but Rox started to siphon some of Tessa's energy nonetheless. She would have to attack Hank first as he presented the biggest threat, though he didn't appear to have anything in his hands, and his robe was open, showing off a pair of blue boxer shorts and a white t-shirt.

"I think I know where they might be," Hank said and held up a piece of paper with three rows of letters and what looked like times beside each one.

"What's that?" Tessa asked.

"I think it might be a schedule or something. Flights maybe," Hank answered.

"How old is Jenny?" Rox asked.

Jenny's mother jumped, like she was just noticing Rox for the first time. "She's seventeen."

"It's not flights. They'd have to register for the unaccompanied minor program, and they'd need an adult to do that," Rox said. "Do they have driving licenses?"

Jenny's mother shook her head, but Tessa said that Chris had just gotten his learner's license.

"Train?" Hank said.

"More than likely bus," Rox said. Only the poverty-stricken and mentally unstable took the bus because of the immense amount of time it took to get from one location to the next. If time was money, and you were broke, then you had all the time in the world. Rox remembered the grind from the bus engine and the stench from the stained cloth seats when she was on the run from Josh. People in bus stations were invisible to one another and to most of society, making it the perfect place to go unseen.

"A bus? Would they even be open at this hour?" Hank asked and looked at his watch. "Hell, it's gone eleven."

Rox stepped back and unzipped her jacket pocket and pulled out her phone. It was nice to be able to interact with technology even if it was uncomfortable. She put the phone up to her ear like she had made a call.

"Po," she said. "What's the nearest bus station that'll be open at this hour?"

"Bus station?" Po repeated.

"Paladin?" Danny's voice cut through her earpiece.

"I need the nearest bus station with buses departing at—" Rox held out her hand to Hank, who passed her the paper so she could read out the times.

"Is this Chris' *other* ... parent?" Jenny's mother asked.

Tessa looked confused at first. "Uh, no. She's a ... she's a friend from college who's come to visit because my dental practice is considering hiring her."

"She a dentist?" Hank asked.

"Just hung up with your ex," Po said into Rox's earpiece. "And the numbers you gave me are Greyhound bus times. They match buses leaving the Manvel terminal, passing through your Bellaire station on its way to Orlando, Florida."

Rox looked back at Tessa. Her son was running away. He was running away with his girlfriend and neither of their parents had a clue. "Any chance you know if they've left Manvel yet?"

"Manvel?" Jenny's mother asked at the same time Tessa shouted, "They're in Manvel?"

"Depends on how long they've been missing. Either they left on the 7:20 bus or they are waiting there until the 6:00am one," Po said.

"When was the last time you saw Chris?" Rox asked.

Tessa's eyes filled with tears again. "Just after we called you. We got the phone and we called you. We spoke to him—"

"Give us a sec," Rox said to Jenny's parents as she guided Tessa to the edge of the porch.

"Wait! What's going on?" Hank asked.

"Did you tell Chris about our arrangement *before* tonight?" Rox asked when they were far enough away.

Tessa nodded. "A couple of days ago. I know you asked us to wait, but—"

"When was the last time you saw him?" Rox asked.

"About an hour after we phoned you."

That was good. It meant Chris and Jenny would have to wait for the early morning bus. "And what about Jenny?" Rox asked when they went back to Jenny's parents. "When was the last time either of you saw her?"

Jenny's mother looked up at Hank who looked down at her. "Dinner?" she said, and Hank nodded. "We had dinner and then she went up to her room with her phone."

"And what time was that?" Rox asked.

"I don't know!" Jenny's mother turned into Hank's chest.

"Seven, seven-thirty," Hank said as he wrapped his arms around his wife.

That was also good.

"Update, Paladin," Danny said into her earpiece.

"Why'd you say something about Manvel?" Jenny's mother said as she lifted her head.

"I have a friend in the police department and he's on the phone," Rox said, remembering to lift her phone back to her ear. "He's helping us look for Chris."

"What's in Manvel?" Jenny's mother asked.

"They might be there at the Greyhound bus station," Rox said. "Tessa and I are going to go look for them."

"I would advise against that, Paladin."

"I'm coming with you," Jenny's mother said and spun around and disappeared inside.

Rox swore under her breath. This was definitely outside of mission parameters.

"Paladin ..."

Wasn't it the kindness of strangers that had saved Ruby and MJ's lives? Two young women on holiday with no reason to help let Ruby borrow a phone so she could call home, and then they also invited Ruby and MJ back to their hotel suite and kept them safe overnight.

"Paladin?" Po asked. "You copying, Lead?"

She heard Danny. He was hard to ignore.

Rox looked back up at Tessa and Jenny's mother who had returned wearing a pair of shorts and an oversized t-shirt. They were two very different women, but no less identical in their love for their children. A love that Rox understood.

There was a sigh in her earpiece. "How far are you willing to go?"

"I—" Rox lifted the phone to her ear. "I ..."

"You've got to establish boundaries," Danny said. "It's okay if they're far out, but once you've reached them, you've got to have the discipline to pull back. If you don't, you endanger everyone who is following you, and trust me, you don't want to live out eternity with their deaths on your conscience."

"I'm ready. Hank'll stay here just in case they come back." Jenny's mother said.

"Where're your boundaries, Paladin?"

Rox looked at the three people staring at her for direction. She put her phone into her jacket and zipped it back up. She looked past Tessa's tears, the fear, and the silent plea for continued help. "After Manvel, I have to return home."

Tessa's breath caught and she visibly paled.

"Do you have a flight or something?" Hank asked.

Rox nodded, but didn't break eye contact with Tessa.

"Well, c'mon then," Jenny's mother said as she pushed passed them and started down the front steps. "We taking your car or mine?"

"Tessa's driving," Rox said. "You can have the front seat. I'll hop in the back."

Jenny's mother used the sole of her sneakers to push the cinder block away from the gate. "She must've propped it open on her way out." It creaked and scratched against the pavement as she swung it closed.

Rox slid into the back row's middle seat and met Tessa's eyes in the rearview mirror. Rox was tempted to look away, but didn't. She had established her boundaries.

Tessa wiped the tears off her cheeks before she pushed

the button to ignite the ignition.

"What's your name?" Jenny's mother asked.

"Tessa. I'm Chris' mother."

Jenny's mother's laugh was filled with nervous energy. "I know that."

"What's your name?" Rox asked.

"Sue," Jenny's mother laughed again. "What's yours?"

Tessa glanced back at her in the rearview mirror.

"Sam."

Sue turned around as Tessa drove off. "Nice to meet you, Sam. Wish it was under different circumstances."

~

## Somewhere

Date/Time: Unknown

Neo sniffed the air and blew out sharply.

"Winter's almost here." Sam sat down on one of the large boulders next to the lake. He stuffed his remaining sock into the toe of his boot and unbuckled his belt. It was a beautiful afternoon with the sun still radiating its last few hours of heat.

Sam tucked his underwear into the pocket of his trousers and placed his folded shirt on top. He reached down to knock the sand from the soles of his boots before he placed it atop of his shirt, and then reached for his bear fur.

First and only rule of living in prehistoric times: without animal fur, you're dead.

After he wrapped everything inside his fur, he placed

his staff on top and waded into the lake until it was deep enough for him to swim. The water was cold this time of year. Not that he had ever experienced it warm, not wherever he was, but soon it would freeze, making this his last swim of the year. Sam had learned to measure the passing of time in seasons, not months. There was no summer – not as he knew it – but this was his third autumn, and the start of his third winter was rapidly approaching.

That first winter had been brutal. A cold like nothing he'd ever experienced forced him on the hunt, and he wouldn't have survived if it hadn't been for Neo. A saber-toothed cat – if that was in fact what Neo was – was a deadly hunter. Sam learned a lot about ambush hunting from Neo. The keys were patience, knowing your prey's movement habits, and then arriving to the ambush site first. And, of course, the importance of being upwind.

Sam was most grateful for the companionship, though. He had never experienced a bond with another living being like he had with Neo. He lifted his arm and traced the triple parallel lines that ran up from his groin and diagonally over his chest to stop just above where his nipple had been. Neo had something similar running down to his hindquarters.

Bears.

Sam's performance shirt and cargo pants provided no protection from the harsh elements of wherever and whenever he had found himself. Building a fire helped at night when he was stationary, but that first winter he was still looking for civilization, and so he had to keep warm while walking during the day, which meant he needed pelt from an animal large enough to provide protection. And it was a good thing he got it because when the first snowfall happened, it was as deep as he was tall.

Sam clenched his jaw and turned away from that memory as he swam out until he could no longer touch the bottom. He dove to keep his mind preoccupied. He counted five, six, seven strokes before his ears began to pop from the pressure change. He held on for another second before he switched directions and headed for the surface. His lungs were burning with the need to expand, and he swallowed, but he didn't inhale until the last few days of the autumn breeze blew across his face.

He did flips in the water until he realized he was still grinding this teeth. He relaxed his jaw, turned onto his back, and formed images out of the small groups of clouds floating by. He decided that he would search for animals this time. At first, the clouds were too thin and moving too slowly to change shape, but he waited, and while he waited he practiced holding his breath. There was no survival reason he could think of for doing so, but he counted to sixty-six, which he considered impressive given he had just finished a series of dives.

Sam almost forgot about the clouds until he saw a tree appear. It quickly dissolved into a flower, and then its petals dispersed, leaving only a stalk that bent into the shape of a crescent moon, which eventually smoothed out into a boomerang. That cloud transitioned out of his view and another floated in with the shape of an old man's face, but with just one eye, and that made him think of a cyclops. He wondered whether cyclops were ever real and if they had been, did they exist in whatever time he was in. Then a cloud passed by that looked like a wolf with three legs, and Sam smiled.

He flipped onto his stomach and swam until he was almost back to shore but still far enough to tread water. He whistled sharply, and it broke the call of the insects in the trees around his side of the lake. A few seconds later, Neo hopped atop of the boulder with Sam's clothes and roared. Everything stilled as Neo searched across the water until he found Sam, and then he leapt down and disappeared to continue whatever he had been doing.

Sam swam back to the middle of the lake and dove down again to look for fish. The water was cold against his naked eye, but it was clear and sunlight allowed him to see what swam around him.

There were a few hours before sunset, and so he started back to shore. He would set up camp and get a nice fire going before it became too dark. The nights brought a frost that left everything covered in a damp, white mist come morning. Sam gazed across the horizon at the mountain that was less than a day's hike away. The clouds surrounding it were too thin and too white to promise the kind of storm he was hoping for, but he wasn't worried. Just as sure as the sun rose and set, a storm always came, and with that storm came rain and thunder.

And lightning.

# CHAPTER TWO

## Then there were four

August 7th, 11:40pm CST (-1 EST)

Manvel Greyhound bus station was not a bus station. It was a 24-hour gas station that also functioned as a stop on the Greyhound bus route. It was situated at a major junction housing fast food restaurants as well as three other gas stations and convenience stores.

"Pull in to the pumps like you're getting gas," Rox said as Tessa eased off the road.

The ride was just under twenty-five minutes and Sue talked the entire time. They learned that Jenny had a lisp when she was younger that led to confidence issues. But they took her to a speech therapist and she eventually overcame it, though when she was tired, it returned. Jenny was also borderline dyslexic, to which Tessa absently replied she didn't know one could be "borderline".

Tessa pulled up beside the pump and pushed the button to turn off the ignition.

"You two stay here. I'll have a look around," Rox said after she'd climbed out.

"Wait, I'm coming with you," Sue said, but Rox put her weight on Sue's door to stop her from opening it.

"Actually, if they see either of you, they could run." That was Rox's second worry. The first was that Sue would see something that Rox couldn't readily explain.

Sue looked her over like she were questioning Rox's story about being a dental hygienist. For the first time, Rox wondered if it would be better to dress more casually on assignments. Most women didn't wear black cargo pants and boots. Their shirts might hug their chests, but not in a way that accented their biceps and made it difficult for an opponent to grab hold. Her attire was made for performance.

"Drone's got 'em," Danny said. "Left of the building."

Rox turned away before Sue could think of a suitable rebuttal and walked as if she were going into the convenience store, but she was only checking the inside. It was large, so she couldn't see into the back, but it looked empty except for the clerk who was behind clear perspex. His head was bent like he was either reading or on his phone.

Rox reached out, but the gas station was alive with kinetic energy. It grated against the back of her neck in a manner she had almost forgotten about. Ever since she had gotten struck by lightning, her ability to manipulate energy had greatly improved, but artificial energy was always uncomfortable.

Another vehicle pulled in behind her as she slowly made her way to the left side of the building. She paused just before rounding the corner and listened but couldn't hear anything over the sound of a door slamming shut. She reached out once more and this time two life forces responded.

A light fixed to the corner of the building was meant to provide visibility, but it was broken or its bulb needed replacing because it gave off a weak glow.

Chris and Jenny were sitting on a bench, Jenny with her back against the armrest and her feet tapping against the metal crisscrossing bars that made up the seat. Chris was saying something when Rox cleared her throat.

"Chris? Jenny?"

Jenny swiveled around and dropped her feet to the pavement. "Are you with the Fellowship?"

"Did she say Fellowship?" Danny asked through her earpiece.

That complicated things. "I'm here because your parents are really worried about you," Rox said as she forced a smile on her face.

"How you wanna do this?" Danny asked.

Jenny grabbed Chris' hand and tried to backpedal, but couldn't because of the bench.

"Did my mom leave yet?" Chris asked.

Rox wasn't sure of the type of relationship Tessa had with her eldest son. Maybe it was a difficult one filled with tension brought on by teenage angst. Rox understood just how difficult it was to communicate with a teenager. Ruby still refused to call her "mom". But Rox was surprised that Chris thought Tessa would leave without him. It meant he had no idea just how much his mother loved him.

"No," Rox said. "She couldn't leave you behind, so she sent Tommy with your stepdad."

Chris looked surprised by that and was about to say something, but stopped as if interrupted.

Footsteps alerted Rox that they had company, and she thought it was Tessa and Sue, but one of the steps fell out of sync with the others, and Rox realized there were more than just two approaching.

In the dark, the three men striding towards her could've passed for triplets: matching clothes, approximately the same height, and their trio of blonde hairstyles were cropped short, like they even went to the same barber. Their swagger placed them in their early twenties, which made them dangerous. The young often thought of themselves as invincible.

The leader identified himself by a loud sucking of his teeth. He stopped well out of striking distance from Rox and looked her over like he was establishing dominance. He had a silver chain attached to his belt loop that caught the faint light coming off the corner of the building. He placed one hand on top of the other and lowered them in front as if he were shielding his most precious bits.

"Trouble," Rox said softly into her earpiece.

"Copy," Danny said. "Pops' en route."

"Thought there was just two of ya," said the leader. He spoke with a drawl Rox had learned over the years to associate with Texans.

"Are you Fellowship?" It was Jenny who spoke.

Rox took a step to her left, attempting to block the two teens from the three men who had just joined them. "Chris?" Rox said, her eyes still fixed on the newcomers. "Your mom is in her car at the pumps. You and Jenny should head over there and let her know you're okay."

"Ah, so you must be the babysitter?" the leader said. "Did mommy send you to make sure Chris is alright?"

The other two laughed.

Rox glanced up at the sky. The moon was exposed, but there were clouds making their way to her.

"Saying a little prayer?" said the tallest of them.

"Pops' ETA, ten minutes," Danny said.

She could have this over in half that time. These boys looked like they took care of themselves – probably lifted weights, definite gym membership – but she doubted they had the stamina for an actual fight. Not like the ones Mika and Danny trained her for.

Rox looked them over. The one who remained quiet was probably the biggest threat. He was the least muscular of the three, but he had a leanness to him that said he was light on his feet and did more cardio than weightlifting.

Chris and Jenny's whisperings grew louder, but neither of them moved. The tension increased as Rox readied for whatever the three boys in front of her were preparing to do.

"Chris? Jenny?" the leader began, his tone harder than before. "You called us all the way out here, ya? The Fellowship don't like to be kept waiting. Go get in the van so we can be off."

"Do they have weapons?" Danny asked. "One for yes, two for no, and three for I don't know."

"Three."

"What was that, *babysitter*?"

"Do you *think* they have weapons?" Danny asked.

"One."

"What is this? Some sort of countdown?"

"Chris," Rox said. "It's time for you to decide. Either you're going with your mom or you're getting in the van. But I should warn you, rumor has it that whoever goes with the Fellowship, they don't come back."

Walter told them the Fellowship were some new group spreading rumors they could do what no scientists could, and that was heal those "afflicted" with evolved abilities. Their claim was complete fabrication, but far too many EOs wanted to be normal to read the fine print.

The leader sucked his teeth at her. "If anybody ain't coming back, it's you."

Rox eased her right leg back so that her stance was wider.

"You've got five minutes until Pops arrives. Can you handle the situation?" Danny asked.

"One."

The leader held Rox's gaze like he was waiting for her to back down or show a sign of weakness. Two years ago, he would have gotten that sign. Her voice would have trembled. She would've glanced over her shoulder or attempted to talk her way out of the situation. But time changed people; time changes everything.

Rox started to syphon the energy from the quiet one, the one who still hadn't spoken a word but who had kept his eyes locked on her the entire time. He was evolved. She didn't need Meita's ability to know that.

"C'mon, Jenny." Chris' voice broke the silence. "My mom'll give you a ride home."

Good. He wanted to go back to his mother, but Rox doubted the Fellowship would be so accommodating.

"Robbie," the leader said.

The quiet one took a step towards them and Rox pulled. Robbie's knees buckled, and his face was the second thing to hit the ground.

"Robbie?" the other boy called, but the leader held him back.

"Get to the car, now!" Rox said. She circled around, keeping between Chris and Jenny and the two members of the Fellowship still standing.

"Bet!" the leader said and reached behind him.

A transparent shade of orange settled over Rox's vision as she took two steps towards her target. The gun made a wide arc as the leader swung his arm out and around, giving Rox the extra second she needed to bring up her left arm and block it before he could level it at her. The punch she delivered to his nose was charged with the kinetic energy from the fallen boy, and it snapped like a whip cracking when she made contact.

The gun fell to the ground and she used the black, matte batons that were attached to her forearms inside her shirt to deliver a chop to the side of the boy's face. Rox kicked the gun, and it spun across the concrete atop a grate and fell through the bars. The leader collapsed.

The remaining one looked unsure what to do next. His gaze kept darting between his leader and Robbie.

Rox advanced.

Danny had stressed the importance of controlling a fight. Every man had to be down for it to be over. Catch the opponent off-guard if you could. Act fast, don't give them an opportunity to formulate a plan. Keep it under thirty seconds, never more than a minute or uncontrollable variables became a factor: a bystander stepping in, a concealed weapon getting drawn, or a downed attacker having the chance to recover, and no matter what happens, never, ever boast until a drink is in hand.

The remaining Fellowship member managed a single back-step before Rox surprised him with a left hook. He fell backwards, and a pain reminiscent of Tusk's fire pierced through the center of Rox's back, followed almost immediately by the crack of gunfire.

There was a fourth attacker.

Rox rolled over, hoping that the bullet was stopped by her compression vest. She formed a glittering shield of kinetic energy as her eyes locked with those of a girl no older than Ruby. The gun was shaking and the young kid holding it was sucking in so much air it was as if she were hyperventilating when she pulled the trigger thrice more, shattering Rox's shield and embedding one of the three bullets into her stomach.

~

**Danny**

August 7th, 11:55pm CST (-1 EST)

"Don't get out of the car to meet them," Danny said into the phone.

Tessa breathed out a sob, and the drone showed her

wiping away her tears as Chris and Jenny got into the back seat.

"Now drive Jenny and her mom home," Danny said. "Stick to the speed limit. And Tessa?"

"Yes?"

"You have thirty-five minutes."

Danny ended the call as soon as she pulled out from the gas station. He was sure Chris had told Jenny about his ability, but that was tomorrow's problem. Right now, if Tessa didn't make it to Curtis in time, no one would be going anywhere and whatever Jenny knew about Chris and his ability was no longer Halo's problem.

Rox's sharp exhalation followed by the sound of a gunshot made a feeling of unease race up Danny's thighs. She didn't have a gun. He had insisted she trained with them, and her aim had improved significantly with practice, but she didn't like them, and because of that, she never carried one.

"Paladin?"

No response. Then three more shots.

Damnit.

"Pops?"

"I heard." Walter's voice was tight. "Will you sit down!"

Walter must've been talking to Shaira. Rox didn't go anywhere without her. The only reason the wolf hadn't accompanied them when they entered the Andersens' was because people tended to reconsider Halo's offer of help when a wolf was present.

"I'm still five minutes out," Pops said.

Danny called her name again, but he knew he wouldn't

get a response. She was down. Possibly dead. For now. He swung the drone back around to Rox's last position. He saw Robbie's unconscious body first, lying face down. The dot over him was white, which meant he was still alive. Next was the leader, white dot. Then he came up to the girl holding the smoking gun over Rox's body. Two white dots. Rox was alive, but she wasn't moving.

Danny flexed his quads to ease the ache that was forming in his thighs. There was nothing he could do to help her, and things were beginning to take a turn for the worst. He was still at the Andersens'. His job was to clean the site of anything that could connect the family to Halo. Curtis had taken Tommy and Glen to the airport, where they would be passed over to Josh who was the only one who knew their final destination. When they landed, Josh would give them an envelope with all the details they needed to start over.

"You got eyes on her?" Walter asked.

"Yeah. She's down."

Walter grunted.

There was nothing Danny could do with the drone. It wasn't equipped for assault. There were no weapons, just a camera, and chances were the girl standing over Rox would be able to bat it down before he could position it to ram into her.

"One of 'em's getting up," Danny said, as a message came in on his other phone. It was from Curtis – a call had gone to 911. A clerk at a gas station in Manvel had reported hearing gunshots. A highway patrolman was less than five minutes out.

"Damnit!"

"What?" Walter asked.

"Police are on their way."

"What's their ETA?"

"Less than five minutes."

Danny could hear the sirens through Walter's earpiece.

"Get down will you!" Walter said. "They're passing me now."

The girl disappeared out of the drone's view, but then the headlights from the van blinded the screen for a moment. Danny repositioned the drone and watched as the girl climbed out and instructed the one stumbling to his feet.

They went for the leader first. The girl took hold of him just under his arms and together they walked him to the van. Next, they came back for their friend who was lying face down. They did the same thing again, and Danny held his breath while they looked back at Rox.

"Just leave her," Danny said. "You need to get out of there. The cops are on their way."

But they ran back to Rox and this time the girl grabbed her by the legs. Danny looked down at his watch, but only three minutes had gone by. There was no way the police or Walter were going to arrive in time. He watched as the door slid shut and the girl ran around the front of the van and hopped back into the driver's seat. She reversed out from the side of the building back in between the pumps, and then turned the van around and drove off.

Three minutes. All of that had taken just over three minutes. Danny switched the drone to follow mode and had it tail the van. As long as they were not driving for more than an hour, an hour and a half tops, the drone would have enough battery to follow and transmit its location.

"Police're here." Walter's voice broke through the silence in his earpiece.

"We need to call it in to Meita. She can get a copy of the surveillance footage from the station and anywhere else that's recorded what happened," Danny said. "Click on the link I'm sending to your phone. It'll open up the map so you can follow the drone."

Danny sat back in the chair at the Andersen's kitchen table and rested his arms on top of his head. This was not how he had envisioned the night's events unfolding. This was a simple extraction. The family's background had checked out. There was still no reason to believe this was some elaborate set-up. Who went to this much trouble? Too many actors. Too many moving parts. No, this was simply a series of bad choices made for all the right reasons that nevertheless led to one cata-fucking-clysmic disaster.

Danny shot up, grabbing the chair before it tipped backwards behind him. He looked around the small, dark kitchen trying his best not to kick anything. He felt his anger rising and he breathed through it. Anger rarely helped anyone in a situation like this. Right now, Rox needed him thinking. He would kick her ass later. He was going to flip her on her back so many times she was going to wonder if horizontal was the new vertical. He would make her do so many push-ups her arms were going to fall off. He was going to punish her for this because she was making his heart beat in a way it hadn't in … ever.

Work with a team long enough, in perilous situations long enough, and inevitably people became emotionally invested in one another. An emotional bond in situations like these were necessary. It's what stopped you from quitting, why you would take a bullet not intended for you or run back into a burning building to pull out the dead body of your teammate. Danny had worked with women before, but never like Rox. Rox was innocent and out of her depth. Mika had trained her in self-defense, and Danny had added a more offensive approach to her regimen, but there was a mental aspect to the kind of work they did that he wasn't sure she fully yet comprehended.

Rox was a woman apart. He still remembered the first time he met her at Wonderland. She was pale and disoriented. She wasn't able to stay upright without Sam's help, and the dark circles under her eyes spoke of a hell he later discovered no human should have to live through. She was just a package then, though, a woman who needed extracting.

A person who survived the unspeakable was one who demanded respect. He knew that because he had survived his share of unspeakables. Rox didn't ask for this life. She hadn't been mentally prepared for it either. But she was learning. He made sure of that.

When Meita reached out to him, Danny was moments away from ending it all. He wasn't ashamed of it, never even considered it a weakness. Who could judge him? Who had lived through the hell and taken the risks and done the deeds he had? But there was something about Eagle Eyes that drew him in. He didn't know her full background, but a person who had escaped death a thousand times knew a fellow traveler when they saw one, and Meita had a story to tell. It was there, in the depth of her stare that said *come with me, and you won't be alone anymore.*

Danny trusted her. Trusted her perhaps more than he trusted anyone else at that moment. She had showed up at the one-room apartment he was calling home and knocked on the door. "I've got a job for you," was all she said. Her eyes didn't stray from his as he stepped back to let her in. She didn't comment on his foul breath, stained T-shirt and boxer shorts, or the gun he was holding. She simply stepped over the pizza boxes and Chinese take-out cartons, pushed aside the empty bottles of liquor spread across his two-seater sofa, and sat down with the grace of a woman having her chair pushed in at a high-end restaurant and not some shitty tenement building where the neighbor's TV was loud enough to be heard. There was a stench about him and his dwelling that even he could smell, but that was the thing about ending it all, nothing mattered. Not one single god-damn thing. Except, of course, when someone believed in you.

Danny shook his head and turned around in the dark, empty kitchen again. He waited, hoping to hear something that would signal this had been a trap. That someone was indeed coming and he could finally let out the frustration he had been trying so hard to contain.

"They're turning off the main road. Looks like they're heading south. Maybe southeast," Walter said.

Danny walked back to the table and looked down at the screen that showed the drone and its locations. He ran his hand over his face and swore. He was at least thirty-five minutes away from where the drone was tracking Rox and the van.

She would be fine. She was used to dying. Said it herself.

Danny spun around in a circle and roared. He didn't want her to die. He wanted a chance to talk to her, not instruct her, but *talk* to her. She was forever rushing from one moment to the next like she were afraid to stop because whatever invisible thing was chasing her would catch up. He wanted to see her laugh, not at herself, but because something tickled her. He wanted to *be* that something.

There was so much sadness in her eyes sometimes that it hurt him just looking at her. He wanted her to see herself the way he saw her. Strong. Brave. Powerful.

But Danny couldn't be in two places at once. If he left the house now and went after her, he would not only be putting himself at risk, but also risking everyone else who relied on him to do his job, and right now that was not going after Rox. Walter had that, and if there was anyone else who could defy aging the way Rox had and still come out on top, it was Walter.

No. Danny would stick to the mission. He would go through the Andersen home, collect all their laptops, phones, and any other devices they had. He would disconnect them from the wireless and bluetooth the way Michael had shown him. Then he would pack a bag for each of the family members with a few changes of clothes, and he would drive all of that to George Bush Intercontinental Airport. He would board a flight to Washington, DC where he would take a train back to Halo.

Just under twenty-four hours. That was how long it was going to take before he saw her. *If* he saw her again. Of course he was going to see her again! This wasn't their first assignment together and neither was this the first assignment where things had gone wrong. Yes, it was the first time she got shot, and yes, it was also the first time she was kidnapped, but she was trained. She would keep her head. She would wait, observe, strike, escape.

"How do you cut the lights off these damn new cars?" Walter said. "They've pulled off onto a dirt path and these lights are a dead giveaway."

"There should be a switch to take the automatic headlights off."

Danny heard Walter swear and then a few seconds later, "Got it."

Walter liked Rox. He was hard on her, but he wouldn't let anything happen to her. He also wouldn't come back without her. They had been through a lot together, Meita had said. Walter was the Dad Rox didn't remember and Rox was the closest connection Walter had to Sam.

Sam. Danny suspected that a lot of the sadness he saw in Rox's eyes was because she was struggling to move on. He understood that. Some people could love many, while others were unlucky enough to only ever love one.

"You need backup?" Danny asked.

Walter was quiet for a moment. "Sweep the house and then go on standby. Don't head to the airport just yet. Shai and I should be able to handle this."

Danny wanted him to say, yes, he needed help, but Walter was right. He and Shaira would be able to handle it.

"Rox'll be coming to pretty soon, and if that's the case, then we should be fine," Walter added.

*Unless she gets shot again.* But he couldn't think like that. They would get her back and then Danny would have a talk with Meita about the Fellowship.

He just found yet another reason to keep on breathing.

~

## Betrayed

August 8th, 2:25am EST

The neon lights on the alarm clock were a minute-by-minute indication of how much sleep Tusk wasn't enjoying. He flipped onto his side and stared into the shadows. An LED strip was placed on the floor along the bathroom wall and was set to sleep mode. It provided enough ambient light for Tusk to make out the chair next to the window. Three days' worth of clothes were thrown over its back. His laptop sat open on the desk beside it. The screen black. Asleep.

Over the years, Tusk had experienced a number of moments when he felt like everything was crashing down around him. There was the time when he discovered Tara's ability to heal, only to discover that her organs and blood samples degraded at a rapid rate. Then there was the time he was prepping her for an experiment, only to return to her room to find her missing. The time Harry got ousted as the leader of Global Frontiers Organization, which began the arduous process of covering their tracks. And, of course, there was the time Katherine and her team closed down Wonderland, followed shortly by Nancy's death – he was stilling grieving her loss. Alchemy was supposed to have been a new start for him, and it was, for a while. He found a new EO with an active ability he was able to replicate. Not in other humans, but he was able to isolate and synthesize the subject's body oils into a sedative one hundredfold more potent than any tranquilizer he had worked with prior. But then GFO discovered his facility in Laos and not only destroyed it, but also turned the local authorities against him, which resulted in his newly acquired head of security being shot in the head. If it weren't for Leona, he wouldn't have made it out alive – or at least un-incarcerated.

But none of those moments compared to the feelings he experienced when he decided to live "off the grid." The intangible constructs of modern society faded away, and with them, the logic that held everything together. It was like being in a freefall with no idea when the bottom would strike. He had learned that erasing his presence entirely was impossible. Even if he could erase every digital footprint he had ever made, people remembered, and people's memories were something he couldn't wipe.

That first year was hard, but then again, it's always hard re-establishing oneself, especially when one didn't have a past they could rely on. Tusk entered a world built on nothing but cash and connections. Credit was only extended after one had spent sufficient time building trust, and that took multiple interactions. Harry had provided the contacts, but it was Tusk who put in the sweat equity. It was *he* who built the trust with the local leaders to ensure their facilities remained off-radar. Tusk managed the doctors, the nurses, the engineers, the tradesmen, the cooks, the cleaners ... he made sure each facility ran independently of the other so that nothing ever linked back to him or to his other projects.

Tusk sat up and leaned his back against the bed's headboard. He was grinding his teeth again, something he hadn't done since those early days off the grid. His gut was trying to tell him something his brain didn't want to hear.

Harry had betrayed him. Tusk didn't want to consider that even as a remote possibility. They had been best friends since college. They held a shared desire to change the world and to create legacy. Harry Carter already had legacy, of course. His family was a Washington political establishment, but Harry wanted to leave his own mark. He wanted his name to be remembered not because of his family but because of what he accomplished independently.

Tusk didn't come from a wealthy family, or a political one. In fact, Tusk came from a cul-de-sac, a family so squarely rooted in middle class there was no way out, just up or down. But Tusk loved science, had a knack for it, and it was his ability to see past the obvious and build a plan for the possible that got him started on his journey.

Tusk could recognize evolved ones. There was no way for him to know what ability they possessed, but he could tell just by being in close proximity to one. That had come in handy many times, but knowing someone was evolved was quite different from isolating the specific genetic sequence that made them so. In fact, despite advances in DNA decoding, the fact still remained that it was incredibly difficult to recreate a specific sequence in another *living* being. The manipulation of stem cells remained the best avenue for turning an un-evolved into an evolved, but even then, the success rate was well below 0.5 percent. There were simply too many variables to account for in a living host.

Tusk squeezed his eyes shut, but the neon numbers remained. He didn't want to believe Harry had sold him out. After all these years? There was so much history between them, so many stories. What did Dr Mallory Fined and AmLife offer him that would make a man betray his oldest friend?

Tusk swung his legs out of the bed and his feet touched the soft carpet. He was staying in a two-bedroom apartment in Georgetown. It was on the top floor, recently renovated, and more than anyone just starting out on their own could afford. It came with a maid who cleaned twice a week and brought fresh flowers and his dry cleaning.

Tusk paced at the foot of his bed as a passing car created slivers of sliding light through his blinds. If Harry had betrayed him, then Tusk really didn't have much time or many options. Dr Fined had a lot more money than he did. She was the daughter of a rich European immigrant who came to the US when she was just a baby. She had access to resources that took him years to accumulate, and still she had more.

What was so wrong about agreeing to her terms anyway? Like Harry said, he would be congressionally appointed.

He would be the voice and the face in Washington for all EO-related issues.

*For now,* a small voice in the back of his head whispered. A woman like Mallory had a plan. Why else secretly embed Leona with him?

Leona had played him for an old fool, and to a certain degree, Tusk was one. But he knew the importance of keeping his research and his findings close to home, and that's why he never shared them. Maybe that's why Mallory approached Harry. Had she realized that Leona was never going to get her hands on Tusk's most prized possessions? That her only way of truly being the "expert" on evolved ones was to hire him? But surely she would've known he would never accept her offer. Tusk was off the grid for a reason. He didn't want to join a committee or a think tank. This was pioneering work, and formal groups had boundaries – ethical boundaries – that could never be crossed.

He thought back to Tara. Harry was confident she was now working for GFO, with Katherine. Harry said he would handle Katherine, but how? And what did that mean for Tara? Had Harry told Mallory about Tara and her abilities? If so, there was no way Mallory would let Tusk continue his experiments on her. She would take over that project without hesitation. It's what he would do.

Tusk sat down in the chair with the clothes hanging off the back and slammed the screen down on his laptop. He would burn everything before allowing his life's work to fall into the hands of someone like Mallory Fined. But then what?

Tusk shook his head and got back to his feet. If Nancy were here, she would know what to do. But she wasn't here. And she would never be again.

His only option was to take Harry's offer and bide his time, but there was no way he was turning over his work to Mallory or her conniving, duplicitous niece, Leona. Everyone thought he was this mad scientist who was too focused on his work to see the forest for the trees, but Tusk saw things with clarity, perhaps more than anyone else. They were in the midst of a global war on who would unlock the genetic code to evolved humans first. Corporations were vying for subjects to test while governments were acting as the supply chain. Tusk wanted nothing to do with either of them because when the code was unlocked, he knew the infighting, backstabbing and betrayals would be explosive. No, he had a plan, and he was sticking to it even if Harry had given up on them.

It was time for Tusk to make some new partners.

~

## Surprise

August 8th, 1:25am CST (-1 EST)

Rox moaned and ran her tongue on the roof of her mouth trying to excite her saliva glands and opened her eyes. She was seated, her arms hanging off to the side. Untied.

She reached out with her energy.

Alone.

A sliver of electricity ran above her head to power

the room's single light source. The dampened hum of a generator pulled at her from behind. It was outside, but she felt its scratch along the base of her neck, seeking a connection that promised pain. Drawing from artificial energy sources did that. It hurt and left her with that inebriated feeling she rarely got from alcohol.

The floor around her feet was dirt, and her blood had seeped its way into the air pockets between each grain. She had been shot. She sat up a bit straighter so she could look down at her chest. Two blackened holes showed where the bullets had been stopped by her vest. The itch signaled that one had gone astray and struck her just below her protective clothing. She had forgotten the burning sensation of a bullet wound, but it all came rushing back to her as she tried to check for additional injury.

Rox would have breathed a sigh of relief if the deep inhalation didn't send pain ricocheting across the center of her back. Four. She had been shot four times. She remembered the girl, the barrel of the gun and the pain of impact. She reached up and felt for the earpiece. It was still there. "Hello?" Her voice was scratchy and sounded faint.

"Paladin?" Both Walter and Danny responded.

"Yeah."

"Did you die?" Walter asked.

No disorientation, no delay in memory recall, and that irresistible itch that encompassed her entire body wasn't there. "No."

"Good. Don't," Walter said. "Shai and I are on foot. I don't know how far away we are, but it can't be too far."

The light flickered overhead and for the briefest of

seconds, the room was cast in darkness. "I'm in some kind of ..." Bunker? It didn't feel like she was underground. She turned around and looked for a window. There was just the one, at the back and too high up for her to look out of without standing on the chair. "A single window." She looked up. "The roof's curved. Metal I think. I can feel a generator out back."

"Does it have a door?" Danny asked.

Walter chuckled. "Sometimes the obvious escapes her; you get used to it."

Rox swallowed her retort. She had just been shot four times. Let's see either one of them get up and move around after that. She reached out with her energy as she walked towards the door. It didn't have a window, so she put her head against it and listened. "I don't hear anything." She grabbed her wrists. The batons were still there. Why had they not taken her weapons? Checked for communication devices or at least tie her up? This was too simple.

"You see anything you can use as a weapon?" Danny asked.

"Still have my batons." She looked around the room. "Think this is some kind of trap?"

No one responded.

The room was bare, like it didn't get much usage. Just a single chair and a desk pushed against one of the walls. She was about to turn back to the door when something caught her attention. A corkboard, above the desk, with notecards and photographs pinned to it. The light flickered again, and she walked through the darkness to the front of the board.

She inhaled through the pain as the door swung open behind her.

"Rox?" It was Danny talking through her earpiece.

She pulled the pin from one of the photographs and turned around to confront the three who had just entered. It was the girl who shot her, Robbie, and some old man.

"Thought you said you shot her four times," the old man said.

"I did!" the girl insisted.

"Why do you have this photo?" Rox asked.

Whatever Robbie's ability was, it didn't make him a fool. He stepped from behind the old man, but kept his distance, his eyes once again locked on her.

"She don't look shot to me," the old man grumbled, and then to Rox, "We'll be asking the questions."

There was a lot that Rox's ability couldn't do. Keenan had taught her how to build an energy shield that would slow down an attacker, but it was useless against a high velocity projectile. She could draw someone's life essence from them until they were unconscious, like Robbie, or dead, like the men who were chasing Ruby and MJ in Laos, but then she had to *do* something with that excess energy. She could drop and do some push-ups, but the bad guys left standing tended not to wait for her to finish her set before resuming their attack. If she took down too many people, she would be on an adrenaline high that was just as dangerous as trying to stop a bullet with an energy shield.

"Who do you work for?" the old man asked.

An orange glaze fell over everything as Rox drew from

Robbie again, sending him face down first onto the dirt floor, permanently.

"What the—"

The girl fumbled with her weapon, but this time Rox was prepared. She raised her hand and a single thread of electricity shot out of her palm and slammed into the girl, knocking her body back against the wall and shaking the roof of the bunker.

The old man's weapon was drawn, but the light flickered out as a wolf's howl pierced the silence.

Danny told Rox that in close quarters, a gun was less effective than a knife or her baton. The key was to keep moving, keep advancing.

Gunfire created a momentary flash of light as Rox stepped to the side and extended her batons. She heard the bones in the old man's hand crack. She dropped to her knee and used her left baton to swipe his legs out from under him. The light came back on and then off again as she brought the end of her baton down into his stomach.

The air burst from his lungs at the same time the door flew off its hinges under Shaira's weight. She was wearing her own compression vest as she walked into the room, her teeth bared and her fur standing like porcupine needles.

"Down!" Rox had to shout it twice before Shaira's growl quieted. The wolf stalked around the room, her body tense and her teeth still visible. She went over to the girl and sniffed, then gave a low growl before coming to rub her body against Rox.

The old man was still winded when the light came back on. Rox retrieved his gun and checked the chamber.

"Sit up," she said, but the old man's attention was held by Shaira.

Rox repeated herself before the man looked at her and slowly pushed up using his one good hand.

"Who are you?" he asked.

"Why do you have this picture?" It was a profile photo of Josh. It was just a headshot, barely captured his shoulders, but he was dressed in a black suit from the looks of it. Perhaps a tuxedo because of the bowtie. His eyes held a sparkle and his lips were curved up like his smile was genuine, and that made Rox think of Samantha, his girlfriend.

"Y-you know him?"

The orange tint that had settled over Rox's vision intensified. She didn't like violence. Keenan said violence was what happened when the "intellectual" argument was lost, but right now that photo represented a danger to her family, and that was something she simply could not abide – she *would not* abide.

"Why do you have his photo?"

Rox knew that Shaira was watching the old man, so she went to the corkboard and read the notecards. It had "Josh Mendez" written in black ink, and the word *evolved* was underlined.

Josh had become somewhat of a public figure for their kind. Ever since they joined Halo, he had become even more vocal about his support for evolved ones.

Walter had disagreed with him, of course. Walter took a more pragmatic stance towards humanity. He believed people only got involved when the war was at their doorstep, and he believed there were far too few ordinary humans being affected by EO troubles to actually "put skin in the game." He said that going public only put Josh and his company at risk, and choosing a side too early, even if it were the right side, could be just as dangerous as choosing the wrong one.

Rox took down the other two photos on the wall. There was an X drawn across the faces. No name cards underneath the photos. "You still haven't answered me. Why do you have this photo?" She walked back to the old man. He was cradling his hand against his chest, his eyes swinging like a pendulum between her and Shaira.

"We think he's evolved," the man said.

"And?" Rox looked up when Walter entered the room. He looked at Robbie, the girl, and then the old man on the ground.

"He talking?" Walter asked.

"He was just about to tell me why he has a photo of Josh."

"Josh?" Danny said into her earpiece.

"Yep." Rox nodded at the old man on the floor. "Talk!"

"We have orders to capture on sight if we see him," the old man said. "But, but we never saw him." He looked over his shoulder at Walter who was now checking the pockets of the two Rox had disposed of.

"Why?" Rox said. "What were you going to do if you 'captured' him?"

The old man shook his head like he was stalling for time. Rox gave a sharp whistle, and Shaira stood up from her seated position. The wolf took a step closer to the man on the dirt floor and bared her teeth.

Rox wasn't going to ask again. She was going to let Shaira work off some of that built-up adrenaline coursing through her body. Rox wouldn't let the wolf kill the old man – she would heal him, at first.

"What's your name?" Walter asked as he came over to stand beside them.

The old man was dressed in green army fatigues like at one point in his life, he had served. The rolls around his midsection announced that his service had been some time ago. He was about Walter's age, if Rox had to guess, but there was a world of difference between the two men.

"Ben. Folks call me Uncle Ben."

Walter nodded. "You served?"

Ben nodded. "You?"

Walter nodded again. "Well, from one vet to another, I'm gonna let my wolf here eat off half your face if you don't answer this lady's questions."

Rox was surprised. Walter had never called her "lady".

Ben looked at the wolf and then back at Rox. "We have a number to call. I can get it for you."

"Where is it?" Walter asked.

"My phone. It's in my pocket."

"Stand up," Rox said. "Slowly!"

Ben rolled over and pushed up to his feet. He used his good hand to reach into his pocket and pulled out his phone. He wasn't sure who to pass it to, so Rox reached out and took it.

"Turn it off," Danny said into her earpiece.

"Don't we want to see who he's supposed to contact?" Rox asked.

"Once we get it back to Meita, but right now, it's better if we turn it off."

Rox held the button on the side until the screen turned black. "Have you heard from PB?"

"I'll have Po check in with him," Danny said.

It was highly unlikely this was some kind of diversion to isolate Josh, but she wasn't taking any chances. Josh was like a … How did she begin to explain her relationship with him? He was the father of her adopted son, Jay, and the first person she remembered since waking up over six years ago without memory. He was a manipulating bastard who stuck his nose into everything, but he was also her first love, or at least the first love she actually remembered, and he was the one person whom she could always count on.

"What do you wanna do with 'em?" Walter asked.

Rox looked at the two unconscious bodies and then back at Ben. She was field lead and it was her responsibility to determine if the Fellowship were a threat to her team or their current mission. "Where's the other two?" Rox asked Ben.

"You mean the other two from the gas station?" Walter interrupted. "I hogtied them inside the little shed next to this one."

Ben's shoulders dropped like he had been hoping they would burst in to save him.

"Any idea how many more on site?" Rox asked.

Walter shrugged, but it was Danny who spoke. "Drone shows no one else."

"What is this place?" Rox asked.

"It's nothing more than a place I use for meet-ups and

mission preps," Ben said, his voice shaking.

"Contact Eagle Eyes," Rox said to Danny, finally answering Walter's question. "Tell her we came across five Fellowship members, and give her the coordinates." Meita would cover their tracks.

"Wait! What are you going to do with us? They're just kids—"

Rox stepped closer so their faces were only inches apart. "And so are Chris and Jenny." She pulled his energy from him and watched as he crumbled backwards. The Rox of two years ago might have stopped, but she was learning that some problems needed more permanent solutions or they simply re-sprouted. The room took on an orange tint as the energy she had consumed needed to be exorcised.

"I hope it's a long walk back to the car."

# CHAPTER THREE

## Towards home

Date/Time: Unknown

His fingers slipped into the cracks of the rock surface, and he pushed up with his knees, leaning into the mountain as he climbed. The wind bit into his exposed skin, reminding him he had never experienced a cold like this. His right ear, the one not flush with the mountainside, was numb from the cold, and the roaring of the wind threatened to take him with it as it flew past.

The sun was just coming over the horizon, but Sam had started his ascent at first light. He hated leaving Neo behind, and he prayed the animal wouldn't follow once he realized Sam wasn't returning. He would be confused since Sam had left his staff behind. He would assume that Sam would be returning for it. But climbing with a bear's fur was hard enough. A staff almost equal to his body length strapped to his back would have definitely tipped his ascent in gravity's favor.

White clouds rushed by overhead. Sometimes, they felt so close he thought he could reach up and touch them, but that was just an illusion. He was at least another hour or two away by his estimate. He had no idea what lay above those clouds or how tall the mountain was, but somewhere up above him was the reason for his climb.

Lightning. Even on the darkest of nights, it would illuminate the mountain against a charcoal gray background, and every now and again, it would shoot out of the clouds and strike the mountain, creating a clap of thunder that made him think of earth shifting.

Sam had begun to struggle with his thoughts recently, but he remembered his training and spoke to himself often. He spoke to Neo, too. But an active imagination was never a substitute for human contact. People needed people. It was in their DNA. Humans created communities. They needed to belong.

He leaned back to see if he could catch sight of Neo at the base below and almost lost his grip when a gust of wind whipped down, trying to separate him from his perch. He screamed out as the fingers on his left hand clung to the crevice, his left arm straining against the pressure trying to push him free. He tried to use his ability, but still it evaded him. Then, just like that, the wind dispersed and he was once again pressed close to the one hope he had of getting home.

Sam leaned into the wall and breathed in the sweet, cold air as he tried to slow his heart and stop his limbs from shaking. Up here, the air was different, almost neutral, lacking any aroma but that of dirt and copper.

He hadn't been able to use his ability since he had woken up, and by his calculations, that was about two years ago. Even if he still had it, how many three seconds were between whenever he was and the time he was trying to return to? No, lightning had brought him here, and he had a feeling it was going to be the same thing to get him home.

A small part of him considered that it might not work and being struck by lightning would very likely be a death sentence. But he had come to terms with that.

Sam tried not to think back to the first time he had attempted to kill himself. It was his father's voice that broke through to him, begging him not to end it and reminding Sam he was the last vestige of his mother.

The tears pooling in his eyes were quickly dried by the wind as he pushed up. His fingertips blindly sought another crevice from which he could gain leverage to continue his journey upwards. His boots were made for performance, but not the climbing kind. The toes were too wide and thick for him to push into the small cracks that he could use for leverage, but Sam didn't dare discard them. The only reason he still had all his toes was because of those boots. The laces had broken not long after he arrived, but he simply tied them back together.

Two years of hunting for each meal meant he had lost a fair bit of weight. But finding sustenance was only part of the reason he was still alive. Neo was the other. They had created a partnership that not only sustained Sam physically, but also mentally.

Whenever Sam allowed himself to reminisce, he'd conjure up an image of Shaira. Did she miss him? Did she think him dead? Walter wouldn't accept his death without a body and neither would Mika. A tightness in Sam's chest threatened to sap his energy at the thought of his younger brother, but Sam laughed through the pain of the memories and the sorrow he knew his absence was causing his family. Had his sister recovered by now? Was she back to her old self? He doubted it. If there was one thing he'd learned in his time here, it was that there was never any return to one's old self. People just moved forward, carrying with them the scars of the past.

"Rox." He hadn't meant to speak her name. He laid his head against the cold face of the mountain for a moment and simply breathed the fresh air into his lungs.

He didn't know how he felt about her anymore. Some days he hated her with the same fervor that made him love her. He tried so hard not to blame her for this. Hell, she was, after all, struck by lightning, too. He had no idea if she still lived. But the memory of her pulses left him yearning for her in ways that made him feel uncomfortable, and those feelings only increased the loneliness and helplessness that threatened to consume him each and every waking moment over the last two winters.

But anger was necessary sometimes. It helped him to find purpose. It focused him. It motivated him to action when too many other emotions left him paralyzed. On days when the solitude threatened to take him under, he got angry, and he let it grow until it rolled out of him in great shouts of fury.

Sam looked up at the bright sky and the clouds still racing overhead. Winter was practically here, and while it was going to get a lot colder, the temperature wouldn't matter if he fell off the side of the mountain. He needed to focus because when he got to the top and the lightning he had been chasing for months came slicing through the sky towards him, his only option was to be ready.

His foot found its next perch, and he pushed up with his knees towards home.

~

**Kelley Michiko Yasuda**

August 8th, 12:00pm EST

Katherine Louise Cheung had been in her current line of work for over twenty years. She liked her job. She believed in what she did, but she didn't always like the people she was forced to work with. The problem, Katherine had come to realize, was that she had little faith in humanity. The overwhelming majority of people were little more than functioning apes, sheep, loud-mouthed ignoramuses put on this planet, and specifically in her country, to test her patience. And what reward would she reap for tolerating them? Nothing, because Katherine didn't believe in an afterlife. This was all there was, and even though she spent the overwhelming majority of her days in meetings taking deep breaths and curving her lips into fake smiles as she painted the "bigger picture" for people who were only interested in what they could hold in their hands, she couldn't see a future doing anything different.

It was her petition for Article 31 that led to a special assembly meeting at the United Nations, where fifty-one members voted to add specific language covering evolved ones under the Universal Declaration of Human Rights. It had been an intense debate. Many nations said that singling out evolved ones meant they were inherently different from normal humans, which was contrary to the overall aim the petition was trying to achieve, and therefore, unnecessary. But it was the ambassador from Kenya who pointed out that while we were all humans, countries often and frequently created laws "singling" out minority groups who, through no fault of their own, were oppressed and/or faced discrimination because of a "majority tribe-like mentality".

That was a victory for which Katherine would receive no accolades. Her role operated from the shadows, which suited her fine because she lacked the personality or the public appeal to create the sentiment for change needed to benefit evolved ones. Besides, there was still more work to do beyond the public's purview.

Katherine tilted her head to the right and curled her lips into a smile. "I get it. No one wants to get in a fight they don't need to be involved in. Especially in your position. But your mother and I go a long way back, Kelley, and she wouldn't have asked you to meet me if she didn't understand the importance of what I'm asking of you."

Once upon a time, women didn't frequent this type of establishment. It was a place where deals were made, ideas for policies debated, careers were launched and a good few brought to an abrupt end.

Kelley sat in the chair with her back straight like she could be the restaurant's owner, but then she lowered her eyes and looked at the food before her as if she couldn't decide which to taste first, the soup or the bread roll beside it.

The decor still screamed misogynist with its dark paneling, male staff, and the "Members Only" cigar parlor off to the side, but women didn't come here for the ambience. Like men, they came here to build alliances.

Kelley picked up her soup spoon and dipped it into the bowl, scooping away from her and then carefully bringing it to her lips. She was nervous, but a woman in her position would be accustomed to the adrenaline rush; therefore, her hand remained steady despite the slight flare of her nostrils.

Kelley was Asian thin, but had a natural tan to her skin that most Asians would never achieve. Her hair was naturally a charcoal black and cut to just below her shoulders. It had a soft curl that would cost a fortune in a salon and never last past the first wash. Her nails were kept short and painted an inconspicuous pink – her lipstick matched. Reputation had it that Kelley was soft-spoken, but no one ever wanted to debate her. She had the mind of a master strategist who was able to take in the big picture, then quickly assess each of the smaller angles before finally forming an argument to support any of them, or none of them at all. She was the type of woman Katherine would love to have on her team but was currently too young to provide the kind of benefit Katherine needed on an ongoing basis. That was okay, however. Kelley could be groomed.

Kelley Michiko Yasuda was half Japanese and half Black American. Her father transferred to Asia with a global financial news organization, and after spending a few years in Hong Kong, then in Singapore, he moved to Japan where he met Kelley's mother, Michiko, who had attended university in the US. Kelley was born a few years later and spent her first ten years in Japan, but when her father died, Michiko took her daughter to America so Kelley could be more exposed to her father's culture.

"He's a senior senator," Kelley said after she took a sip of water.

Katherine nodded. Harry Carter was indeed a senior senator. The world was privy to that bit of information.

Katherine continued to stare at the young woman seated across from her, not making direct eye contact – that would be too aggressive – but looking at Kelley's nose, her mouth or the bangs that were swept softly to the side, but would fall back in front of her left eye whenever she tilted her head. It was a nervous tilt, an unconscious tell that Kelley more than likely had no idea she performed.

Most people were largely the same. It didn't matter which country they originated from; they all wanted the same things for the most part. However, it was the little things that created the nuances. For example, North Americans were a gregarious lot. They chatted easily with just about anyone from anywhere. They were easygoing and friendly. Silence between them created discomfort, and so they would say anything to fill it.

Silence to Asians, however, was golden. It was where ruminations sat, the truth lied, and the path to unhinging your enemy, especially the Westerner, was stretched out before them.

Katherine, like Kelley, danced between the two cultures seamlessly, instinctively using the strengths of both to their own personal advantages. The true challenge came when sitting across from someone who knew the unwritten rule book from which the other operated. Katherine was certain that Kelley's mind was playing chess with itself, constructing the most plausible scenarios if she sided with Katherine, and if she did not. The problem Kelley would run into would be one that couldn't be strategically resolved. Her problem, of course, would be her conscience. It was an easy no-brainer *not* to help Katherine, especially at the risk of making an enemy out of Harry Carter. But Kelley was a minority living in a majority, and one thing history would have taught her was that discrimination against one *always* led to discrimination against all. If Kelley turned her back on the evolved ones, it would be akin to turning her back on her heritage. And that, Katherine believed, would be against everything her mother had taught her.

Katherine's watch vibrated, alerting her that she had an incoming call. To answer it would be to signal to Kelley there was something more important than her decision to help, but truth be told, there was nothing more important than Kelley's decision.

So they sat, neither of them saying anything as they worked through their individual thoughts.

"I need time," Kelley said.

Katherine nodded, curling her lips into a smile. She liked Kelley's mom, Michiko. Michiko had a sharp wit that Katherine believed came with having to juggle multiple languages and different cultures in one's head simultaneously. She was grateful to see that sharp wit had been passed down to Kelley.

"Of course." Katherine lifted her napkin off her lap and placed it beside her plate of untouched salmon cakes. "I hope that I never have to reach out to you, Kelley, not under these circumstances at least. But if the need arises, my associate, Henry, will contact you, and then you will need to make your choice."

"How will I know this Henry?"

Katherine smiled. "He will tell you the story of why your last name is not the same as your father's and is instead your mother's maiden name."

Kelley reached up to tuck her bangs behind her ear. "What do you have on my mother?"

In truth, Katherine had nothing on Michiko. The two Asian women – one Japanese, the other American – bonded while at university and kept in touch off and on over the years. Katherine had attended Kelley's father's funeral, but doubted the young girl remembered. It was probably best that way. Kelley's choice had to be one based on belief and not out of family obligation. Obligation, at some point, ran out. Belief, on the contrary, lasted generations.

"Nothing," Katherine said. "I simply asked for a favor."

"Does she know?" Kelley asked. "What you do?"

"I think it's best she knows only what she needs to know, don't you?"

Kelley nodded like she were slow to agree. "Don't contact my mom ever again."

Katherine inhaled a slow breath. "To not contact her

ever again would be more telling than to contact her, Kelley. She and I are friends."

"My mom has nothing to do with my decision."

Katherine leaned forward. "I couldn't agree more." She pushed back her chair as if readying to stand. "The bill has been taken care of. You're welcome to remain here for as long as you like."

Katherine smiled before she turned and walked away. She passed the placard that read "Ladies" and continued to the door labeled "Members Only". Katherine was not a fan of cigars, but she had smoked her share. She went to the cloakroom and gave her ticket to the attendant.

"One moment." He disappeared behind a velvet curtain so thick and faded it made Katherine wonder if it had been there since the establishment first opened. He returned and passed her the shawl she had checked yesterday. He waited until she had it wrapped around her shoulders before he extended a box of cigars sheathed in gold paper. He tipped his head as if giving the slightest of bows to her. "These were on hold for you just as you requested."

Katherine curled her lips into a smile and said thank you. Instead of walking through the doors into the main parlor, she followed the clerk behind the counter and waited silently as he unlocked a side door that led out into the alley.

Washington, DC in August was beautiful. It was the end of summer, but the heat still lingered like it wasn't ready to give up its turn to cooler weather. Katherine hung her handbag in the curve of her elbow and inhaled a deep breath. Gold wrapping meant she was being followed; therefore, it was likely her meeting with Kelley was exposed. There was nothing she could do about that now. She doubted anyone would approach Kelley, but she may be surveilled, though that might prove troublesome given Kelley's position. In a perfect world, Katherine would never have to approach the young Chief of Staff, but the world they lived in was far from perfect, and women as talented and as smart as Kelley didn't get to sit on the sidelines.

Katherine turned onto M Street and tucked the cigar box under her arm. She flipped open her bag and pulled out her mobile phone. After a few seconds, Henry answered.

"How was your lunch, ma'am?"

"I've had better," she said. "But I've also had worst."

"I'm sorry to hear that. For those prices, I'd expect each meal to be exquisite."

Katherine gave a genuine laugh. Three years ago, she wasn't sure the word "exquisite" existed in Henry's vocabulary. But a lot had changed since then. He had changed.

"Henry?"

"Yes, ma'am?"

"Have you located the missing package?"

"I'm afraid not, ma'am, but know that I won't stop until I find it."

Gold wrapping plus nothing more on Meita … Katherine slowed her pace and lifted her face up to the sun. It really was a gorgeous day. "Cancel my appointments for this afternoon. I'm going to yoga."

Henry coughed like he was swallowing something that had gone down the wrong way. "Okay. I'll let your appointments know."

"One last thing."

"Anything."

"In my safe, you'll find the details for my three o'clock."

"I'll handle it personally, ma'am."

She ended her call and flipped the phone over so she could remove the SIM card. She pulled her silver nail clippers out of the zippered compartment in her handbag and clipped the card in two pieces. She dropped one piece between the bars in the grate at the edge of the curb and carried on down the street like she was simply enjoying a long walk after a meal.

The thing about most major cities in the US was that homeless people were drawn to them. They often had more social services to help those in need, and they had the added benefit of creating camouflage for those wishing to remain unseen. An older man dressed in a surplus army fatigue jacket that smelled like it had been worn throughout the summer sat talking to himself a few blocks later.

He looked up at her as she approached, not sure if she were going to shoo him along or offer him a few coins towards a hot meal. "Take this. Get yourself something to eat."

The man looked up at her in confusion. She doubted he had ever been given a phone before, and he appeared hesitant to take it. He looked Katherine over like he was trying to decide why an Asian woman dressed in an expensive suit would give him anything, let alone a phone. "It stolen?"

Katherine shook her head. "No, it's mine; I just don't need it anymore."

"The police ain't gonna come looking for me, is they? I ain't looking for no trouble."

Katherine thought back to Rox and the years she had spent on the street. How long had she gone without a hot shower? A hot meal? Or the simple act of being noticed? "Some really bad people have found me, and I need to disappear."

"I don't want no trouble, I said."

"No. They'll know I gave it to you, but that just means they'll also know that I know they're on to me." Katherine wasn't sure he followed her logic. "Look, you don't have to take it. I'll just leave it here, and it'll be your choice." She placed the phone on the ground beside him. "Take care of yourself."

"I need to be saying that to you," he grumbled. "You ain't got nobody to call who can help you?"

Katherine stopped and looked back at him. By any modern standards, he had very little, arguably nothing, yet his question showed that he cared. Maybe not enough to do anything, but inside of that coat was a human being, and she was surprised just how easy it was to forget that about certain kinds of people.

"Is there anyone I can call for you, sir?"

He picked up her phone and turned it over in suspicion. "Don't reckon nobody in all my life has ever called me sir." He looked up at her and nodded his thanks. He was taking the phone. "You take care of yourself, hear? These streets, they eat a sweet, pretty thing like you for breakfast, and spit ya out 'fore lunch."

Katherine smiled. "Not if I eat them first."

~

## Threats and yoga

August 8th, 3:00pm EST

Keenan stepped through the sliding doors from customs out into the main terminal of Baltimore/Washington International Thurgood Marshall Airport. He resisted the temptation to inhale deeply. In this part of the airport, the air was heavy with auto exhaust fumes and aviation fuel.

Keenan did not like air travel. Too many pollutants, too many constraints, far too many people. He preferred the train. When he was young, he would have never dreamt of being able to cross the Atlantic Ocean in just over eight hours. In fact, when he was young, he had no knowledge of how expansive the world was. It would be a few lifetimes before he learned of the existence of other countries and cultures beyond his borders.

At this hour, the airport was busy with travelers and their entourages. There was a queue at a coffee shop with impatient customers waiting for their sugar-based caffeine fix and pre-wrapped, processed sandwiches. Keenan went to the adjacent newsagent stand and looked at the books on offer, some pulp, some meaty, but all of them promising an escape from the present. He remembered a time before books, when stories were recited and then remembered, and the storyteller was lauded. Then there was the advent of motion pictures, which gave birth to the cinematic revolution. The art of storytelling changed and people feared it meant the death of books. But the pen was more powerful than most recognized.

Keenan picked up a newspaper and inhaled. There was something about the smell of the ink against the fabric of paper that reopened his nasal passages and helped him to purify the surrounding air. He looked over the edge at the people either on their way out or just arrived.

Americans. They all took such pride in being different from one another. When he was a child, to be different was to be ostracized. To be a part of a village increased one's chances of survival. Each member had a role to play, and more than likely, that role would be passed down through the generations. Individuality was frowned upon and often exorcised from the community. Most of history was written similarly. But then America emerged, and with it a vocal advocate for individuality that superseded the collective needs of the majority.

In all his years of living, Keenan had never experienced another nation quite like this one. He had even lived here for a while. He did not like it, though – too brash – but America, he decided, had a way of earning one's respect, even if done so begrudgingly.

"Mr Kenan Amara Ward Browne?"

Keenan slowly lowered the newspaper. There was only one person alive who knew the name he had amalgamated over the years. Keenan was born during a time when names were practical and purposefully short. Villages were made of family and extended family, which meant there was little confusion about who was who. Often, a given name was enough. The only distinguisher would be by trade. There was no registry of births or deaths. Life was simpler then. It was also harder. "And who is asking?"

"Ms Cheung sent me."

Keenan nodded, but did not move to follow. He reached inside his suit jacket to check his phone. No messages from her, and his phone had switched over to one of the local carriers. He was confident that no one could have learned his full name without Katherine, which should put him at ease and bring validity to the story of the gentleman standing in front of him, but Katherine had sworn an oath of secrecy, one he had extracted from her using the old methods. Few people knew about his relationship with her, and they both agreed that was for the best; therefore, there were only two paths that could have led to this moment: either his existence had been extricated from Katherine using enhanced interrogation techniques or she had sent this man to collect him.

But why him? Why not someone Keenan knew and trusted?

"If you could just come with me," the man said as he approached, trying to keep his voice low. "I can explain everything."

Why not Rox? "What is your name?"

The man nodded, like it was a good question. "Henry. I work for Ms Cheung."

*Henry* … "I am afraid you have the wrong person."

"Wait." Henry stepped forward like he wanted to take hold of him, but then thought better of it. "She needs your help."

He had no doubt that Katherine needed his help, but

the question was why send Henry and not Rox? Maybe it was Rox who was in trouble. He had been training her for two years now and she was a fast student. An impatient one as well, but she was still new in her abilities and no one exhibited a mastery of impatience like the young.

Keenan felt a certain responsibility towards Rox. She was older than he was when he first gained his ability, but he understood what she had gone through, what she was still going through – the memory loss and confusion, the need for answers even though there were none. But science had come a long way since he first became a healer. At that time, the world he knew had not yet developed science. Superstition was God. Rox may not have the answers to her questions about why, but at least now she knew *what* she was.

Keenan took in Henry's attire. Katherine would not have sent him dressed as he was. He was wearing jeans that left enough room for extended leg movement and a pair of sensible black shoes that would enable him to run. But his suit jacket hugged his shoulders like the stitching would rip with any sudden, exaggerated movements, and the length hung a little too high above his waist. It obviously did not belong to him and was more than likely a hasty purchase (or misappropriation) in a failed attempt to look the part of a driver. But a driver Henry was not. Everything about the young man announced he had a job that required him to be in top physical condition. He took care of his body and his skin was healthy and taut around his face and neck. He lived a lifestyle that involved a heavy cardio routine because no matter how much air

Keenan syphoned from under Henry's nose, he was able to stay upright and focused.

"Do you know who I am?" Keenan asked.

Henry looked confused and reached up to wipe the sweat from his forehead. "Kenan Amara Ward Browne?"

"The rise in your heart rate and the increase in body temperature are because I am interfering with your vascular system. I am not one you should deceive, young Henry."

Henry took a step back, but then stopped. "They found her. And I don't know what they're going to do if they get her. But she told me that I was to meet you here and you'd know what to do."

"Then let us go," Keenan said. "But Henry, if you betray me, I will suffocate you and then I will do the same to everyone who shares your bloodline."

Henry hesitated, but then slowly nodded. "Um … okay?"

"I do not do threats. I either do or I do not." Most people would make such a threat as a mere scare tactic, but Keenan had lived long enough to know that wiping out an entire bloodline was often the only way to ensure there would be no future acts of vengeance.

Henry nodded again, but this time with a hint of a smile on his lips. "She said if you said that, I am to tell you that she went to yoga."

A powerful wind blew through the terminal and picked up the edges of the newspapers resting on a crate. Henry glanced over his shoulder at the rotating doors leading outside, but Keenan's focus was elsewhere. A gray filter settled over his vision, eliminating all shades of color. "When was the last time you spoke to her?"

Henry turned back to him. "Almost two hours ago."

Keenan reached back in his suit jacket for his mobile. He needed to get in touch with Rox. If Katherine was in danger, then they all were in danger.

"How far are we from Connecticut?"

Henry shook his head. "I don't know. Three to four hours to New York, and then another two hours I guess from there? Six? I say six hours. Why?"

"Because Katherine hates yoga."

~

## Soulmate

August 8th, 4:00pm EST / August 9th, 4:00am SGT
(+12 EST)
Bedok, Singapore

Dr Dottie Dotz rolled over aware that she was in some kind of lucid dream that made it possible for the voices to communicate more easily with her. They were whispering that someone was coming, but each time she asked who, something in the dream made it impossible for her to hear. First it was the swarm of bees that built a nest in her ears. Despite the absurdity of that, it made sense in the confinement of her dream, and so she went about shaking her head from side-to-side until they were dislodged. When the last of the honey dripped free, an elevated train flew past using the clouds as tracks, its whistle preventing her from hearing once again. Next, she found herself standing adjacent to a tree that produced cars. The rhythmic sound of a chainsaw cutting the branches on which the automobiles grew drowned out the voices' words.

This, Dr Dotz had come to learn, was the voices' way of expressing their desire for a more conscious audience. But she was tired. She didn't know the exact time, but she knew it was too early for the morning sun, which meant she had at least another hour – perhaps two – before she needed to start her day. The voices would have to wait.

Over the years, she had asked them repeatedly to respect her privacy, as well as her need for uninterrupted sleep, but they rarely listened. Her relationship with them was mostly one-sided.

The voices had been with her for twenty-six years, and in that time, she had never once learned how to effectively block them out. When they first started talking to her, she thought it had something to do with puberty and her changing hormones, but as the voices became more insistent and began to tell her the answers to questions before they were asked, she knew something was wrong. Initially, she sought help from her family, who turned to a respected psychiatrist and family friend. In hindsight, the medication she was prescribed did nothing to quiet the voices. It just made it more difficult for her to sleep, to think even. Her thoughts became elusive, like they were close enough to formulate, but too far away to verbalize. In fact, while she was on the meds, the voices increased their interactions with her, often interrupting her mid-conversation. Five years ago, she weaned herself off the medication, and that was when everything changed.

*He's coming.*

*I heard you! But if you're not going to tell me who,* Dotz responded, *I'm going back to sleep.*

But it was too late, and they knew it. She was awake.

"Wanna talk about it?" Mal asked.

Her eyes slid opened and she reached for her husband, but the space beside her was empty. He was sitting in the chair in the corner of their bedroom, dressed and waiting, like he knew the sequence of events about to play out.

"Did I wake you?" she asked.

Mal stood up and laid a pair of trousers and a matching t-shirt at the end of their bed. "Not really."

Which meant she had.

*He's coming.*

Dotz sat up and rested her forehead on the heel of her palm. *I'm up!*

*Don't be late.*

*For what?*

"They being cryptic again?"

Hearing voices was not like most people thought. They didn't tell her she was special or some kind of messiah, neither did they tell her that she should harm herself or anyone else. In fact, the voices were great to have around as long as she wasn't trying to have an intimate moment with her husband. Or trying to sleep.

*He's coming.*

"Yeah," she finally answered. "You've said."

"Is it urgent?" Mal asked, accustomed to the interruptions.

It was hard to determine what was urgent with them. Their understanding of time was different than hers.

*You must be there first.*

Dotz pulled back the covers and stood up into a stretch. "When *isn't* it urgent?"

"What are they saying?"

She grabbed the trousers he had placed on the bed for her and began to dress. "Something about 'he's coming'."

"Who's coming?"

She sat down hard on the edge of the bed and sighed. "I wish I knew."

Mal turned on the lamp. "Do *you* think it's urgent?"

A tired smile slipped across her face. There were just as many times when they had shared time-sensitive information with her as they had led her on a fool's errand. There was never any way of knowing without following through with their wishes.

Mal sat down beside her, and she laid her head on his shoulder.

"Well, we're up. What'd'ya want to do?" he asked.

She sighed. "We need anything from the grocery store?"

Mal chuckled. "I was thinking we could watch a movie."

"At this hour?"

"There's that new all-night cinema."

She had forgotten about that. She lifted her head and kissed her husband on his cheek.

It would be their fourth anniversary soon. Sometimes, she couldn't believe her luck in finding a man so attentive, but she knew luck had nothing to do with it. She had been engaged to Mika when she met Mal, and while the voices had liked Mika, they liked Mal better. They had warned her that Mika wasn't meant for her and had his own path with someone who would love him more. It had been an awkward break-up, mostly because Mika didn't believe her when she explained her reasoning to him. They both said things they later regretted, and now, they mostly tried to stay out of one another's way. But that was surprisingly hard to do when his uncle was her mentor, not to mention their families had known one another for generations. There wasn't a birthday celebrated when they weren't forced to endure each other's presence.

Now they were a team. Southeast Asia's own version of Halo, headquartered in Singapore. It was exhilarating work, and they were developing an amicable relationship. Slowly.

"Alright, what shall we see?" Mal stood up and turned to face her so he could pull her to her feet and then into his arms. "Though, I'm not sure we have a lot of choices. Shall we just head into town and see what's on?"

Dotz stood up on her toes with the practiced ease of someone who had been in ballet for over a decade and kissed her husband on his lips. "What would I do without you?"

"I'm hoping you never have to find out." He raised an eyebrow and nodded back toward the bed. "Bed or movies?"

She laughed and shook her head. "They'd never let me enjoy it. Not now that I've purposefully ignored them."

Instead of the look of disappointment she knew any other guy would have given her, he nodded as if he understood. Perhaps the voices were right, and she *had* found her soulmate.

*You don't want to be late.*

Mal stepped back out of her embrace to help her dress. Afterwards, she followed her husband out of their HDB flat into the night-time humidity of Singapore.

It was dark, but the streetlights and road signs gave off enough light to remind them they were in a metropolis. They lived in Bedok, a popular neighborhood for its close proximity to good schools as well as restaurants and shopping. At this hour, everything was closed, so they decided to cross over the main road and walk along the side of Bedok Reservoir. Singapore was one of the safest nations on the planet, and that was something Dotz never took for granted. The voices shared enough with her that she was aware just how fortunate she was to have grown up on this tiny red dot.

"Have they said anything else?" Mal asked.

The voices had quieted, and Dotz wasn't sure if it was because they had lost interest in whatever they had been saying or if they had realized she wasn't giving in to their wishes at the moment. Either way, she was grateful for the temporary reprieve. Sure, they would come back and she would have to eventually figure out *who* was coming, but then again, it was equally likely they could whisper something entirely different to her.

She walked hand-in-hand with Mal until daylight arrived and the streets grew a little busier with people at the start of their morning routine. Mal signaled to a yellow taxi at the traffic light. Its green "TAXI" sign was lit.

The driver asked where to, and Mal told him Orchard Road.

Dotz rested her head against Mal's shoulder and

yawned as he pulled out his phone and searched the movie times.

*He's coming soon. Don't be late. He won't be alone.*

## Boxed In

August 8th, 4:30pm EST

The drug they gave Meita made her mouth dry, and for some reason that made the clattering of her teeth more painful. She rubbed her hands down her arms and tried to keep moving, but her muscles ached. The room tilted a little, and she wasn't sure if it were imagined or real.

She tried to make sense of her surroundings, but there was little to go on. Someone had stripped her of her clothing and left her naked. Her toes had lost feeling some time ago, and her hair had been released from its tie to fall loose and tangled around her head.

Meita knew this was meant to demean and disorient. Take away her clothing and that made her less human and more of an animal. A uniform would mean they were trying to chip away at her individuality and confidence. Keeping her cold weakened her resolve, not to mention tightened her muscles and made it harder for her to be in good physical condition to successfully escape. Extreme bright lighting was a classic sleep deprivation technique that would reduce the speed of her thinking as well as the quality of her decision-making. Currently, however, she was in the dark. A blackness that prohibited her from using spatial awareness to form a sense of time and place against her surroundings.

It was getting harder to fight the drowsiness that came in powerful waves. Each time she drifted off, the row of lights in the ceiling would switch on and the brightness would jolt her out of her slumber. It was far too bright for her to keep her eyes open, and she would cover them with her hands as a shield against the pain.

Meita ran through the list of people who knew about her let alone those who had the means to actually capture her. The last thing she remembered was sitting on the Metro, the train heading to … Where was she going? And how did they get her off public transportation? She would not have gone willingly. She would've fought back, and that would've have brought the authorities. They had to have found a way to inconspicuously incapacitate her. But how?

She shook her head, trying to clear away the fog, but instead set the room spinning. She desperately wanted to lie down, but there was no furniture and the floor was deliberately kept too cold to be a makeshift bed.

Meita wasn't sure how long she had been here, but she was sure wherever she was represented trouble. There were protocols in place that would alert the right people if she went missing, but knowing she was unaccounted for and finding her were two very different scenarios.

She shook her head again, but this time welcomed the shift in equilibrium. It broke her train of thought and allowed her to refocus. The dark was designed to kill hope, to leave her feeling alone and isolated. *It was working.*

When was the last time she checked in? Henry would contact Katherine if she was late.

A giggle slipped up her stomach and out of her mouth at the thought of Henry. He was far too nice to immediately report her missed check-in to Katherine. Instead, he would more than likely give her a few extra hours before he "ratted" her out.

Cold tears slipped down her face as she paced the cell with her hands out in front of her. She had to keep her heart rate up. Her fingertips smashed into the wall in front of her as she counted twenty. Twenty paces. That was it. She decided to go the other way and counted eight. Twenty-by-eight, complete darkness when there was not blinding light, and freezing cold.

Meita was being prepped, and there was nothing she could do about it. Her eyes would have adjusted by now if there were any sliver of a light source. No, whoever had her wanted her as close to sensory deprivation as possible without actually pushing her over the edge. She had read the studies, depriving someone of their senses for even a short period of time could have irreversible consequences. So, they weren't trying to kill her – not yet anyway. They just needed her a little broken so she would tell them whatever it was they needed from her. That meant they were going to keep her in this room long enough for her to *at least* consider helping them. That's when someone would come for her. They would open the door and let the light pour in like whoever was standing at the door was her savior. They would sit her down at a table with food. Water that she would be hesitant to drink, but whoever sat across from her would assure her was safe. She would drink because she would be severely dehydrated, and at that point, what more would she have to lose?

Then the questions would start. They wouldn't be direct questions – nothing too overt. They would paint a picture that showed her what the world was like for whoever they represented. It would, of course, be the opposing side to her current viewpoints. She might be asked about the evolved ones she had helped to relocate with Halo. But why? Did they inadvertently move someone of significance?

Meita's mind went through the list of families she had helped Halo with during the past two years. She had stayed away from anyone who had connections, whose disappearance would be noticed. Most evolved people who had strong community ties didn't need to be relocated because they were able to find help within their community. It was the families that were alone, mostly those living on or just above the poverty line. There were a few families like the Andersens, but they were the exceptions. The mother had been in the wrong place at the wrong time, but even they lacked family. Both Tessa's and Glen's parents were dead. They had no siblings and hadn't made good friends with their neighbors. Relationships weren't the only key to happiness, they were the key to survival.

Meita stopped pacing in the dark. Could this be a nightmare? Some type of dream her subconscious had dreamt up?

Another bubble of laughter rose up and out. She leaned back against the wall, but stood back up. It was not only frigid but also wet. She looked over her shoulder before she remembered that she couldn't see anything.

But how did the wall get wet? Condensation? Could there be a vent up high somewhere? But how were they keeping the floors so cold if there was a vent at the top near the ceiling?

Meita pushed up on her toes and placed the tips of her fingers as high as she could to run them along the walls. They were probably watching her. In the dark? Thermal imagery. They wouldn't be able to make out her facial expressions, but they could see where she was standing. But it was cold. Her body temperature was dangerously low. Maybe there were reverse motion detectors that automatically turned the lights on if she remained still for too long. Or a heart rate monitor that when slowed, would also trigger the lights. There were any number of surveillance equipment the room could be rigged with.

Meita shook her head to clear away the negative thoughts and waited until the room stopped spinning. She had to prepare herself. This wasn't just a physical game they were playing with her. In fact, it wasn't a game at all. They were physically dominating her so it would be easier to mentally overpower her. Whoever was out there was going to come for her at some point because the only way to assess just how much longer they needed to leave her in this box was to take her out of it and see how she responded.

She thought of her dad and another trail of fresh tears made their way down her face. She would make him proud. She wouldn't betray her country or her teammates.

Death was nothing to fear.

# CHAPTER FOUR

## Father figure

August 8th, 7:30pm EST

"Do you understand what I'm saying to you?" Walter asked her as he changed lanes.

Shaira groaned and laid down her head on the seat like she would rather be elsewhere. Rox looked out the window at the darkening orange sky. They had about a quarter of an hour before darkness fell. She liked this part of the US. It was the trees and their many colors to come.

Michael and Ruby hated it, for different reasons of course, but they both joined forces to complain about the colder months, preferring the humidity of Singapore and the ease of city living. Sometimes, Rox missed it too. Singapore seemed like a lifetime ago. She wondered how Mika was doing. She didn't often hear from him, and she wasn't sure if it was because he was busy setting up Halo throughout Southeast Asia or if that was his excuse to avoid her.

"I'm just saying you still gotta lot of years left in you," Walter continued. He chuckled as a way to make light of the topic. This wasn't the first time he tried to let her know he was okay if she "saw" other people. Specifically, other men. But how did she explain she wasn't waiting for Sam, it was just …

Rox laid her head back on the rest and looked over at the closest person she had to a father. When they first met, Walter had taken an instant dislike to her. At the time, the feeling had been mutual, but over the years they had developed respect for one another. One would go so far as to say a *love* for each other. Although he never apologized for manipulating her into helping him rescue his daughter, Val, from one of those evolved research facilities, Rox no longer expected him to. Having children herself now, she understood his motivations, and she didn't blame him.

"Your silence is making it weird," he said.

"You bringing it up is what's making it weird." Rox chuckled.

"I'm just saying with Ruby and Jay at university now, you're going to find that you have a lot more time on your hands is all …"

"Just stop." She laughed at him.

"I'd hate for you to miss out on something, you know. Something staring you right in the face but you can't see it, you know … cause … you know, you're still living in the past." He took his eyes off the road to glance over at her.

Rox cleared her throat and went back to gazing at the sky. Dusk. They were still a little over an hour from home. *Home.* Two years ago, that was exactly what she thought she had. A family. Now? So much had happened she wasn't sure of anything anymore. Discovering her ability to heal was the closest definition to immortality humankind currently had was unsettling. Knowing she would witness her children grow old and die, well, that changed things. She wasn't sure whether to love them less or love them harder.

Walter told her family was messy. *Nobody's neat and tidy,* he had said. *They're complicated and flawed, and they hurt you bad sometimes, but they represent home.* And home was where the healing happened.

Last year, Meita had helped to officially declare Tara Alexandra Harding deceased. It was a bit surreal having a funeral for herself, but Bethany said it would be good for Michael and the kids. Not long after, Rox adopted Jay. She couldn't remember what it was like to give birth, but she was sure signing the papers that made a child hers in the legal sense was just as joyful because the love was the same.

"I just keep hoping that I'll feel … something," she said. With Sam, there was this physical draw, like a pull to be near him. She felt him before she saw him, and he said it was the same for him. When they touched, a peace settled. The quiet hum of the electricity she had spent over six years learning to live with eased. She hated that she'd forgotten what his kiss felt like.

A sad smile spread across her face and she reached up to touch her lips.

"What I had with Sam's mother … that was special," Walter said. "You know, she and I created Halo together. Back then, it was more of an idea than anything else, but we knew we didn't want our boy growing up in a world where his kind would be feared. Or hunted."

Walter's first wife, Sam's mother, had died. Walter later remarried and had twins, Mika and Val, but he never shied away from speaking about his life with Sam's mother. "You don't try to recreate what you had with someone else," he said. "We mourn, and then we move on to create something new."

"Do you think he's … alive? I mean, wherever he is?" Rox understood that on some level, until Walter had a body, he would always believe his son was alive and fighting to find his way back home. But it had been two years, and the video footage showed Sam disappearing as if there had been a fracture in the fabric of time and space, and somehow, he had slipped through it.

"Some days." Walter cleared his throat. "Most days."

They had been through too much for the silence between them to be awkward anymore, and so they both allowed their thoughts to distract them.

"Sometimes," Rox said, "sometimes, I just wish I never left Josh's, you know. I wonder what it would've been like if I had stayed with him."

"Hmph." Walter didn't say anything more for a while, and then, "You were never meant to be in his shadow, Rox."

She sighed. He was right, and she knew it, but she couldn't deny that life was easier then. Training was easier. The only lives her decisions affected was her own. But then, would her relationship with Josh be as rich as it was if she had stayed? "Those were simpler times," she said.

"Simpler ain't always better, I'm afraid."

Rox closed her eyes and let the steady speed of the car relax her thoughts. She was tired. Mentally, that was; her body was fine. The gunshot wound had already healed, and they had stopped and eaten three times since he and Shaira rescued her. The bullet was still in her, of course, and that raised some questions when she went through the scanner at the airport, but she stuck close to the truth and said it was a gunshot wound. A manager got involved, and she was taken to a separate room where a female agent had her remove her clothing to ensure she wasn't concealing any weapons, but then she was able to board the next flight.

When she landed at LaGuardia, Walter was already waiting for her. He said Danny called to let them know Josh had delivered "the package" to its final destination. No one knew where that was, not even Meita.

How many families have they relocated in the last two years? Not nearly enough.

Rox lifted her head and turned to Walter. "Did Danny tell Josh we found his photo at the Fellowship bunker?"

Walter nodded. "Yep. Danny said he's not too worried about it though."

"Josh thinks because he can hear a person's thoughts he's invincible."

"Well, makes sneaking up on him awfully hard, I'd say."

"Not if they send someone like Meita or Ruby," she countered. "Then he's just an ordinary person." Like Rox, evolved ones like Meita and Ruby were rare. While they didn't have any active abilities, they could spot an EO just by looking at them. Both of them said it wasn't a tangible feeling they got or something about the way an EO looked, it was just instinctive. The added bonus, however, was that they were immune to any EO abilities.

Josh couldn't read their minds and Rox couldn't heal them or steal their energies.

"He'll be fine," Walter said, but there was concern in his voice. "Danny mentioned he hadn't been able to reach Meita."

It wasn't odd to not hear from Meita for a day or two, but Rox still hoped it was nothing more. Finding the photo of Josh in the bunker had unsettled her.

"Why don't you lie back and try to catch a nap. Danny'll be waiting for you when we get there," Walter said.

She didn't need the reminder. Danny had probably worked himself into a fine state. He would be on the front porch waiting for her. Arms folded over an impossibly broad chest with a smile on his face that proclaimed whatever he had in store for her was going to be extremely painful.

"You think he'll go easy on me if I tell him the bullet is still inside?"

Walter's laugh roused Shaira from her slumber in the backseat, and the wolf snorted. "Sweetheart, I reckon if you ask him, he'll do just about anything you like."

"You ever had him throw you?"

It took a moment before Walter's smile faded. "No, get to my age and people tend to keep their distance." He looked over and winked. "'Fraid of what an old man like me can do to 'em."

Rox shook her head, laughing quietly.

"I think he just doesn't want to see you hurt, Rox," Walter said. "I think that's why he's extra hard on you."

"Extra hard?" she said. "He hurts me!"

Walter smothered his laugh. "You want me to have a

word with him?"

Rox glared at him. "You better not. I can take him." She could not take him. Well, not without her ability.

She was surprised when Walter just nodded. "I believe you." This time, there wasn't a hint of a smile on his face.

~

## Unexpected

August 8th, 9:00pm EST

The sound of the tires on gravel lifted Rox out of her nap. She sat up as the car slowed, and Walter lowered the back window so Shaira could jump through. The night air was still warm with a hint of a cool breeze every now and again. The moon was almost full, and that made it too bright to see the stars. Clouds floated by now and again with the promise of a shower sometime through the night.

The copse of trees that lined the path leading to the main house was beautiful in its lushness. She understood Walter's draw to Halo. In the fall when the temperature dropped, the leaves painted the property in beautiful shades of reds, oranges and browns. Some days, when the sun was at the right height, she could swear the trees outside Sam's window looked like they were on fire.

In the winter, it always snowed and while the trees were bare, it was like a divine peace settled over the property. Sitting in the living room and just listening to the wood crackling in the fireplace was something everyone did together after dinner. The house would smell of cinnamon and other wintery spices that would weave their way into the fabric of everyone's clothing.

"Looks like someone's waiting for you," Walter said, as he stopped the car in front of the house.

Rox didn't need to look to know it was Danny. Michael had taken Jay and Ruby for their freshman orientation at university, and MJ and Emma had decided to go along. No one else would be interested in their return because everyone else would have received an update from Curtis.

Rox was about to reach for the door handle when Walter stopped her. "Listen, he means well. Remember, it's his job to train you."

Danny was sitting in one of the rocking chairs on the porch, his laptop on his lap and his fingers moving across the keyboard. He knew they were there because he would have heard, if not seen, the car pull up and the engine turn off.

Rox nodded at Walter. "I know. I'm just tired I guess, and I could do without another one of his lectures followed by an S & M session in the training room."

Walter chuckled. "Maybe instead of fighting, you could just try talking."

Did he think she enjoyed being pummeled on the mat? She never felt fast enough nor strong enough, and her core was forever in need of strengthening.

"Rox ..." There was a look on Walter's face she had never seen before. "Sweetheart ..." This was the second time he had called her *sweetheart.* "It's a hell of a thing for a man to know that a woman can best him." He held up his hand to stop her from interrupting. "Yeah, I know, women's lib and feminism and all that, but men, we're wired to protect. It's in our DNA, and a few generations of women earning the bacon ain't gonna change that. Wait, just hear me out."

Rox had her own thoughts about why men were so slow to get on the equality train, but she did as he asked.

"Sometimes, a man shows he cares by being hard. By making sure you're prepared for what's to come in case he can't be there to protect you."

Rox thought about that for a moment. Was Danny planning on leaving them? Was he only around until everyone felt confident she could effectively replace Sam? She still couldn't believe Meita suggested – and Walter agreed – she was the best candidate for the job.

Walter scratched his forehead and smothered a yawn. It had been a long day and he had driven from New York. "That was a tough call you had to make about saving the boy. You did good out there."

She wasn't sure what to say, so she nodded her thanks.

Their car doors slammed shut, and Danny placed his laptop on the floorboards. Were those reading glasses he took off? He lifted himself out of the rocking chair and passed Walter a bottle of beer as the old man went up the steps. Their bottles clinked together before they took a sip, and then they slipped into an easy conversation about what everyone had gotten up to earlier in the day. Rox felt a little annoyed Danny hadn't brought her one.

Maybe Walter had gotten it wrong. Maybe Danny hadn't been waiting for her. Perhaps, for once, he would let her rest before he went in for the full "debrief". Rox sighed. She liked Danny, but he confused her. There was a sadness about him, like he was trying to keep everything bottled inside for fear of losing something if it slipped out. It was an exhausting way to live. Walter had counseled her on the same thing a few months ago.

Halo was a motley crew of people who had no other place to go and were simply trying to do good. Curtis was a widower and former police detective who finally announced his feelings for Bethany, their in-house medical doctor and field psychologist. She was Walter's niece from his first marriage and had been with Halo since the beginning. Walter's wife, Marissa, handled the day-to-day management of the place, making sure they always had supplies. She also took care of the kids' logistics to and from school and all their extracurricular activities. Michael had agreed to work for Halo not long after Tusk kidnapped Ruby and MJ. It was obvious he was reluctant to join, but he realized that no security team in the world could keep them as safe as their mother (or Halo), so he stayed. Rox's relationship with him was complicated. They spoke, they were cordial and could even share a meal together, but her return meant he had to bury Tara a second time. After they held a mock funeral for Tara, he stepped down from his role of running his virtual reality and social media company, V-R. It was a painful decision with no easy – or right – choices, and so, much like everyone else, Michael adapted. He was currently working with Walter and a local architect to build an annex to the main house and a few other smaller homes at the back of the property. He couldn't move away from Halo, but she had a feeling he'd settle for smaller accommodations if it meant he had his own space again.

Then there was Josh. Josh was a part of Halo, technically speaking, but he split the majority of his time between his organization and his self-appointed "in principle" role of spokesperson for evolved ones. He was doing a lot of good by educating the public about EOs. He even had a new girlfriend, Samantha Ingpen, a reporter for a national news agency. They had been dating for less than a year, but they seemed serious, and Rox was happy for him.

Rox looked up at Walter where he was still chatting with Danny. Walter *was* Halo. She wasn't sure any of them would ever be able to replace him. He didn't just breathe life into the team, he gave them a purpose. She had never known a man as simple and as complex as him. When they first met, all they did was argue. Nothing she did was right in his eyes, but then Sam disappeared.

Grief either brought you together or tore you apart.

The screen door whined close, leaving her alone with Danny. He was at the top step with his arms crossed and his attention now fully on her. She was expecting him to say something like, "Well that was a shit show," or "You had to go and get yourself kidnapped. Again," or "It's a good thing you can heal."

He usually made her list all the mistakes she made from the moment she decided to operate outside of mission parameters because he believed that self-appraisal led to self-awareness, which was the bedrock to survival.

Rox waited for the barrage of carefully-worded, but nonetheless passively-aggressive criticism he was going to share; instead, he just stood there, watching her.

"Drive okay?" he asked.

Rox was not prepared for this. He was always so serious, like her life depended on each lesson he imparted and each word that left his lips. She supposed in some ways, it did. He was training her for nightmare situations, after all.

Maybe this was a new tactic.

"Kids will always be my weakness," she blurted out. "I can't ... I mean, I've lived it, you know."

He nodded, but she didn't think he understood. Did he have children? Had he ever been married? She knew so little about him. Was there another side to him? A more human side?

"Anyway, thanks for sending the drone after me," Rox said. "I know it wasn't protocol—"

"Rox?" He was leaning against the post, his arms still crossed, but his stance relaxed. Eyes that usually held sadness now twinkled. The tips of his hair were curled like they needed trimming, and he was dressed in a pair of gray lounge trousers and a long-sleeved white shirt that looked nice against his skin tone. Was this the first time she had seen him in anything other than his workout gear? He was a lot less menacing with bare feet and a slight grin on his face. In fact, he looked quite attractive the way his muscles stretched the fabric of his shirt across his impossible—

"Oh ..." It came out as a whisper.

Blood rushed to her face. Her skin grew hot, so she lowered her gaze, but then she was staring at his feet. His bare feet. She looked at the rocking chair he'd just vacated behind him on his right.

She crossed her arms over her chest, but then felt like that was a defensive stance, and so she lowered them. But Danny had his arms crossed over his chest, so she recrossed them.

Damnit. She felt like an idiot. Of course, Danny was attractive. Just because she always saw him as some sort of asexual drill sergeant didn't mean he was one. She shook her head at how silly she was being, but then stopped when she realized he was watching her. There was no way he hadn't noticed how rapid her breathing had become.

This was ridiculous. She was *being* ridiculous. She lowered her hands to her hips and looked into his eyes. Gone was the sorrow that normally sat there and in its place was *his* attraction to her. How the hell had she missed that?

Danny slowly came down the stairs and stopped on the bottom step. For a moment, they both just stared at one another, waiting.

Rox hated herself for thinking it, but Sam was gone, and Walter was right. She had a lot of years left in her. Her ability didn't allow her to see the future or to predict the odds, but she could heal, and it was time for her to let her old wounds scab over.

For the first time in two years, she lowered her guard and took a step towards someone who didn't exist just in her memory. "Danny?" It came out much softer than she had planned.

He lowered his arms and closed the distance between them. "Tell me if this isn't what you want."

She could smell the soap on him and the glass of whiskey he'd had from Walter's private cupboard. It had that smoky, woodsy aroma that reminded her of …

Rox reached up to caress the side of his face, and the stubble from his beard tickled her palm. She ran her fingers into the wet strands of his hair, and his eyes slid closed. Rox pressed up on her toes until their lips met. Their first touch was tentative, and they stood still like two school kids experiencing their first kiss. But then Rox opened her mouth.

Danny leaned into her with a moan.

She cleared her mind of all thoughts of the past and what could have been, and instead focused on what was in front of her – *who* was in front of her.

Strong hands circled her waist to spin her around and lift her up to the bottom step. He was still a little taller than her, but not by much. Their kiss deepened now they were closer in height, and the stubble rubbed against her face, strangely exciting her.

He pulled her closer, and she pressed her body against his. She had forgotten how good it felt to be seen, to be wanted, and to be held. She ran her hands up the inside of his shirt and felt the muscles of his abdomen before making their way around to his back.

His hands gripped the belt loops on her cargo pants, and he pulled her against the length of him. For a moment, they both forgot to breathe when they realized they wanted the same thing.

Danny reached up to wrap her braid around his fist and tugged her head back. His stubble made a burning trail over her chin and down her neck where he took small bites followed by warm kisses that involved his tongue.

Rox lost sense of place and time when she felt the warmth of his mouth descend down past her neck, across her chest to finally close over the fabric covering her breasts. His teeth gave a slight tug, and she inhaled sharply. His knee parted hers, and she didn't mean to, but her hips flicked against his thigh.

"Put your legs around me," he said, and then his lips were back on hers as he lifted her up.

In this position, she could feel him pressing against her, and it took a moment to realize he was walking. She broke off their kiss and looked over her shoulder to see where they were going. His teeth latched on to the bottom of her ear, and she inhaled in pleasure.

Danny carried her to the picnic table at the side of the house. It was under the shade of an oak tree that still held a few planks in its bough from the treehouse that Walter and Sam had built when Sam was young.

Rox turned away from that memory and focused on the feeling of the hard wood against her back as Danny lowered her to the table. A cool breeze flew between them, and Rox opened her eyes to find him looking down at her. She raised up on her elbows, missing the warmth of their chests pressed together.

"Rox?" There was a vulnerability in his tone that made her think of his bare feet. He was asking permission to make love to her, and that warmed her heart.

She pushed up until she was sitting with him pressed in between her thighs. She looked at the sky and felt the clouds floating by. They weren't heavy with rain, but the ones coming after held more energy. Those were bringing the promise of a shower.

When she felt the heavier clouds respond to her draw, she looked back at Danny as she ran her hands under his shirt again, lifting the edge up and over his head. There was just enough light to make out the contours of his chest and the small circular scar under his right nipple. It felt smooth, like heated wax. A thick line of scar tissue ran horizontally on his left side. She took her time, kissing each one of the smaller ones dotted across his chest, enjoying the way he sucked in his breath each time her lips lifted and then returned to his skin.

She couldn't tell if it was insecurity or raw need she saw in his eyes, but either way, the twinkle was a nice change. It suited him. Her hand traveled lower and her fingers splayed across his abdomen. He sucked in another deep breath and his jaw tightened. They stared at one another as the palm of her hand covered his belly button. Then the rain began to fall, and she went lower.

Danny's eyes slid closed and his head fell back as her fingers slipped beneath the elastic waistband of his pants. His fingers found the hem of her shirt and pushed it up until the rain was sliding down her back. She had to let go of him when he lifted it up and off her, but she quickly reached for him again.

"Rox." He lowered his head and took her nipple into his mouth along with the fabric of her sports bra. She threw her head back and the rain fell across her face and down her neck.

Danny pushed her back onto the table and used his knees to press her legs farther apart. He reached down and undid the button on her cargo pants. When he got the zipper free, she released him so she could push them down to her ankles. Thunder rocked the sky as she fumbled with the shoestring on her boots and pulled them off her feet.

She went to reach for him again, but he grabbed her hand. "Did you make it rain?"

She shook her head. She couldn't *make* it rain. All she could do was reach out and draw on the kinetic energy of the clouds passing by. The clouds would release the rain when they were ready. Sometimes it was before they reached her and sometimes it was after; that she had no control over.

He helped her pull her pants free and then instructed her to lift her arms so he could remove her sports bra. "Ever made love in the rain?"

"Not that I can remember," she answered honestly.

"Wrap your legs around me again."

Rox looked confused at first, but then she scooted to the end of the table and did as she was told. The rain fell against her shoulders, soaking her hair and wetting their skin as she felt him press against her entrance.

She held his gaze, grateful for the twinkle. Without closing her eyes, she nibbled on his bottom lip as she lowered down until she could feel him deep inside.

Danny's hands grabbed her waist and just held her there for a few seconds as he deepened their kiss. Rox squeezed her insides as he raised her up and brought her down against the length of him. Her entire body vibrated with pleasure, and for the first time in a very long time, she simply let go. She broke off their kiss and let her head fall back. She felt each raindrop as it slid in between her breasts and down her belly to where their bodies joined.

His mouth found her nipple again, and she called out his name, but he answered with a deep, long thrust. His gaze was locked on hers as she rose up and down on him. Her breathing quickened, and for a moment she wondered if the rain was such a good idea. She felt the kinetic charge in the air and it excited goosepimples along her spine. The hair on her arms rose as she felt the pressure between her legs rising. "Danny ..." she cried out, but he released her nipple and his lips captured hers.

Rox forgot about the Andersens, she forgot about Halo and the pile of cases that were next to impossible to get through. She didn't think about any of the disappointment and unmet expectations she had to adjust to since leaving Josh over six years ago in search of her identity. Instead, she closed her eyes, let her head fall forward and simply let the rain and the storm clouds heighten her sense of pleasure.

A shiver ran up her spine when Danny lifted her and moved them to the nearby grass. She turned her head to the side and inhaled the sweet smell of nature. He gripped her hips and lowered his head to the crook of her neck and let go of whatever he was holding back as he plunged into her again and again.

Lightning cracked across the sky as Rox wrapped her legs around his waist and raised her hips to meet each of his thrusts. She wasn't sure if it was the rain or the way their bodies fit so perfectly together, but she needed more of him. She needed him deeper, and without thought, she tucked her arm around his elbow, and then rolled him over onto his back without them separating.

Rox put one hand on his chest for balance and the other traced the raindrops that slid down his body. She set the pace as she arched her back and lifted, only to slide back down again. Her eyes slid closed but then opened to see his face locked in concentration as he squeezed her hips. A smile started at the corners of her mouth as she realized that he was close, and that increased her own pleasure. She picked up the tempo with a flick of her hips each time she rose that elicited an uncontrollable groan from him.

Her climax was building like the storm making its way across the horizon. Danny must have sensed it because he released her hips and put his finger on the tip of where all her nerve endings met, and Rox came undone. Thunder stole her cries as she slammed down into him one, two, three more times, her head thrown back, her eyes closed and the fingers of one hand interlaced with his.

A few moments later, Rox felt him convulse beneath her, and she smiled a slow, happy smile. She lowered her head to his chest and felt his heart beating against her ear. She placed a kiss there as Danny ran his fingers down the center of her back.

They lay in silence, listening to the steady drops of rain fall against the leaves and then finally down to the grass. Her breathing was beginning to slow, and she could feel his doing the same. Neither of them felt the need to say anything, and somehow that made the moment more special.

She stifled a yawn as she thought back to how many hours of sleep she had gotten that day. It wasn't much. Ever since Shaira and Walter met up with her at the Fellowship bunker, they had been in transit on their way back to Halo. She caught an hour or two on the flight from Texas to LaGuardia, but her body was craving a deep sleep. And food because her stomach let out a loud rumble.

"Someone's hungry," Danny said.

"Starving, actually," she said as she smothered a yawn.

"You wanna head inside?"

She shook her head. She wanted to enjoy this for a few minutes more. The rain would stop soon and all their responsibilities would be there waiting for them as if their moment had never happened.

A strong gust of wind blew in the opposite direction of the clouds and a chill raced down her spine. The rain stopped as she sat up and looked towards the front of the house.

"Change your mind?" Danny asked.

A wolf's howl pierced the night just as Rox heard her name.

Danny leaned up onto his elbows and looked at her. "You hear that? Sounded like someone called you."

Someone did call her. She looked down at Danny, and for a brief moment, she thought about lying back down and ignoring everything. Why was it that when she finally decided to let go and live, truly live, responsibility came calling? She wasn't ready to walk away from this moment. In fact, she was struggling to find the words to communicate all the emotions running through her. Pleasure, gratitude, joy, fatigue … hope. She hadn't felt like this since … maybe never.

Rox lowered her head until their lips were touching. She didn't rush their kiss, but she couldn't let it last as long as she wanted because she heard her name again.

"I really enjoyed this," she said.

"Me, too. Something wrong?"

Rox nodded. "My trainer's coming."

He looked confused. "I thought *I* was your trainer."

She kissed his nose and stood up to grab her clothes. "You *are* my trainer. In fact, you're one of three."

"One of three?"

Rox slipped her sports bra over her head as Shaira came trotting around the house. The wolf stopped before reaching them and lifted her head to sniff the air.

"Yes, one of three, but you're the only one who gets 'special treatment'," Rox said as she slipped her panties back on and winked at him.

They heard the car's approach and waited for the headlights to breach the darkness.

"Your trainer?" he asked.

"Yes." If Keenan were here, then there was trouble. Their arrangement was simple, she had spent the first six months training with him, but then afterwards, she would only go to England one month out of the year. Those first six months were hard, but they got into a routine and it was working. Only a handful of people at Halo knew about him, and that was limited to only those who had met him.

A light inside the house switched on and they heard the whine of the screen door as it opened.

The car came to stop in front of the porch next to Walter's rental.

Keenan was the first to get out. He looked her over before visibly inhaling. “Forgive the interruption,” he said to her, and then looked up at Walter who was standing on the porch with his arms crossed over his chest. “Greetings, my friend.”

Walter nodded. “What brings you ‘cross the pond?”

“I am afraid that I bring trouble with me.”

Walter looked at the man who had just stepped out of the driver’s seat.

“Henry?” Rox asked. “What are you doing here?”

Henry turned around in a circle before looking at her. “Is this Halo?”

“Where’s Katherine?” Rox asked.

“That is what I was hoping you could tell me. She did not meet me at the airport as expected. Instead, she sent him.” Keenan thumbed over his shoulder without looking at Henry.

Walter chuckled. “Long way to drive just ‘cause your date stood you up, don’t you think?”

“Anyone mind filling me in?” Danny said as he came to stand beside Rox.

Keenan studied Danny for a moment before he slowly nodded his head, and then looked at Rox. “Good choice.”

Shaira brushed against Rox as she made her way over to Keenan, who reached down and patted her side. “Hello, dear friend.” Then he looked up. “Has anyone seen her?”

“No,” Rox and Walter said at the same time.

“Why come here?” Rox asked.

“Because she said she went to yoga,” Keenan said.

Rox inhaled sharply.

"Shit," Walter said. "How long ago was that?"

Keenan looked back at Henry, who was standing there silently watching the exchange. He glanced down at his watch. "Eight hours ago."

"Has she been in contact since then?" Rox asked.

"No," Henry said.

"Meita?" Rox asked.

"She missed her check-in," Henry said.

"When was that, because I've not been able to contact her either," Danny said.

"She made her last check-in last night, but today, nothing," Henry said.

"What's the protocol when a check-in's missed?" Danny continued.

"Meita? Contact Katherine. Katherine?" Henry pointed to Keenan.

"Me," Keenan said.

"He your trainer?" Danny asked, and Rox nodded.

"Well, no sense standing out here in the middle of the night. Let's get inside where we can get something to drink," Walter said.

"And eat," Rox added.

"I cannot be sure that I have not been followed, my friend," Keenan said. "I am truly sorry."

Walter held the door for him to enter first. "Ah, don't worry about it, mate," he said in his best British accent. "Never had two healers at Halo before. Sure it's gonna be lively."

Keenan laughed at his attempt. "Your hospitality is much appreciated."

"Just returning the favor."

Henry followed them inside and said he needed access to a laptop or computer. "I need to get online and do some stuff for Ms Cheung."

"Rox, you go ahead and take everyone into the kitchen. I'll call Michael to see what we have lying around that we can let Henry use," Walter said.

"Make sure he and the kids are okay," Rox said. Michael was staying at a hotel near Jay and Ruby's university for a week to make sure they settled in alright.

Ten minutes ago, Rox was lying on Danny's chest thinking about how the day had taken a sudden turn towards the unexpected. While she enjoyed their time together and liked the idea of spending more time with him, there always seemed to be something demanding her attention just around the bend.

Katherine was missing and Meita had missed her last check-in. Rox thought back to the photo she found in the bunker at Fellowship.

"You spoke to Josh, right?" Rox asked Danny.

He looked confused. "About the Andersens?"

"No, about the photo I found and how he should be careful."

Danny nodded. "Why?"

The kitchen at Halo was industrial-sized, but Marissa did a wonderful job to make it feel homey. Cookie jars lined the counter on one side and electrical appliances like a coffee maker and a toaster were still easily accessible on the other. The table was the kitchen's center attraction. It was large enough for everyone to sit and have a meal as a family. Marissa always had a bouquet of flowers on it and it was only removed at meal times. Out of all the rooms at Halo, it was the kitchen that made the house more than a dormitory and turned it into a home. It also transformed them into a family.

Rox walked past the table to the large bay window that looked out on the side of the house with the picnic table. The rain clouds had moved on now and the moon was once again visible.

She closed her eyes and reached out with her thoughts. She wasn't a mind reader, but Josh was. Not long ago, she had spent over a year learning how to block him, but a lot had changed since then. They had changed. But one thing remained constant and that was she never had to think about him for long before he was there, inside her thoughts, communicating like they did in the old days. She wasn't sure how he retained that connection to her, and truth be told, she wasn't sure she cared anymore.

*¿Amor?*

~

## Mi amor

August 8th, 10:10pm EST

Samantha Ingpen was a beautiful, intelligent woman with an easy sense of humor and quick wit. She was an investigative journalist for the nation's oldest and largest news agency, and she hosted their online video channel where she interviewed some of the world's most influential people. Samantha had a relaxed way about her that made it easy for her guests to open up. In fact, that's how Josh met her. Her thoughts were uncomplicated, and she believed her calling was to pursue the truth and bring it to light. It was that belief that drew him in.

She sat across from him now with a smile on her face and her head tilted to the side so she was looking up through her lashes at him. He didn't need to read her thoughts to know she had paid special attention to her appearance for their date. For work, she divided her attire into two segments, above the waist and below. Above, she wore professional tops with simple designs so as not to clash with the graphics screen behind her. Below, she was in jeans and a pair of comfortable shoes. Whenever they had gone out, she put in the effort to have her bottom match the top, but this time she had gone to the hairdressers.

Samantha had lips that were plush and painted red. They were kissable, and Josh had a feeling he was going to do just that before the night was over. He leaned forward and took her hand in his. He allowed their fingers to interlock as he debated, not for the first time, just how much of his identity he was going to share with her. It was still early days, but he liked her. She was kind but tough. Most people mistook kindness for a weakness, but she exuded both strength and compassion, and both were attractive qualities.

"What are you contemplating?" Samantha asked him as she rubbed her thumb over the back of his hand.

"How beautiful you are." He reached over and pulled one of her curls before letting it spring back in place. "I love what you've done with your hair."

She blushed, and Josh felt a warmth spread throughout his chest. It was different from what he had felt for Rox. This felt less consuming, more balanced.

Why was he thinking of Rox? He released Samantha's hand and sat back.

*¿Amor?*

*Josh!*

*Is everything alright?*

Samantha looked at him in confusion.

"I have a call," he said as he reached for his phone like it had been vibrating. "Be right back."

The restaurant they were in was less busy at this hour, but that was only because most of its patrons had moved on to either a nightclub or some other source of entertainment for the evening. That meant the long hallway that led to the restrooms was thankfully empty.

*Where are you?*

*Miami, why?*

His ability to link minds was usually limited by proximity. He didn't always need to see someone to read their thoughts, but they had to be nearby, and if he touched them, then the connection was even stronger. But it was different with Rox. He could link with her over vast distances, and he always knew when she was thinking of him. That had made getting over her difficult. If he were honest with himself, he wasn't sure one ever got over someone they were connected with the way they were, but he had learned to live with her without being *with* her. He still loved her, but that was alright because she felt the same. It was there, sitting as the foundation of everything she felt for him. He was her first love, and he doubted she would ever really get over him, but she had moved on. It had taken him awhile to accept that he had to do the same.

*You think Katherine and Meita's disappearance has something to do with that photo you found of me?* he asked after reading her thoughts.

*I don't know. But something feels off.*

There was a moment of silence while he processed the thoughts she had opened up to him.

*Yeah, not good that Keenan shows up out of the blue like that. Especially if he thinks he's been followed.*

*What do you think? Tusk and his men have found Katherine, and maybe Meita, and now he's after us?*

Josh doubted it. Tusk wouldn't be able to find Halo, let alone Katherine. If he was behind this, he would've had help.

*Ruby and Jay are good. I spoke with them earlier, and Michael is staying nearby for the rest of the week, so stop worrying about them,* he told her. Her brow would be creased and her lips curled in worry over them. Josh had done a lot of things wrong in his life and regardless of the reasons, he had hurt people. But he knew that asking Rox to adopt Jay was the best decision he had ever made.

*I don't think we should just dismiss the Fellowship,* she said when she realized he hadn't given them much thought.

*Danny and Curtis both think it was a coincidence that the Andersen boy contacted them, but I agree with you.* Walter mentioned the Fellowship once before. They were gaining more publicity by spouting nonsense like they could make evolved ones "normal". Until yesterday, they were nothing more than some special interest group preying on the ill-informed. But maybe there was more to them. *Hey, are you alright?*

*Yeah. Bullet's still in me, but I'm sure at some point I'll have it removed.*

He chuckled. *You know, not many people can say that.*

*Not sure I want to be able to say that. Listen, think you can keep it low-key tonight?*

She was worried about him, and that warmed his heart in a way that was wholly new to him. The door to the men's bathroom opened behind him, but he didn't bother turning around. Instead, he moved further down the hallway without looking over his shoulder. He was about to tell her he was fine and she need not worry, but thoughts about death and EOs bounced around his head with a singular purpose.

*What is it?*

Reading thoughts created a two-way connection that allowed others to read his. Most people didn't know that because he never stayed connected to anyone as long as he did with Rox.

Josh turned around into the blade of a knife cutting through his shirt and skin like it wasn't there. Its blade slicing neatly between two ribs just above his heart.

Rox screamed his name, but he blocked it out as he grabbed the wrist that was holding the weapon. Instead of trying to push him away, Josh brought him in closer and used his other hand to punch up into his assailant's nose. The bone popped as his attacker cried out.

Josh latched on to the man's mind to stop him from moving, and then reached back out to Rox. *Call Samantha.*

*Josh?*

*Call Samantha!*

The attacker stumbled backwards, which meant Josh didn't have as strong of a grip on him as he wanted.

*Who are you?* he asked the man.

*Theodore Bails*, but his friends called him Tater.

*Why are you trying to kill me?*

The word "Fellowship" flashed in Tater's mind, and the hatred that followed in his eyes alerted Josh that Rox was right. They were in more danger than any of them thought.

*Ask him why they want you dead*, Rox instructed.

"Because your kind shouldn't exist," Tater said. "You're demons. Abominations. And if you don't repent, the world will burn."

Josh tried to say something, but pain sliced across his chest and stole his concentration.

"Josh?" It was Samantha. "A woman named Rox called me and said you were stuck in the bathroom."

Tater tried to turn his head, but Josh tightened his grip.

"Oh my god!" Samantha took the shawl from around her shoulders and quickly rolled it up as she looked for some way to press it around the knife handle sticking out of his chest.

*You can't just leave him*, Rox said.

She was right. But Samantha was there, and while she knew he was evolved, she didn't know what his abilities were. She had never asked, and he never volunteered. It was one of the reasons he liked her as much as he did.

*If he gets away, they're going to just try again.* Rox told him. *And we need to send a message that there will be consequences.*

He chuckled and then instantly regretted it.

"We need to get you to a hospital," Samantha said, and then as if noticing his attacker for the first time, she looked at him. "Who's he?"

Josh gritted through the pain. "Name's Theodore Bails. But his friends call him Tater."

*You're starting to weaken. I can feel your hold on him slipping,* Rox said. *And your thoughts are fuzzy. You need to end this.*

*When did you get so blood thirsty?* Josh asked.

He followed her train of thought back to the beginning, or at least as far back as her memory stretched. She recognized the change herself, but what struck him most was just how comfortable she had become with it.

He grabbed the knife's handle, but both Rox and Samantha shouted, "*No!*"

The blood spread across his shirt forming a red stain that was only increasing in size. *Got any other ideas then?* "Because I could use you right now, *amor.*"

"I'm right here," Samantha said. She lifted his good arm over her shoulder and started him back down the hall, but he stopped her.

Tater stood behind them. Hands at his side, and his muscles pulled tight like he was on the precipice of action.

Black spots danced across the hallway in front of Josh. He couldn't hold Tater much longer. *Do you understand why I made you train now?*

*What? You want to have this conversation now? While you're bleeding out?*

Josh attempted to laugh, but instead coughed through the pain. *This is why I trained you. Why I trained Jay and everyone else I cared about.*

Josh lifted his arm from around Samantha and yanked the knife from his chest before she could stop him. He tossed it to the floor in front of Tater.

Blood pumped out of Josh's wound, but he held on long enough for Tater to pick up the knife and bring it up to his own throat.

Samantha gasped, and Josh watched as Tater dug the knife in and slit from ear to ear.

*You will* not *die. Do you hear me?*

*Anything you wish, mi amor.*

Then everything went black.

# CHAPTER FIVE

## Penance

Date/Time: Unknown

Sam blocked the stinging pain that shot through his hand and ran up his arm to settle in the space just beneath his shoulder blade. His fingertips and palms were a patchwork of cuts. The holds he found on the face of the mountain were almost always jagged edges. He was grateful for the bitter wind because the cold helped to staunch the flow of blood that had threatened his grip on more than one occasion.

The sun had set over an hour ago, but luck was on his side because the moon was almost full. Clouds floated across the sky in rapid groups. When they blocked out the light, he used those moments to rest. He would secure himself into a one-handed perch and tuck his free hand under his armpit. But warm fingertips reignited the pain, and so he continued in darkness until his right foot slipped and his trouser leg caught on the edge of a rock. Cold air blasted through the protection of his cargo pants and ran up his thigh to settle in the pit of his stomach. If he wasn't so cold, he would have laughed. Two years of living exposed to rain and snow and his trousers had held up. So had his shirt. They were made for performance, just not the rock-climbing kind. The hole in his pants meant every sharp point his leg passed over carved a new pattern into his skin, and soon blood was running down his leg into his sock. He suddenly thought of mountain goats and wondered if any were nearby. Could they smell blood? Were they carnivorous?

Sam's stomach growled, and he stopped to catch his breath. Those first few weeks here, his stomach complained constantly, but then his body adjusted and his stomach shrank and eventually stopped protesting its desire for regular feeding. It had been a long time since he had three square meals a day with snacks in between. The human body didn't need that many calories as he had come to learn. In fact, he had survived just fine on a diet of fish and berries. Animal meat from a rabbit or a deer was a rare treat he enjoyed when he got lucky and caught something in his traps or when Neo hunted. The military had prepared him for a lot, even how to survive in isolation, but there hadn't been a course on how to survive as a hunter-gatherer. It was in the moments when he thought back to his childhood with his Dad that he was the most grateful. Walter knew how to trap and skin a rabbit. Sam had only ever watched. There's a lot to be said for learning by doing, and so it took Sam a month of failed attempts before he snared his first rabbit. Burned rabbit fur was disgusting, but once he got past that, and if he didn't leave the meat too long over the open flame, it was downright heavenly.

Sam looked down into the darkness that represented death. He wasn't afraid of heights, but he knew somewhere down there Neo was waiting for him. He hated leaving him. If it hadn't been for that animal, Sam was sure he wouldn't have made it. Neo had stood watch over him on those early nights when he had fever from poorly cooked meat or berries that shouldn't have been eaten. They had fought a bear together, and while both of them had scars to remember it, if it hadn't been for their teamwork, neither of them would've survived. Sam never figured out why Neo didn't just attack him that first night he woke up here injured and confused, but he reasoned the saber-toothed cat needed companionship just as much as he did.

By Sam's calculations, he was in his second year here – wherever that was – and in that time, he hadn't seen another person or anything that could help place him on the spectrum of the human timeline. He had survived mostly through sheer willpower. And luck. A lot of luck.

Sometimes, when his thoughts would get the better of him, he imagined he was living in a post-apocalyptic world and he was the last human alive. Other times, he played out the scenario of being transported back in time before humans. He had mixed feelings about coming across a dinosaur.

Some days he would scream so loud his voice would hurt and eventually give out. Neo didn't like that, but Sam needed the release sometimes. All that doubt and fear and frustration could eat a man alive as he had come to learn, and so he found ways to cope. Screaming was one of them.

He just needed to hear the sound of a human voice outside of his own head.

Sam leaned against the cold face of the mountain and breathed through his moment of panic. His body shook with a combination of fear and hypothermia. He dropped his bear skin just before the sun had set. He hadn't wanted to, but a gust of wind slipped up inside the skin and almost pushed him off, so he stood there for a moment trying to adjust to the bite of the cold before he accepted there was no adjusting, just climbing.

It was too dark now to make out how much farther he had to climb before he reached the summit. The next bank of clouds brought thunder with it, and that gave him hope, but he was tired. He wanted to drop his arms below his head and give them a rest. His thighs burned and the tips of his toes had blisters from his boots, the soles of which were too thick to make climbing easy. Each hold he found, he had to fight to keep from slipping off.

Light flashed above him, and for a moment, Sam froze. He remembered the bright glare and the deafening vibrations from the lightning that had struck Rox. That was different. That one had a hum and a pull on him he had never experienced before. But then again, how many times had he been around actual lightning? So how could he know the lightning that just flashed above him was different than the one that hit Rox and transported him back in time?

Some days he was convinced she was dead. He had witnessed her getting her throat slit open, and her blood running across the floor like spilled paint. Shaira had taken a chunk out of her shoulder and had killed her. Perhaps one of his greatest shames of all was the time he had cradled her in his arms and shot her with so much tranquilizer that her heart stopped.

Tears pooled in his eyes, but the wind quickly dried them. Maybe this wasn't an actual place or time. Maybe this was his penance for all he had done. Maybe he would reach the top of the mountain and lightning would strike, and he would be transported back. Back to the time when he first woke up here with a thin line of drool running down the back of his neck.

The clouds cleared and the contrast made the night seem brighter than before. Stars appeared across the sky like candles being lit one by one on an elderly man's birthday cake. He thought he saw a ledge not too far up ahead on the right. Would it be big enough for him to lay down?

Sam looked back down into the darkness where he had abandoned the only friend he had known in this place. Guilt threatened to loosen his grip, but he screamed instead. When his throat grew too dry and he started to cough, he stopped and caught his breath. Then he screamed some more. Some days, Sam believed in a God while other days he questioned the benevolence of an omnipotent being who would do this to him. Maybe life was simply random and there was no one looking out for him. Or maybe he had a different definition of "looking out". Maybe Sam's definition meant that only good things happened while that Someone's definition was more simple – he lived, and what happened to him was largely dependent on the choices he made.

Where would he be if he hadn't fallen for Rox? What if he hadn't gone to Singapore but instead left her alone to repair her relationship with Michael? Would he be here now? Would another path have led to this same mountain?

A howl pierced his thoughts and Sam looked up. It took a moment for his brain to reconcile the direction of the sound and the fact that it was ahead of him. He shook his head and dismissed it as a trick of the wind.

He tested his perch with his left leg and then stretched over a narrow gap to his next foothold with his right. A shiver raced through him as he made his way to the ledge that he hoped wasn't a mountain mirage. He just needed to close his eyes and give his muscles a chance to relax. He would continue on just as soon as he woke up. *If* he woke up.

~

## The graft

August 9th, 8:30am EST

"Gentlemen," Dr Mallory Fined said as she stood up from the table. "I will leave you two to discuss the details. I have to get to the office."

Harry stood, which forced Tusk to scramble to his feet or appear rude for remaining seated.

Mallory winked at the senator and then pressed her lips into an insincere smile at Tusk before she followed the staff out of the dining room. Tusk rolled his eyes and sat back down.

"Don't be like that," Harry teased him. "She's a remarkable woman."

Tusk stopped himself before he rolled his eyes a second time. It was obvious that Harry was sweet on Mallory, and it was equally obvious that she was using his affections to her advantage.

"She was fair, wouldn't you say?" Harry asked. "More generous than you'd given her credit for."

Tusk wondered if it would be rude to ask for a few drops of whiskey in his coffee?

Harry Carter had a sprawling ranch on the outskirts of Northern Virginia where he preferred to conduct his private meetings. It was his second home and set on so much land that Tusk had no idea of the acreage, but he did know it had been passed down through the generations and now belonged to Harry. And one day when Harry was gone, it would pass on to his children.

Tusk didn't have children, but even if he did, he had nothing to leave them other than his work. While his work was far more valuable to mankind than anything contained within the walls of Harry's ancestral home, Tusk's children would have to start from the beginning like all those who didn't have families who had made their fortunes on the backs of others.

The Science, Space, and Technology committee had approved the National Science Foundation grant, and just like that, AmLife had become the global leader in the genetic decoding of evolved abilities. It didn't matter that no scientist on the planet had been able to successfully neutralize a cell's natural repair process to stop it from generating unintended consequences that led to off-target mutations in the "un"-evolved; therefore, it was pure ignorance to think that in a few years, AmLife would be able to decode what made some humans "evolved".

But politicians were less interested in facts and more interested in what had more public appeal, and over the last two years, there was renewed interest in evolved ones. People wanted to know why some were chosen and others were not. No matter the nuance (or the fact that evolved ones were not "chosen"), the general public was divided into two groups: those who were afraid of evolved ones and those who wanted to *be* evolved ones. Sure, those afraid could master their fear and learn to live with them the same way they had learned to live with others from a different race or religion, but it was the group who wanted to be evolved that presented the greatest threat to his work.

Tusk had spent more than three decades dealing with governments, companies, and individual investors who, for one reason or another, had a special interest in evolved abilities. Governments wanted evolved soldiers; companies wanted evolved employees; and individual investors wanted to be evolved. Tusk had one investor who funded an entire facility just to get him to "unlock" the ability for humans to fly. The investor had donated well over $300 million, not to mention tissue samples, bone marrow, spinal fluid ... Tusk was sure he would have amputated a limb if he said it would help further the research that would one day enable the investor to sail through the clouds without the aid of an aircraft. But

Tusk had needed the money, and so he didn't explain the physics behind aerodynamics and why no human – evolved or otherwise – would ever be able to fly. Bone density, tissue mass, physiological structure, center of gravity and just plain old Newtonian gravity meant the human body would have to mutate on such a massive scale to get even a millimeter off the ground without assistance that the heart, liver and lungs would never survive such a metamorphosis.

"She's given me her word, Cliff. She'll be fair to you. She's going to make sure your name is included."

A woman dressed in a maid's uniform entered the room so quietly that for a moment, Tusk wasn't sure she was there. She came in with two fresh cups of coffee, milk already added, and placed one in front of each of them, and then quietly removed the other three on her way out.

"Any word on Katherine?" Tusk asked, changing the subject. Trying to convince the man who had been his business partner and best friend for more than half his life that the woman he decided to get in bed with was going to stab both of them in the back, just at different times, was impossible. Harry had given up on their shared dream. He saw a quicker path to achieving his goals of legacy, and Tusk understood his friend well enough to know he wouldn't compromise that for anything as noble as loyalty. It was every man for himself now.

Harry swore. "Bitch has gone underground. But that's alright because we've got her number one."

Harry had lived in luxury while Tusk had taken all the risks. Perhaps it was a good thing Harry chose to betray him for the seductive promises of Dr Mallory Fined. At least now Tusk saw his friend for who he truly was. "Who?"

Harry smiled like he had beaten the house. "Remember that photo you sent me a few years back?"

Tusk was silent for a moment and then shook his head.

Harry sucked his teeth like it should've been obvious to whom he was referring. "When you finally told me about Tara, and her ability to heal? When we traced Major Sam Watts and Josh Mendez?" Harry snapped his fingers a few times. "The empath. We were searching for the empath!"

Singapore. Chiang Rai. Pak Tha. Yes … he vaguely remembered a woman in a photo that Leona had found. "The immigration photo? The woman we couldn't identify?"

Harry nodded. "Well, we've identified her."

"That was years ago!"

"She was at GFO when I was there, but I had her on low-security stuff mostly. Anyway, a guy I pay to do personnel checks and stuff like that just happened to mention that people like her – people with no past and no identity – usually work for special interest companies, you know, to support whatever's trending on the Hill."

Tusk thought about that for a moment. But why would a woman working for a special interest company be interested in *his* Tara?

"That's when I ran her through the database of GFO employees from the days when I worked there." Harry sat back in his chair. "And you'll never guess what I found."

Her. It was obvious Harry had found her. "Who is she?"

"Meita bint Tariq al-Shaikh." Harry drank a few mouthfuls of his coffee before he continued. "And she's going to tell me everything I want to know about Katherine Louise Cheung."

Tusk wasn't exactly sure what had sparked the intense hatred Harry felt for Katherine, and before now, he had never even bothered to wonder. The simplest explanation would be pride. Harry had been removed from his position and replaced by Katherine, but after all this time he should've gotten over it. What did she do to him that made him want to hold a grudge for this long?

However, in Harry's defense, she had systematically dismantled their facilities, but then again, there had to be something more to the Harry-Katherine story. "Any idea where she's at?"

"Meita? Yeah! A few miles offshore on a container ship locked inside one of the shipping containers we use to question terror suspects."

Tusk sat back in total surprise. How did Harry manage that? "Was she involved in the shutdown of our Pak Tha facility?"

Harry shrugged. "Don't know, yet. But I'm guessing she's had a hand in all of the facility shut-downs." He finished his coffee. "It's a good thing I copied GFO's personnel database when I did. Never thought I'd need the damn thing."

Tusk looked out of the dining room window onto a perfectly manicured bush that ran a circular perimeter around a cherry blossom tree. He knew it was a cherry blossom tree because he had sat at this very table, in the same spot during the early days of spring many years ago. Cherry blossoms were one of Tusk's favorite flowers, and he remembered back to when he and Harry first started working together. They were just two young men with ideas. Neither of them could have guessed that all these years later, they would be here, seemingly sitting on the same side of the table.

"You think I can get in to see her?" Tusk asked.

Harry looked surprised, but Tusk shrugged it off. "Just thinking she's got to be evolved if she's as good as you say she is."

"Why? What're you thinking?"

"Just like to find out what her ability is and if she's evolved."

Harry leaned back and crossed his legs under the table. He placed his elbows on the armrests of the dining chair and twiddled his thumbs over his lap before he nodded. "See if you can get her to talk while you're there. I want to know where Katherine's slithered to."

Tusk fought to keep his expression neutral, so he gave a slow nod and exhaled a steady breath. "Sure."

Harry looked at his watch. "I'm going to be late." He wiped his mouth with his napkin and then placed it over his half-eaten plate. He got up and went to the sideboard to the left of the table and opened a drawer. He took out a small notepad and a pen. He scribbled something down before he tore off the page. "Here. This is where you need to go and what you need to say to gain access. Just tell them you're my lead scientist. The password's on the paper, but it's a one-use kind. After you use it, they will erase it and come up with a new one. So make sure you get what you need before you leave."

Tusk looked down at the paper and then quickly folded it and put it in his pocket. "Thanks, Harry." He stood up so that the two friends of more than three decades could shake hands.

"Find something that'll help me locate Katherine, and we're even." Harry laughed. "Listen, I've got to go, but Manny'll take you wherever you need to go."

Harry left the dining room, and Tusk sat back down and took a slow look around. Everything seemed like it originated in a time that was hostile to modernization. A portrait of Harry and his parents when he was younger hung over the fireplace. Vases and urns that did nothing but act as props to create an atmosphere of sophistication and wealth decorated the mantelpiece. Did anyone other than Harry and his wife sit in this dining room at the same time? The table was ridiculously long. It was large enough to hold every person Tusk had ever met and still have room for additional guests.

Tusk looked down at his white plate with a blue and gold trim on which his croissant was served. There were two separate, matching dishes for his butter and jam. His coffee cup and saucer were also part of the set, as well as the cutlery. The curtains that framed the window overlooking the cherry blossom tree was a similar blue with a gold sash. Who the hell coordinated their dinnerware with the interior design?

The kind of people who already had legacy and would do anything to maintain it.

Tusk looked at the cherry blossom tree again. At this time of the year, the arc of the branches reminded him of a weeping willow the way they curved down. Little buds were still visible, but they were not yet as vibrant or as colorful as they would become after winter.

Tusk put a piece of the croissant into his mouth and slowly savored its flavor, much as he did with the coffee. The only time he ever ate pastry as good as this was when he was in Harry's presence, when Harry chose the dining location and paid the bills. Tusk was never going to own a home like this. The place where he would be forced to hang his lab coat would not have a cherry blossom tree outside any of its windows. He was too old for such fanciful dreams, and he was far too familiar with failure to think what Harry strove for would ever be attainable to him. Tusk had started at the bottom. Sometimes, he feared he was going to end up there as well.

But Tusk was finally old enough to spot a con when he saw one, and Dr Mallory Fined might as well have the word "grafter" tattooed across her forehead. He didn't doubt her intellect, but he did doubt her motives, and he couldn't decide which one was worse.

~

## Volunteer work

August 9th, 10:30am EST

Leona ran her thumb over the pads of her fingers in frustration. No matter what path she considered, none of them allowed her to get close to Josh Mendez. Not close enough to get a blood sample or to get him out of the hospital without getting caught. It was the man named Kevin who presented the biggest obstacle. He watched over Josh like he were more than a hired guard. That made her wonder, and she rubbed her fingers again.

"Excuse me," a nurse said as she rushed by.

Leona needed to keep busy, or at least look like it. She was dressed in a candy striper uniform with a hospital badge. If anyone stopped her, she was an intern at AmLife, the genetics company everyone was talking about. Part of her intern assignment was to spend a total of forty-eight hours assisting nurses in a hospital environment to bring that kind of "patient first" experience back to the company. Leona's friend who helped her create the backstory and the badge said that nurses were often overworked and underpaid; therefore, any offer of help would go unquestioned.

A nurse and a hospital security woman came out of a room they were prepping for a new patient. That new patient was Josh. He was being transferred out of post-op ICU.

Leona ran her thumb across her fingers again and wondered about Josh's ability. Everything she thought never gave her the right feeling. According to one of the nurses, he had almost died from internal bleeding, which meant he was nothing like Tara, Tusk's pet obsession.

Leona just didn't see it. Sure, being able to heal oneself – and others – was an extraordinary gift, but being able to predict the future was equally powerful. Imagine what she'd be able to accomplish when she was out from under her aunt's thumb.

If it were up to Leona, she would've remained undercover with Tusk a little longer. Sure, Pak Tha was an unmitigated disaster, but Leona was able to sense the attack before it happened and got her and Tusk out just in time. By doing that, she had gained his trust, and it was only a matter of time before he would lower his guard around her enough to trust her with something that would ultimately gain her access to his research.

But Aunt Mallory wanted her out, said it was taking too long. Before she left, Leona was able to take a sample from one of their most promising patients. Dream Weaver's body oils created a powerful sedative more potent than any benzodiazepine, even if it didn't last as long. Tusk had only just been able to successfully create a synthetized version using Dream Weaver's DNA when Katherine and her crew came and destroyed the facility. Leona had passed that sample to her aunt, but wasn't sure if it was enough for AmLife to reverse engineer it.

Leona was surprised when her aunt made the announcement about being so close to unlocking the genetic code to evolved ones. They weren't anywhere near that, but Senator Harry Carter said it didn't matter how close they were. What mattered was how they managed people's perceptions.

Leona didn't understand any of them: Tusk and his paranoia and irrational need to be the man who redefined humanity; Carter and his obvious carnal lust for her aunt and his desperate attempts to remain relevant; and her aunt, Dr Mallory Fined, who wanted to create an empire that would make her the most respected scientist and businesswoman in the world. It all just seemed ... ironically juvenile. The fact that all three of them were entirely too old to make any lasting effect on mankind was lost on them. Most research showed that if a person hadn't made their mark in the world by the time they were in their mid-thirties at the latest, they weren't going to. All three of them were well past that. No one was going to remember their names, except for Carter, but only because his last name was already lasting. *He* wouldn't be remembered.

Leona was the future of evolved ones. She was the future of AmLife. She had Fellowship – yes, it was a fledgling organization, but an eager one willing to supply her with test subjects who were evolved. While Tusk was out there taking evolved ones against their will, he had overlooked the population of EOs who didn't want to be evolved. The best thing about them was she didn't need to kidnap or trick them into her facility. She simply partnered with an organization that promised to help those with abilities to get rid of them. And if you added to that the number of ordinary humans just dying for the opportunity to gain abilities, there were enough subjects knocking at her door that she didn't need to go looking for them.

Leona had little respect for her elders. They were worse than children who spouted in nonsensical hyperbole to advance their own agendas. All three of them were predictable with their loyalty-to-self mentality. That's where the Fellowship showed its true value. People were always more afraid than they admitted, and all you had to do to ignite that fear into action was to give them a target they could blame for their anxieties. For all the evolution mankind was going through at the moment, tolerance was not one of them. Tolerance had to be taught because instinctively, humanity was hardwired to fear things that were different. It was why everyone gravitated to their own like-minded thought bubbles. People who believed in one religion socialized with others of the same religion. Those who were of the same race naturally socialized with their own kind. Educated people hung out with those who were also erudite, and those who weren't drifted towards their intellectual peers. All of humanity was one large species divided into smaller homogenous populations, with each group afraid of the other. Well, until the emergence of evolved ones. Their very existence united populations and gave them a new, common enemy to fear. Public sentiment was once again piqued, and no one knew which way it was going to sway.

Leona walked down the hall towards the waiting room on the left. She passed a security guard making his rounds with a cup of coffee in hand. She ran her thumb across the pads of her fingers, and again saw there was no way for her to get to Josh without being noticed. Could she make up a story sufficient to explain her presence in his room? Even if she could, it was unlikely she would be able to convince Kevin to leave his side. He remained the one problem she couldn't resolve.

She opened the door to the waiting room and stuck her head in like she was looking for someone in particular, but she was attempting to hear what the tall and skinny, brown-skinned man was saying. She wasn't sure who arrived first, him or Kevin, but it was obvious they knew one another when she saw them talking. It could be a coincidence, two friends running into one another at a hospital. It happened. But her ability told her otherwise. They were both here because of Josh.

Leona was about to turn around and leave when she caught a of glimpse of someone familiar. She turned back and stared at the woman sitting in the corner. The left side of her blouse was covered in blood and she had dark rings under her eyes like she hadn't slept. Where had she seen that face before?

Then it hit her. Samantha Ingpen. The news journalist. And who was she talking to?

Leona pulled the door shut and continued down the hall. She ran both thumbs over her fingers to determine if anyone had noticed her and breathed a sigh of relief when her ability confirmed she was safe.

Leona needed to figure out how Josh had managed to survive while the man she had sent was found dead at the scene. She was waiting for a copy of the autopsy report from a contact that one of the Fellowship members had inside the local police, but it hadn't come through yet. She was beginning to think that whatever Josh's ability was, it made him hard to kill.

The phone in the front pocket of her uniform buzzed. It was her aunt. Leona rolled her eyes as she headed for the stairwell. Another nurse was there talking on her phone one storey down, but when she looked up and saw Leona, she waved and then carried on down the stairs as her voice trailed off.

"I'm at the hospital," Leona said.

"I know. I told you to go there. Any update on him?" her aunt asked.

"No. He's got a guard."

"And you can't get rid of him for a few minutes?"

Leona shook her head in frustration, but kept her tone even. "He's not left his side since he came out of ICU."

"Well, it may not matter anyway. Carter has agreed to my terms and Tusk is onboard."

Leona was positive Tusk was *not* onboard. He was old, paranoid, and grumpy, but he wasn't a fool. While she didn't like him, she'd be naive to underestimate him. A man didn't spend over thirty years living on the wrong side of the law, running unethical and immoral scientific experiments on innocent people in over half a dozen countries, and not learn how the game was played. Oh, she was sure Tusk said he would cooperate, but Leona didn't need to run her thumb over her fingers to know he was up to something. Tusk's life was his work. There was no way he would give that up. Ever.

"I've got some good news for you," Aunt Mallory said.

"Yeah?"

"That woman who attacked you and Tusk two years ago in Laos?"

The one Leona couldn't get a read on? The woman Leona hadn't seen coming, and until now wasn't sure even existed. "Yeah?"

"I've got her."

"What do you mean you've 'got her'?" Leona had

nightmares about that woman. In her dreams, her face was always covered in smoke.

Her aunt laughed. "Settle down. She's somewhere secure. Right now, she's incapacitated, but later on this afternoon, I'm sending one of my lead doctors in to have a chat with her."

Leona wanted to be there, and her aunt must've known it because she warned Leona to stay away.

"Why?" Leona asked. She needed to see her. She needed to put a face to the woman who invaded her dreams.

"Wait until we've got her compliant," Aunt Mallory explained. "Then you can have a heart-to-heart with her if you'd like."

That was exactly what Leona would do. No one ever left her with feelings of intense unease – not even Tusk, and she couldn't read him either. "You got her name?"

"No. Remember that sample you took from that Dream Weaver woman?"

"Yeah?" Had her aunt's team replicated it?

"Well, I was able to produce more of it. It's not as potent as the original sample, mind you, but I'd say it works pretty damn well."

"Is that how you got her?"

"Mm-hm." There was pride in her aunt's voice. "And after my team is done with her, she's all yours."

Leona had never taken a life before. She'd been put in enough life-threatening situations to know how to conduct herself, but to actually pull the trigger, wield the knife, or squeeze the life out of someone was an area in which she lacked experience. But this woman … every time Leona dreamed of her, it always ended the same way. A dagger. Dripping blood. Smoke covered faces and death. Leona's.

She ran her thumb across the pads of her fingers and thought of the faceless woman.

Once again, nothing happened.

## Mysterious ways

August 9th, 12pm EST

Katherine didn't believe in God. Most people assumed that was because she was of Asian descent and therefore a Buddhist. Katherine wasn't a Buddhist. She was a Catholic who had converted to atheism when she no longer needed to rely on her parents for financial support.

She grew up attending Holy Mass and catechism classes. While going to confession four times a year was not a requirement, her parents made her do it to prove they were a "good Catholic family". They had hoped that if they attended Church regularly – essentially buying into the local religion and adopting its belief system – they would be seen as more than just the "immigrant" family from China (they were *not* from China), and Katherine wouldn't get teased so much at school for looking different.

Her high school graduating class had a special service for them at the church, and she had attended, as did her parents and most of her classmates' parents, but as Katherine sat in alphabetical order in the pew so that every student could be called up in an orderly fashion by their surname to receive a special blessing from the priest, she had a bit of an epiphany. Religion, she realized, wasn't for her. It wasn't that she was ungrateful for the special blessing, it just seemed a bit irrelevant to the trajectory of her life. She remembered leaning forward and glancing down the aisle to look for the kid who everyone knew was gay but was struggling to come out to his parents for fear of their reaction. Would the special blessing work for him? Would it work for the popular kids who were vapid and, in Katherine's opinion, had enough *blessings* as it were? The smart kids who got teased and ignored, were they destined for better futures because of the words the priest said for them? Would those words be enough to anoint the jocks, whose only hope at an education lay in a scholarship and good, strong bones that wouldn't snap underneath a pile of bodies?

What was the priest's special prayer anyway? That they all do well and continue to love God as He loved them? That they go off to college and then get good jobs and pay their tithes and taxes? More importantly, what about the kids in her class who weren't there at the service? Were their futures rushing to a dead end before they even got started because they weren't in attendance?

All of a sudden – or perhaps because she had finally stopped to think about it – it just seemed like a huge waste of time and effort when, in the end, she couldn't truly, empirically answer if prayer changed anything. Didn't good things happen to bad people and vice versa?

As they called up the students to form a neat and

orderly line, Katherine was only partially paying attention because she was preoccupied with thinking through the repercussions of what could happen to her if she stopped praying. What if, instead of praying for what she wanted, she simply went out and tried to achieve it? What if she didn't ask for assistance but, instead, looked for those who could assist her? It wasn't that she was becoming anti-God as she received her special prayer; instead, it was more of an analysis of a pathway she had never allowed herself to consider before.

Katherine chose one of the empty pews in the back of Mary, the Mother of God Church. It was quiet at this time of day with only a few trickling in during their lunch break. Church was better when it was quiet like this. Even though she hadn't believed in God for many years, Katherine was of the mindset that if a higher power did exist, it would do so in absolute silence. One couldn't hide from the truth in silence. It sat there like the sun in the sky on a cloudless day.

The pew creaked as she sat down, and she ran her hand along the back of the dark wood, impressed by its shine. On the backs of the pews in front of her were rows of Bibles, hymnals, and prayer books. Most of them were worn, but they all remained in relatively good condition. In fact, now that she thought about it, churches were kept in surprisingly good condition considering the amount of wear they got.

As she sat there enjoying her silence, Katherine was struck by the comfort she felt after stepping through the church doors. It was like walking into someone's embrace after a long, tiring day. *Peace, be still.* It was one of her mother's favorite quotes from the Bible. Katherine couldn't remember from which book it was taken, but Mark 4:39 came to mind. She shrugged to herself. It could just as easily be Matthew or Luke for all she knew.

She closed her eyes and allowed her shoulders to relax. She sat there for a while and gave in to the natural rise and fall of her breath. The tension in her jaws released as the weight of the last twenty-four hours settled into the pit of her stomach. She knew Keenan was safe because if Henry didn't get to him, the news would have reported an incident. Keenan would never again be taken without a fight.

One of Katherine's friends had taught her how to meditate when they were in college, but she hadn't done it in years. She always felt too busy to sit around and do nothing. But Katherine breathed in slowly through her nose and exhaled the same way. She counted each exhalation until she was lulled into a peaceful rhythm that helped her mind to focus on the here and now. She caught a whiff of incense and furniture polish that brought back memories of a time when life was simpler, when God was real to her.

Gravity pulled her head forward and jerked her out of a sleep she had no idea she had fallen into. She wiped the side of her mouth and looked around. To the right, on the same pew but with a good amount of space between them, sat Father Ong.

Father Thomas Wáng (Ong being his romanized surname) was either divine intervention or serendipity. He and his family owned the local butchers where Katherine grew up. She had never really known him back then, but she knew his daughter. They weren't best friends, but they were close in the way that immigrants stuck together, even if they weren't immigrants. Katherine never knew the details of what happened, even with her connections she couldn't get the full report without huge sections redacted, but Father Ong's entire family had been killed in a gas leak at their home. It was not, of course, a gas leak. Ong was a double agent and his cover had been blown overseas, and as retribution, he and his family were hired out to an assassin.

Father Ong would call it His Grace, but Katherine saw it more as one of life's great ironies that Ong wasn't in bed with his wife when their house exploded, taking out a few of the neighbors' windows on either side. Instead, Ong was in the bed of another man's wife in the next town over. The police rang his phone and when he answered, all he could think about was that he had been caught. It took him an unbelievably long time to realize his wife hadn't pulled some elaborate prank to punish him for his indiscretions. This was real. His family was dead, and it was his fault.

He negotiated a deal with the US government and they relocated him to Washington, DC. He had to start over, assume a new identity, become a priest.

When Katherine first recognized him, she had approached him to say hello, but she could tell by his reaction that something was afoot. She did some digging and uncovered his story. Now, he worked for her. Sometimes.

"You looked like you needed the rest," Father Ong said.

Katherine nodded slowly. "Thanks for letting me

have it."

Ong sucked his teeth and waved her off. To thank him was to insult him, but she didn't try to retract her expression of gratitude as that would only prolong the offense.

"You need communion?" he asked.

"Only if you promise to give me the good stuff."

He tried to hide his smile, but in the end just laughed. "This is not a house of ill-repute, Katherine."

"No, but it is a church, and where there is a church, there is wine."

He rolled his eyes. "There are some denominations that frown upon libations."

"Yeah, but they're one of the watered-down versions. They believe in birth control."

"Don't be blasphemous, Katherine. It's unbecoming of you."

"It's only blasphemy if it's untrue."

He chuckled and used the back of the pew in front of him to push to his feet. The file indicated Father Ong was in his eighties, but he looked younger. Asian genes. "Follow me. I will pray for your soul."

"I'd rather you pray for my life. We can worry about my soul after the fact."

Katherine stood and followed him down the side aisle. It was a beautiful church, decorated in gold and royal blues and crimson reds. Portraits of angels and sculptures of saints lined the walls.

"Do you know why a church invests in stained glass windows?" Father Ong slowed and glanced over his shoulder. They were about the same height, but it was the way he cut his eyes upward and the way his eyebrows descended to meet in the center of the brow that told Katherine he was serious about his question.

She wanted to say it was a great way to preserve stories, but wasn't that what the Bible was for? "Beauty?" she answered.

"Light," he corrected, and then turned back around to continue down the aisle. "And light represents heaven, spirituality, genesis. He said, 'Let there be light.'"

Katherine nodded, remembering her catechism classes.

"And these scenes ..." He stopped in front of one and they both looked up at the light from outside. "Are meant to remind us of His grace and His unwavering love."

Father Ong didn't join the church out of free will. When she first read his report, she thought his US handlers had chosen this life for him as a way to paint him in a corner, a sort of symbolic gesture that *Someone* would always be watching. But now, all these decades later, when she looked into the depth of his eyes for the sorrow or guilt she knew from experience should be there, she saw nothing but joy ... or maybe just some kind of resigned peace.

They turned the corner and went through a heavy wooden door that slid quietly shut behind them. No matter how many times she came here, she was always struck by how modern it looked in comparison to the main sanctuary. A thick, plush carpet the color of eggplant covered the pathway throughout the hall. Their steps were silent, and she looked over her shoulder as a sense of unease settled. What if she were followed? What if the protocols she put in place to lose a tail hadn't worked? She would be putting this entire church in jeopardy. She doubted Harry would ever sanction anything to harm the parishioners, but that didn't mean priests like Ong and a few others wouldn't meet with some unlikely, but explicable, demise.

He opened the door and allowed her to step inside before he closed it behind them. His office was pretty much the same as the last time she was there. Black leather chair with a tall back, glass table with ornate silver legs. His computer was new, or recently dusted. It lacked the wear that keyboards and screens showed when they were often in use. A filing cabinet that stretched lengthwise instead of vertically was pushed against the wall behind his desk, and Katherine wondered what sort of files priests kept.

"Trouble?" he asked as he sat down.

She nodded and took one of the two seats across from him. There was a window in his office, smaller than any out in the main sanctuary.

"What do you need?" he asked.

"To get a message to Halo."

He sat back and crossed his arms over his chest as a slow smile spread across his face. "How long have you known?"

That he was evolved? After she first read his file, she did some checking into his background herself. Thomas Wáng was born without documentation in a small province in Indonesia. The first record of his existence was dated in the late 1800s, stating his age as nine years old. His "official" name at that time was Wongso Jianghe. Katherine was forced to do some research on the Chinese-Indonesian-Dutch history to put it all together, but her best guess was that Father Ong's origins were Chinese, but his family had somehow made it to Indonesia where they settled. For him to still be alive meant he was either evolved or he was a descendant of the first Wongso. She had never really known which was true, but then again, she didn't feel like it mattered. If she had to guess, she would have said he was a descendant who had committed some crime and had been on the run from the Indonesian government when he had signed on to become a double agent. But now, looking at him, that mole under his left eye would have to be an incredible coincidence given the boy in the photo in the report also had the same one. Could it be?

"Not long," she said, which was technically true. "Do you heal?"

"Oh no! Nothing so grandiose as that," he said. "I age very slowly."

She nodded like she understood, but she wasn't quite sure she did.

"And you? What is your ability?"

Katherine sat back in her chair and sighed. "I have none."

He was surprised by her answer. He leaned forward and looked her over like he needed an answer only her appearance could provide. "Then why?"

That was a long story she didn't have time for and he hadn't yet earned the privilege of hearing. Instead, she leaned forward herself and placed her palms on the glass of his desk. "Senator Harry Carter took one of my agents, and I want her back."

"But I'm a priest. What can I do?"

Katherine chuckled. "Surely by now, Father, you've learned that the Lord works in mysterious ways."

~

## Home

Date/Time: Unknown

He was perched on a ledge wide enough for his left foot to rest, but only the tips of his toes on the right. He was leaning against his side, his hands out at awkward angles clinging to knots on the surface of the mountain as the wind cut through him with such viciousness he was now numb to it. His body was wracked with involuntary tremors in an attempt to generate body heat, though no amount of movement could warm him.

He had been climbing for two days and still had not reached the top. And that wasn't the worst part. The worst part was that it was a clear night. The sky was so bright with the moon and stars that his path was visible as far as his eyes could see. But Sam was weary. He was hungry and thirsty.

He had cried twice, his thoughts running away and creating disastrous stories about what was to come. He thought a lot about Jessica, his daughter who had spent far too few hours alive. He also thought of his wife, who was so consumed with grief she took her own life. And, if he were being honest with himself, he'd always considered her suicide an act of cowardice. Was it not far easier to kill herself than to piece herself back together after the death of her only child?

Yet now, on what would otherwise be a beautiful night, he was able to see things from a different perspective. His wife had lost her parents when she was young and was raised by her grandmother, who had died just after she graduated from college. His wife had no brothers and sisters, just like both her parents, and so she didn't really have anyone to tether her to the living. *He* should've been that tether, but he didn't know how to be that back then. Not when he was too consumed with his own anger and guilt. It was his job to keep his family safe, and he had failed at that. Jessica had only been alive for two hours and eleven minutes.

Sometimes, life just wasn't worth living without the right people in it. Jessica was the right person for his wife, and as Sam clung to the side of the mountain, so cold he couldn't feel it anymore, he realized he understood her decision. His right people weren't here either, and no matter how much he loved Neo, the animal wasn't enough. He wanted to see his father again, and he wanted to see the woman he was in love with. The woman who had become the best part of his dreams as well as the worst part of his nightmares. She, of course, would've moved on by now. She was, after all, a survivor. It was one of the things he most admired about her.

Sam never thought of himself as an emotional man but there was no hiding from the truth in silence, and the stark truth was that he was going to die. The irony that that was his plan wasn't lost on him. He was going to climb to the top of the mountain, get struck by lightning, regain his power, and be transported back to his time. But stuck there on the mountainside on a clear and cloudless night, nowhere near the top, was not how he envisioned his life ending.

He had survived food poisoning, dysentery, a bear attack, and a gnawing hunger that at times reduced his intellect to no greater than that of his animal companion. And after two years of isolation, he was going to fall prey to the elements. He wasn't sure if his father would be proud of him for surviving as long as he had or if he would be angry as hell at him for dying in the manner in which he was going to.

But his father hadn't always been the man everyone saw. There was a time when Walter was absent, gone on missions, returning home but not really being there. When Sam's mother died, it took Walter twelve days to make it back from a classified location. Twelve days was an eternity to a boy who had just lost his mother. It was Bethany and her mom who took him in when child protective services threatened to put him with a foster family. Walter had missed the funeral, and the pain of having to go through the ceremony without his father gave birth to an anger that remained with Sam for years.

For a while after her death, he and his father existed in the same house but had little interaction. Then one day, it was like Walter was done grieving and decided to show up and help Sam get through his own pain. Since then, they had become close. His father wasn't just his best friend, but also his mentor. The thought of never seeing him again made him climb this mountain. Storms and lightning were always passing over its peak. He thought if he could reach the top at the right time, he would be able to return home.

So how had he messed up the timing?

The sky darkened, not by much, but enough to be noticed. Sam looked up as a cloud covered the moon, and then quickly raced on. He looked around and hadn't noticed he had kept climbing. During the last two days, he had made it a habit of keeping on the move. He wasn't sure how his leg muscles hadn't seized, but there he was, pressing up for the next handhold.

Was that a ledge? A proper ledge wide enough to fit his entire body?

If he was lucky, a bird's nest would be there. He would be able to build a fire with the flint still in his pocket.

Sam reached the ledge and collapsed on his stomach as his muscles shook out their fatigue. There was no nest, so he curled into a ball with his back against the wall so that one part of his body was protected from the elements. He had to tuck his head in from the wind which was threatening to push him down, back over the ledge.

That's when he realized he wasn't alone. Living in the wild had sharpened his sense of proximity to other life forms. Whether it was a rabbit or a deer, he had learned to pay attention to his sixth sense.

But Sam was tired. His body had no more to give; therefore, a fight was out of the question. He prayed whatever animal had found him would make it quick, puncture a major artery, so he would bleed out. A loss of consciousness would be fast. He was so cold, he doubted he'd feel it anyway.

Whatever was there was drawing closer, and Sam didn't have the strength to lift his head. But then it growled, and the sound was familiar.

He moved much slower than he wanted, but when he pressed his palms into the cold stone to push himself up, eyes that sparkled in the darkness greeted him.

Sam opened his mouth to speak, but his throat was far too dry to make any sound.

Neo's chest rumbled like that of a cat purring. Then it turned around and ambled back the way it came, farther up the ledge.

Neo stopped and looked over its shoulder before disappearing around the bend.

If Sam had the energy, he would have laughed. But instead, he pulled himself forward on his arms and knees, praying that wherever he was going, there would be warmth. Food and water could wait.

~

## Loyalty

August 10th, 1:00am SGT (+12 EST)

The lights on the footpath at Fort Canning were turned off to discourage use during the night. Dr Dotz and Mal had spent the entire day in the park. They had walked from the north end at Canning Walk all the way down to Hill Street at the bottom. They left briefly to get lunch from Ya Kun's, and that's when the voices began to speak to her again.

An hour ago, she and Mal left the south side of the park and walked up to Fort Gate. It was too dark to make out, but a mark still remained in the stone from two years ago.

The voices had led her here a few times over the past two years, and she was now wondering if that had something to do with why they directed her here tonight.

"You think it's going to rain?" she asked Mal, as she laid her head in his lap.

He nodded. "Inhale."

She did, and she smelled the rain making its way closer to them.

"Should we go?" she asked.

He smiled at her and tucked the tips of her hair behind her ear. "You tell me."

She rolled over into him and gave him an awkward one-handed hug. "I love you."

He chuckled. "Why? Because I'm the only man who'd spend the entire day in the park with you because 'voices' told you to?"

"Exactly." Dotz laughed until it ended in a yawn. "I'm sleepy."

"Rest." Mal ran his fingers across her forehead, and then down over her eyes until they were shut. "I'm sure the voices will have something to say to you soon enough."

For the first time in over eighteen hours, Dotz closed her eyes and drifted off into a deep sleep.

***

Sam thought he was dead until he inhaled a mouthful of Neo's fur. It made him gag, and he rolled out from under the large animal. The instant drop in temperature was jarring and pulled him to full awareness. It was still night, but the stars were gone.

Neo had led him to a clearing large enough to hold half a dozen tents if he were part of an expedition. However, there was still more mountain to climb and he didn't need to see it to know it was there.

The ground rumbled, and it took Sam a moment to realize it was the sound of thunder. Thick, gray clouds rushed by, and not all of them were above him. He had never touched a cloud before, but it had texture, like cotton candy dipped in water just before it melted. The wind picked up and with it came a howl that whistled down the side of the mountain like an angry ghost. He lifted his arms to protect his face from the dust and scree cutting their way across the clearing.

Neo made that purring sound again in his chest as he rubbed his body against Sam's legs. In the past two years, they had grown quite close, but never did Neo show the kind of affection he had expected from a domesticated animal. It made what Sam was about to do even more difficult. Sam was about to leave his best friend, his only friend over the last two years, to a life of solitude because whether Sam's plan worked or not, death was the only outcome.

Sam reached down and rubbed his hand through Neo's fur. "Never before has a man had a more loyal travel companion." His voice caught and he lifted his head up to the sky to stop the tears from falling.

But then it didn't matter because it started to rain. The clouds surrounding him released the water vapor they were holding. He had never seen rain at its origin. A section of cloud broke off from its host when it attempted to pass through him. It grew smaller and disappeared once it had released all its water. Then the sky lit up from behind him and he spun around just as it flashed out. Thunder roared, and he covered his ears as the ground trembled.

At sea level, his plan seemed like a solid one. It even made enough sense for him to give it a try. But up here, soaking wet and his teeth and body once again shivering in an attempt to generate warmth, it no longer seemed like such a stellar idea. What if he needed Rox? She was there when he lost his ability, shouldn't she be present when he attempted to regain them? In the end, it didn't matter. His heart rate increased without the need for him to alter his breathing. The hair on his entire body rose as he watched lightning jump between two approaching clouds. This was his moment. He was either going to curl into a ball, wait out the storm, and most likely die from exposure, or he was going to close his eyes, lift his hands as far above his head as he could, and stand perfectly still.

~

## Salvation

August 10th, 1:58am SGT (+12 EST)

*Help him!*

Dotz jumped awake just as the air around them stilled. Sound ceased. The hair on her arms lifted and she turned to look at Mal. He was already on his feet, searching for the threat on its way.

*Help him!*

"Get behind me." It wasn't a request, and she quickly followed Mal's instruction.

*Dontseedontseedontseedontseedontsee.*

The air started to vibrate as raindrops the weight of pebbles crashed down around them. The air thickened, and instinct told her to run, but the voices kept up their litany of *dontsee*'s.

Then it clicked.

"Close your eyes!" But sound had been neutralized by the vibrations. No drops of rain. No wind. No voice.

She yanked on Mal's arm, and he spun around just in time for her to cover his eyes with the palms of her hands as she squeezed hers shut. A bolt of lightning thundered down and flashed behind her eyelids. She cried out from the concussive explosion that restored sound. Pain sliced through her ears as she was pulled into a warm embrace. A cold blast of energy washed over them that pushed Mal into her.

Then there was silence again.

She stepped back from Mal's embrace and pinched her nose. Scorched earth and a thick smoke that hurt her eyes greeted them.

*Help him!*

At first, she thought it was the rain distorting what was in front of her. She pulled out of Mal's arms, but he didn't release her hand as she started towards the smoking figure laying just outside of Fort Gate.

They both stopped a few feet away and waited for more of the smoke to clear. When it did, the first thing Dotz noticed was the animal lying on its side, its head facing her.

It was the curved teeth that caused her to take a step back.

"Mal," she said in stunned surprise, but her ears were still ringing.

Then she saw an arm lying underneath what had to be at least three hundred kilos of fur and solid muscle. She waited for it to move or give some sign of life.

*Help him!*

She ran towards the animal and began pushing. "Mal!" Tears ran down her face as she finally understood why she had been brought to the park. It hadn't been a wild goose chase. Someone was in need.

It took far longer than she would have preferred, but Mal was able to pull the animal off the man's chest. Dotz pressed her fingers against his wrist before lying her head on his chest to listen for a breath. Two seconds. Four seconds. Five. Six. And then, an inhalation.

She lifted up so she could stare at his face. It wasn't the face of anyone she'd ever seen before. Caucasian and gaunt. He looked homeless. But Caucasians weren't homeless in Singapore.

Mal tapped her shoulders, shrugged and mouthed. "Who is he?"

Dotz looked back at the stranger and searched for something familiar. She couldn't think of anyone she knew with a beard this unkempt or this red. Red? Red enough to be seen in the dark.

She looked back up at Mal.

"Sam!

# CHAPTER SIX

## Number One

August 9th, 1:58pm EST

The man who met Tusk when he boarded the vessel looked nothing like someone working on a container ship. He was dressed in black and had a gun holstered at one hip and a knife far too long to do anything but extinguish life on the other. His face was hard, like his eyes had witnessed too much to ever smile again. He had a deep, pale groove running down the side of his face where Tusk assumed a knife not too dissimilar from the one at his hip must have parted his skin. He had introduced himself as Black, and later, Tusk met his partner, Brown, who had an equally unappealing expression, but some of his sour appearance could be due to the sizable red knot just under his left eye. Tusk wasn't sure if their names were some kind of inside joke, given Black was pale with matching hair and Brown was the exact opposite, but they were both equally frightening, and he had an uncomfortable suspicion that if he had to defend himself against either of these two, he would be dead before he knew it.

Tusk finally made it to the top of the rope ladder three containers high, and tossed his doctor's bag up and over before climbing up onto his feet. He looked over his shoulder and immediately regretted it. A fall from this height meant instant death, and from the look of his escorts, they would just simply roll him overboard and not think twice about it. His fear must've shown on his face because Black laughed.

"C'mon, man," Brown said, and so Tusk followed.

The container holding Katherine's number one was balanced across two rows of containers stacked three high. A thick hose ran through a cut-out hole at the bottom of the one holding Katherine's lead. The closer he got, the colder the air grew. There were also multiple cables crisscrossing their way to a multi-source outlet that supplied some type of power inside. Could one of them be connected to a camera? He hadn't thought about being recorded.

"Look here," said Brown. "We don't care what you do when you get in there, but do not get close." He pointed to the knot at the top of his cheekbone.

Tusk nodded. "I-is she restrained?"

Black laughed at him again, but Brown answered. "Is now."

"We'll be right out here waiting for you," Brown said. "You're approved for twenty-five minutes, and not a second more. If you wanna come out early, give us a knock, yeah?"

"Or a scream," Black said with another laugh.

He could tell that neither of these men were evolved, but Tusk wondered what it would mean if men like these could become evolved.

"Yeah," Brown chuckled. "That'll work too."

Tusk had worked with men like these before, big on brawn, but not much else. They had a mission, and they'd do anything to achieve it.

Tusk inhaled a deep breath and remembered that it was he, not Mallory, who had gotten mankind this close to unlocking evolved abilities. "No cameras," Tusk said simply. "I don't want what's going to happen in there recorded."

Brown shrugged his shoulder like he didn't care. "No cameras then." He bent down and pulled a plug from the power source and flicked open a pocket knife he had in his pocket. He did something with the plug and then turned back to Tusk.

It was the fuse from the power cable he assumed controlled the camera. Without it, even if he plugged in the camera, it wouldn't work.

Brown lifted his arm and pressed a button on his watch that gave a beep. "Time starts now, Doc." Black opened the door behind him and a loud screech made Tusk jump. He turned around just as a blast of cold air smacked him from the inside of the container. He would've commented on it if at the same time the light coming from within didn't blind him. He squeezed his eyes shut and turned his head away.

"Let me turn that down." Brown leaned over the power source again and yanked another power cord free. The light coming from the inside instantly diminished, but thankfully didn't go out completely. "She's all yours."

The air coming up from the floor was cold enough for Tusk to see his breath when he stepped inside. He could make out a woman sitting, her arms tied behind her back and her legs tied to the chair. Her head was hanging forward and her hair was loose and disheveled. He couldn't tell if it was wet or had gone days without washing, and therefore greasy. But it was the fact that she had no clothes on that caused Tusk to suck in a deep breath.

He jumped when he heard the lever that locked the container door lower.

He turned back to Katherine's number one and her head was up. Despite the tremors racking her body from the intense cold, there was fire in her eyes that said all she was waiting for was an opportunity.

Tusk wasn't sure what he had expected to find. It wasn't like he was unaccustomed to less than five-star conditions or seeing people in restraints. He preferred to restrain his subjects to ensure they didn't interfere with his experiments, but he never tortured any of them, and by the looks of this woman, she had experienced a "personal" encounter with the Black and Brown duo.

For a long moment, he stared at her, not sure what to make of the red and blue bruising on her face or the one eye that was practically swollen shut. But then he heard her teeth chatter and watched as she clenched her jaw close in an attempt to regain control.

He walked around her once, and then back the other way to see if she had any other injuries that weren't apparent. The hatred in her eye was palpable, but he dismissed it because her emotions were for her to sort out. He was here to make sure she remained alive long enough to deliver a message.

"Listen, I don't have long." He stopped in front of her and took two steps back and then stooped down to unzip his bag. He pulled out a pen light so he could check her left eye. It looked pretty bad.

"I know who you are." Her throat was dry and so it came out as a whisper.

He looked up in surprise, but then realized if she were indeed Katherine's number one, then of course she would know him. She was the one responsible for Alchemy, and more than likely Wonderland, Watership Down, Mockingbird, and possibly all the other ones.

Tusk snorted. "And I know who you are."

She opened her mouth to reply, but was struck by a coughing fit that sprayed blood across her chest and lap. When she finished, she looked up as if nothing had happened. "Let me guess. You fix me up so they can beat on me again?"

Blood in her lungs, he surmised. There was a crimson-colored bruise just under her heart. From its size, a few ribs were broken and one of them may have punctured a lung. But there was that fire in her eye again when he lifted his gaze. She had a level of pain tolerance that not many could claim. Cracked ribs and a punctured lung meant each breath was agony. Perhaps that was the reason why her voice was so faint. It wasn't because her throat was dry, it was because she wasn't getting enough oxygen to speak any louder.

"I am here to help."

The surprise on her face meant he had said the last thing she expected. But then she smiled, and he was sure she would've laughed if it were not for the pain that lanced through her side. She moaned, and he thought she was going to lose consciousness.

He took a step closer and clapped his hands as loud as he could. "Hey, stay with me. What's your name?" He already knew her name, but he needed her to trust him, even if just a little.

She shook her head, but then he shined the penlight in her good eye, attempting to over-stimulate one of her senses. "All I want is a name."

She nodded like she was going to comply, but then once she felt steady enough to speak, she told him to fuck off. Or at least that was what he thought she said to him. He hadn't considered that she wouldn't believe he was there to help. For all the facilities he had run and the experiments he had conducted, he was surprised at himself for not being more prepared.

Tusk wasn't sure if Black and Brown were telling the truth about the cameras, but he was running out of time. "Was it you?" he asked her. "Who blew up Alchemy?"

She looked confused. Would she know the names of his facilities? "Laos. Two years ago. Pak Tha?"

A smirk settled on her face and it was obvious that it caused her pain, but she held it.

Tusk sighed. So few people understood the importance of his work. Mostly, it was because people were notoriously short-sighted. But if the choice was saving millions of lives by sacrificing a few hundred, well, who would choose the alternative? He was going to reverse – or maybe even halt – aging. His research was going to show humans how they could heal their own ailments. Was that not worth a few lives? A few hundred even?

"What about it?" she asked.

"I can't get you out of here," he said. "But I can tell your team where you are."

He reached into his bag and pulled out a sealed syringe packet along with its hub and shaft. He looked around for a clean place to put them, but realized there was no table or similar surface, so put them on the cold floor since they were still wrapped in plastic. He pulled out a vial and rubbed it between his palms upside down. "Listen, I don't have much time but this will help with the pain." He placed the vial in his shirt pocket and then opened the syringe packet so he could screw the hub onto the syringe's barrel.

"What are you doing?"

He didn't have time to go through the ins and outs of his plan. Hell, he wasn't sure he fully understood it, but if he had any hope of retaining ownership of his work, he was going to have to dispose of Dr Mallory Fined, and for that, he would need help.

He flicked the vial a few times and then inserted the needle into its rubber top.

"What are you giving me?" She wasn't able to get up, but she pulled as far away from him as the restraints around her arms and legs would allow.

Tusk knew there was no point in trying to explain it all to her; he didn't have the time anyway. It would be up to her from now, but he was going to give her the best chance she had without exposing himself before he was ready.

"I can't stay here to help you. You've got to fight through the drowsiness, okay? Do *not* give in and fall asleep or this will all be for nothing."

She didn't say anything, but she didn't need to. She was busy trying to work out if this was some kind of trick.

"I'll cut through your restraints, but you've got to pretend like you're still tied to the chair when they come in."

He stepped back and had a good look at her. The ribs, the eye, the lack of blood flow to her extremities because of the restraints all meant she was in no condition to fight, not that he had any advice to give her about Brown and Black anyway. Sure, she was muscular, it was obvious she took exceptional care of her body from the definition along her arms, shoulders, abdomen, and legs, but even in top form, she would be lucky to take out just one of them, let alone both. In her current state? Tusk sighed. But the simple fact was that she was his only hope.

"When you get free, you need to notify Katherine. Harry's onto her, but the real threat is coming from Dr Mallory Fined. Do you understand?"

She raised her eyebrows for a moment like she was listening, so he continued.

"She's the head of AmLife. She's partnered with Harry to be the leader in genetic manipulation of evolved abilities."

"I don't understand," she said, her voice hoarse.

"You don't need to; you just need to remember. Dr Mallory Fined of AmLife. Say it."

She stared at him for so long he lifted his hand to snap his fingers. But then she said *no* and pursed her lips.

If he was in one of his facilities, he would have ways to make her comply. But, in the shipping container with cold air pumping in through a pipe at the floor and a light so bright it hurt the eyes even when they were closed, he lacked the tools needed to get her to see things from his perspective. “Listen, you and I have sat on opposing sides for quite some time now. But trust me when I say there is a threat to the both of us. She’s not only got the financial backing I always had to scrape together, she’s got Senator Harry Carter backing her. You know what that means, don’t you?”

She lowered her head, and he wondered if she was considering what he had said or if she decided she didn’t want to hear anymore.

Tusk looked at his watch. He wasn’t out of time yet, but he didn’t have a lot left. “Harry is working with Mallory to steal my research. I believe that unlocking the genetic sequence that creates evolved humans is the biggest discovery we will make since mankind’s learned to control fire, the domestication of animals, agriculture, and vaccinations.”

“And what do Harry and Mallory want to do with your research?”

“I believe they want to figure out how to create evolved ones to weaponize them, and perhaps create a new marketplace where evolved genetics is sold to the highest bidder.”

She snorted and then winced against the pain. “How’s that any different to what you’ve done and the pain you've caused?”

What did she just say? Was she serious? He had never maliciously harmed one of his patients. Oh sure, some of his experiments had wreaked havoc on their pain receptors, but still, it was done in the pursuit of knowledge, never pain for the sake of it. But looking at her now, the fire still burning bright in her one good eye, he realized that regardless of the intent, pain was pain to the recipient.

"You've ripped people away from their families, against their will, and then you stuffed them into boats, transported them using human trafficking channels to one of your facilities so you can run experiments on them." Her speech was delivered in between wheezing breaths, but then she laughed. It was a silent one, but she bore the pain to make her point. "I don't see how you're any different."

Tusk felt his anger rising. If she couldn't see the difference between him and someone like Mallory, then maybe she was exactly where she was meant to be. "I did what I did in the pursuit of science! Not currency."

"Yeah? Based on the financial records I've uncovered, you weren't exactly altruistic."

He took a step closer to her. "I had to generate revenue somehow! There isn't money just lying around for those who are trying to progress mankind. I did what I had to do. I won't apologize for that."

"You kidnap children," she rasped. "You murder people just so that you can watch them come back alive. You're no different than—"

The only person he had ever come across who could return from the dead was Tara. And while he suspected that Katherine and Tara worked together, Meita just confirmed it. Tara was worth more than all the evolved ones he had ever worked on combined. Her ability to heal could eradicate cancer, heart disease, and people with diabetes would have a new lease on life.

When he looked back down at her, she was staring at him with disgust. It was his turn to smile. "If you think I'm bad, then wait'll you see what Mallory does."

That got her wheels turning because she finally shut up. He didn't want to spend the rest of his twenty-five minutes convincing her he was there to help.

"We have a shared enemy now whether you like it or not. You can either help me, and in turn, I will do what I can for you, or you can sit here and wait to die by the likes of Black and Brown out there."

Her jaw tightened at the mention of their names.

"What's your name?"

Her lips sealed into a thin line again.

"I gotta give Harry something or he might get suspicious if I go back empty handed."

"Maybe he'd just think you're incompetent and couldn't do the job."

He snorted. "I think we both know that if I wanted to *make* you talk, I could. The fact that I've come in here as I have should be proof enough of what I have been saying."

When she didn't reply, he decided it was time to take their conversation to the next level. "Listen," he said as he wrapped his hands in her tangled hair and pulled her head to the side. "This won't last nearly as long as you need it, but it's the best I can do." He stuck the syringe of toradol into her neck and slowly pressed the plunger.

She screamed out, and he quickly glanced over his shoulder to make sure that Black or Brown weren't coming in.

When all the liquid was emptied into her blood stream, he pulled the syringe back out and quickly unscrewed the hub away from the barrel and put them into a small plastic case in his doctor's bag.

"What did you just—" But then the euphoria hit her and her head fell forward.

Everyone reacted differently, and so Tusk looked down at his watch and waited. Thirty-five … Forty-five … Fifty-eight, fifty-nine … He leaned forward and smacked her. The sound reverberated around the refrigerated container. "Hey," he snapped his fingers right near her ear.

She looked up at him, but it took her a few moments to focus. Then tears flooded her eyes as she squeezed her lips shut like she was trying to remain quiet.

"I didn't know you were going to be …" he gestured to her nudity, "and so I didn't come prepared with a way for you to hide this." He stooped in front of his bag again and pulled out a pair of surgical scissors and cut through the zip tie that was restraining her hands behind the back of the chair.

He wasn't sure if it was the toradol or the fact he just released her arms, but she had a sort of stupefied expression on her face when she looked up.

"Rub your wrists, and make sure you do windmills with your arms," he instructed as he released her legs. "You're going to need circulation in your limbs if you have any hope of taking on Black and Brown."

Tusk turned away from her and emptied the entire contents of his bag out onto the floor. Then he reached his hand in and began to remove the lining from the inside. He pulled out a Walther PPK and passed it to her. "The safety's on and I'm told it has a sensitive trigger."

Even high with the toradol pumping through her, she handled the weapon with an expertise born of habit. Whoever she was, she was no stranger to a handgun. She released the magazine and slipped free one bullet to inspect it. "These are live rounds." Her words were slurred, but she was surprisingly steady on her feet given her punctured lung.

"Blanks won't do much against those two I'm afraid. Where are you going?" he asked when she headed towards the back of the container.

"You told me to circulate," she said. "So the best way to do that and keep warm is to move around."

He nodded. "Now, I've just armed you and set you free. You gonna give me your name or something I can take back to Harry?"

She lifted the weapon and pointed it at his head. Her arm immediately began to shake and she added her other arm to help steady her aim, but her face contorted in pain.

"You won't have time to take aim anyway," he said. "Not against those two."

He started to repack his bag. "Dr Mallory Fined. AmLife." He looked back up at her.

"This could all still be a trick," she said. "Some kind of elaborate trap."

"If you are Katherine's number one, then I think you know me well enough to know that I don't do elaborate. Elaborate takes too much time. I like to get in and get out."

She laughed.

"Listen, I gotta go now." He stood facing her.

"I need you to do me a favor."

He raised an eyebrow. "And what would you call this?"

"The right thing. Now about that favor."

"Name. I need your name."

He watched her try to take a deep breath, but in the end wheeze through a few shallow ones before answering. "Meita bint Tariq al-Shaikh."

She told the truth. That mattered.

"How did you find me?" she asked.

He shrugged. "Harry used to run GFO, he looked through old employee records."

Meita was surprised. "He's not supposed to have access to that."

He gave her a sad smile. "I have to go. Remember, Dr Mallory Fined—"

"Yes, head of AmLife. They're trying to steal your work." Even though her voice was barely above a whisper, her tone gave away her thinking. "Hey?" she called. "I need a favor."

Tusk laughed. He gestured to the gun in her hand and the chair from which he recently liberated her.

She shook her head. "An actual favor."

Under different circumstances, he might actually like Meita bint Tariq al-Shaikh. It was the fire that refused to be extinguished in that one good eye. It reminded him of Nancy. "What is it?"

"I need you to send an email to Henry Teasdale at GFO dot com." She spelled out his name.

"The message?"

"Eagle Eyes is at yoga."

There was a bang on the outside of the container and she went back to her seat as quickly as she could and sat back down. Meita put her hands behind her back, but didn't relinquish her weapon.

He liked Meita. He hoped she would make it out. He doubted her chances, but people survived worse situations with far worse odds. For some reason, he thought of Nancy and how Rox bested her. Maybe one day he would be able to talk to her about it.

The creak of the bar that locked him inside lifted. He walked to the door as it opened. He was greeted with a gun pointed at his forehead.

"Shit," Black said as he holstered his weapon. "I guess next round's on me."

Brown was laughing as Tusk stepped out. The contrast in temperature sent a chill down his spine. It was amazing that Meita was still alive.

"So, Doc," Brown began. "You get what you needed?"

Tusk looked over his shoulder at Black who was peering into the container like he was looking for something. "Not a lot, but enough." He returned the fuse for the camera cable to Brown.

"Bitch is feisty, ain't she?" Black said, but he still hadn't taken his eyes off her.

"She was mostly silent with me," Tusk said.

Black tore his eyes away from the inside of the container

and over to him. "Nah, you're too soft. Woman like that needs a little something harder."

To Tusk's great horror, Black reached down and grabbed his crotch. He glanced back at Brown who was busy studying him.

"I'm going in," Black said.

What? Now? This was too soon. He needed to be further away when she was forced to attack. "Why?" he didn't mean to say it aloud, but he realized his mistake the moment he did.

Brown nodded with his chin for Black to go ahead.

Tusk stepped away from the door as Black disappeared inside the container. He wasn't sure what would happen, but he looked over the side of the container at how far he would have to jump. He'd never make it.

The faint sound of a gun firing echoed from the inside, and when he looked back up, Brown was pointing a gun at his forehead.

"Knew I couldn't trust you." Brown spat on the container beneath them. "You're too fucking smarmy for me."

Tusk held up his hands, his bag still in his grip. Smarmy?

"Turn around and open the door," Brown shouted at him.

He knew better than to hesitate. Brown was looking for any excuse to shoot him, so Tusk turned around and reached for the handle.

"Drop the bag."

Tusk nodded and dropped his medical bag on the floor and used both his hands to open the door. Brown came up behind him and used his body as a shield as he pushed him inside.

Another shot fired and Tusk curled down onto himself, not sure who was firing and if he had been hit. But then there was a thud behind him and he looked back.

Brown was lying on his side, his weapon still in his grip, a hole the size of a macadamia nut on his temple.

Tusk turned back to see Meita about a foot away. She was shivering so badly he was surprised she was able to get off two true shots.

She asked him a question, but he couldn't hear her. The gunfire had been too loud; he had been too close.

He shook his head.

She pointed to Black, and then Brown and then mouthed something. When he still didn't understand, she pointed to their bodies again and then shrugged her shoulders, which caused her pain.

*How many more!*

Tusk shook his head. "I didn't see anymore. I think this might be it."

She nodded and then looked between the two men she felled with an ease that he had not expected. He looked her over again. This was training. Habit. This was Katherine's number one.

Wait. She could be like him. He studied her as she bent down in front of Black and immediately straightened up in pain. She bent her knees and leaned from the waist, trying to keep her upper body as straight as possible as she began to untie his shoe laces. He could tell from the way her brow was pulled tight that she was trying to think her way through the next sequence of events. The toradol he had given her was blocking her pain receptors, but not entirely it seemed, plus it didn't come without side effects. Her body would be filled with adrenaline, which meant she should be high, her judgment impaired, but instead she appeared calm. Unsteady, but calm, like she had been through this before.

Meita unbuttoned Black's pants without relinquishing her hold on the gun. She struggled to lift him into the sitting position because even though she was numb to most of the pain from her cracked ribs and punctuated lung, no amount of pain meds could increase her lung capacity. Her breathing was changing and she'd begin to hyperventilate if she didn't take it slower.

"Sit down," he told her.

She paused and looked up at him.

"You're going to kill yourself before you deliver my message. Sit down. I'll take off his shirt. That's what you want, right? His clothes?"

She nodded, and he pulled Black by his arms into the seated position. But then his head fell to the side and bits of his brain slipped out of the hole on the other side of his head where the bullet had existed. It landed on the floor with a plop, and Tusk realized that wasn't a sound he was unfamiliar with, and obviously, neither was Meita.

She pulled the shirt over her head very slowly and pushed her arms through the sleeves. "Where's the scissors you used to cut me loose?"

He went back outside the container with her close behind him. She closed the door and secured the lock in place. One of their knives was in her hand, and one of their guns was in the other. A pair of trousers were tucked under her arms.

*She was fast.*

He unzipped his bag and passed her the scissors. She took five slow, deep breaths and then cut the legs off Black's trousers, turning them into shorts. They were far too big, but he had an idea. He took the scissors from her, went over to one of the power cables, and cut off a good length and passed it to her.

She threaded it through the belt loops and then tied it into a knot. For the first time since she came out of the container, she stopped and had a good look around her. They were too far out to see land, and he surmised she had no idea where she was. "We're at the mouth of the Patapsco River."

It took her a few moments, but she finally nodded. She was still shivering, and now that they were outside in sunlight, he could see the blue tinge to her lips. He looked around for something to wrap around her shoulders, but there was nothing.

"How'd you get aboard?" she asked.

He explained he was brought here by the coast guards, and as soon as he climbed aboard, he was met by Black. She nodded like she understood.

"You think they're still waiting for me?"

She nodded and passed him the gun she had taken off Black or Brown. "Put this in your bag."

"Won't they know something's up when they see me returning with you?" Tusk asked. "I mean, I don't mean any offense, but you don't look like someone I can just bring to shore without questions."

The corner of her mouth lifted into a smile as she pointed to the rope ladder leading down the containers. "You go first."

"What? Down?" Was she crazy?

"You wanna stay up here?"

Fair point.

"Listen, the coast guard won't know anything. I'm willing to bet they are just following orders, and those orders were to transfer someone to this shipping vessel. I doubt the captain knows what's going on here. Start climbing down. If them banging on the door meant you had to go, then we're already late."

Tusk slipped the bag onto the crook of his arm and then slowly lowered himself over the side of the container until his foot touched the rung of the ladder. His heart raced just like it did when he escaped from Alchemy, and Wonderland before that.

It was slower coming down, but when his foot touched the deck, he breathed a sigh of relief. He looked up and saw Meita was visibly shaking. "Look at me," he instructed when she touched down.

He widened the skin around her good eye. Dilated pupil. Feverish to the touch. He needed to get her somewhere safe if she was going to hold up her end of the bargain. "Hold on to me." He pulled her arm around his shoulders and started towards the next ladder where the boat was. "Just a little further." She would have to find the strength to climb down yet another long ladder. He hoped she was right and the coast guards didn't know anything.

He got them to the side and he peered over the railing.

Waiting below was the boat. He wasn't sure if he should breathe a sigh of relief or a take a deep breath filled with apprehension. When he looked back at Meita, her eyes were sliding shut, and so he gave her a good firm slap.

She jolted awake.

"Listen, I'm going first. You follow me down. Don't wait for me to get in the boat before you start. Start as soon as I'm on that third or fourth rung. You got me?"

She nodded, but he wasn't sure if she was going to be able to hold on that long. From this height, a fall into the water would break every bone in her body.

"Meita?" He snapped his fingers in front of her eyes and then again in front of her ears. "If you fall asleep now, you're dead."

She nodded again like she understood, but her head was slipping forward.

"Do you know Tara?"

Her eyes widened. He had found his mark.

"I've never had a subject like her." He knew it was a low blow, but it had the desired effect. Her brow creased and the fire in her eye roared with life.

~

## Failsafe

August 9th, 2:15pm EST

Henry missed the edge of the bed when he sat down and slammed onto the floor. The room shook and the floorboards protested against the sudden drop in weight, but it held. If he wasn't already numb from exhaustion and worry, it would've hurt. He ran his hand over his face and leaned his head back against the foot of the bed. The bed he had missed sitting down on.

He just didn't know what to say. He was hoping that the unidentified caller would've been Katherine or Meita, anyone but who it was presenting him with yet another problem he had to solve. "Are you sure it's him?" he asked.

"Where is Katherine? I want to speak with her."

Henry wanted her to speak with Katherine as well, but she wasn't exactly available at the moment. Who knew if she was even alive. He looked around the room that Walter had put him in and wondered how events had spiraled so quickly out of control that he wound up here. He had heard of Halo before he joined Katherine a few years back, but he didn't know they really existed until he began working for her. Funny how much of his life had changed in the last three years.

"Is Meita there?" she continued. "Walter? Rox?"

This woman seemed to know everyone by name, which was either a sign she had done her homework or she was someone they could trust. "Can you please hold for a moment?"

He pressed hold on his phone and then put his head down in between his knees and took a few deep breaths. It had surprised him just how much he had come to like his job even though it wasn't an "at will" type of employment arrangement. Katherine had explained to him quite clearly when she forced him to work for her that he should take each day he awoke as a sign that he had done well the day before.

Henry had spent those first few months in perpetual fear. Katherine wasn't an easy woman to work for. She was direct. She cared nothing for his feelings, not that he was the overly emotional type, but she had a way of cutting a man down to his marrow that left him feeling … inadequate. It wasn't until she explained to him just what kind of facility he had been guarding and the kind of "research" he'd been inadvertently supporting did he begin to understand her. And that understanding eventually led to respect.

He had lost a lot of colleagues the day she'd phoned him when he was still working at WD-11. He still remembered the briefing when Connor had told them they were expecting intruders. Two men with extensive combat training were coming to help someone escape. They weren't sure who that "someone" was, but they needed to be on high alert. Chances were the intruders were going to infiltrate from the cliff side, but they were to be taken alive if possible. The lead scientist – who Katherine later explained to him was named Dr Clifford Tusk – wanted them captured because they were more useful that way.

Henry lifted his head and laid it back on the bed. He hadn't known. None of them knew. But none of them cared either. It was a job. The pay was great, the benefits were amazing, and they even got paid when they were on rotation. He was told it was a facility dedicated to curing mental illness and that the patients all suffered from some type of degenerative brain deficiency that made them create elaborate stories they confused with reality. But if he were honest with himself, he hadn't wanted to know the truth. The money was too easy, and it was twice as much as he had made in the military. He'd never had that much disposable income. In fact, he'd never had any disposable income. The fact that all he had to do was walk the perimeter and make sure none of the patients escaped should've been a huge sign that something was wrong, especially since he was given a military-grade weapon, but again, he just wanted the paycheck.

Then Katherine came along. She gave him an opportunity and a purpose. She rode him hard, and not in the physical sense. She made him stop and think about every single sentence he was going to say before he said it. She would ask him how he knew the data he provided her was accurate. Hell, she would ask him if he was certain the coffee he was bringing her had no milk in it. At first, he didn't know how to respond and neither did he know whether to take her literally or not. Then Meita took him to lunch. It was Meita who showed him how to relax around Katherine. It hurt to think about what she must be going through to miss check-in.

Now Sam's body had surfaced. What would Meita do if she were here?

A slow smile spread across his face. Well, she wouldn't be sitting on the floor feeling overwhelmed for starters. She would take control of the situation.

"Hello? Dr Dotz, are you still there?" Henry asked.

"Yes, I am. I was just asking if I could speak with Katherine or Meita or maybe Walter, if he's there. Sam is his son and I'm sure he'd want to know he's been found."

Henry cleared his throat and got to his feet so he

could pace around the room that reminded him of his grandmother. She would douse woodchips she collected from the firewood in different smelling oils and place them around the house. Cinnamon. Vanilla, and another fragrance he couldn't remember.

"I'm afraid everyone's indisposed at the moment. I'm all ya got. But here's what I can do for you. Firstly, I need a photo confirmation of his body, another of his face, close up, with today's newspaper showing the date."

He heard Dr Dotz inhale.

"Listen, ma'am," Henry said. "I don't mean to offend you, but I have protocol I need to follow. I sure as hell hope you do have Sam's body. I know his father, in fact all of us, would like nothing more than to put him to rest properly. But if I take that promise to them and come to find out you don't actually have him … well, I'm sure you can imagine the devastation I'll be making them live through a second time."

Then she laughed. Henry wasn't expecting that. It sounded like a tinkle really, like what he imagined a fairy would sound like if fairies were real and one of their kind laughed.

"I don't think you understand," she said. "He's alive."

Henry stopped pacing. He quickly scanned his memory of the reports he had read. They all said he had disappeared and was "presumed dead". "What do you mean 'alive'?"

She explained to him that Sam had a pulse, his pupils responded to light, but he was unconscious at the moment.

"Has he seen a doctor, ma'am?"

"Oh no!" Dr Dotz explained that if she took him to a

doctor, there'd be a lot of questions and she thought it was best to just get him back home as soon as possible.

Henry thought about that for a moment. Mika was on assignment somewhere in Cambodia. Then he remembered Guy Koh, who was in charge of Halo Southeast Asia. "Is Mr Koh available?"

There was a moment of silence and then an older gentleman's voice spoke. He asked to speak to Katherine. Henry paused. He remembered her saying that Koh was Mika's uncle and that if Mika was ever in trouble, they could trust him. They weren't allies, she'd said; the man was a friend. Katherine went through a lot of pain to distinguish between the two.

"She's at yoga, Mr Koh."

The line went silent again. "Oh, I see. And Ms al-Shaikh?

The fact that he understood what that meant was promising. "Likewise."

"Understood," Mr Koh said. "Shall I send my two agents to accompany Major Watts on his return journey?"

"That would be appreciated," Henry said. Though he wasn't sure he understood what that meant. Was he offering to help? If so, in what capacity?

"They, of course, would require authorization from you to assist with whatever help Ms Cheung needs in terms of returning from yoga. Can you do that?"

"Absolutely." Henry had no idea what that meant either, but he was certain Meita would've said yes, and so he said yes.

"Excellent. I'll leave the travel arrangements to you to organize then. When Mika calls for his next update, I will be sure to pass on the good news about his brother."

"When's he scheduled to have his next check-in?"

"Seventy-one hours."

That would have to be enough time. "Can you, um, can you still send those confirmation photos for me. As soon as I receive them, I'll send through the flight details." Flight details he could handle. Giving "authorization" to foreign assets to "assist" with yoga was a little above his pay grade, but he needed the help.

"Consider it done."

*Sam was alive.* Henry wasn't sure what to make of that. He started for the door to tell them the good news, but stopped. He caught a glimpse of his reflection in the mirror resting on top of the dresser. This room reminded him of a time when life was simpler. He had spent summers in a room like this. All it was missing was the green paint and the baseball card collection.

Baseball was his grandfather's favorite sport, and it became a way for the two of them to bond. Cracker Jack boxes and Budweiser. That's what Henry remembered most about his childhood. That and his father not returning from the war. His grandfather wasn't the same anymore. Sure, they still went to games, but it wasn't the same. It was like his father's death had taken the joy in baseball with him.

Henry wanted to tell Walter his son was alive. Especially when his phone pinged and he received the photos he had asked for. It didn't look like him, though. A lot had happened in those two years he was missing, and from the looks of it, not all of it was good for Sam. Most of his face was covered in facial hair, but that wasn't what gave

Henry cause for concern. It was the hollow cheeks and the severely cracked lips. Dark circles appeared to be tattooed beneath eyes that were more sunken than Henry recalled. He had a feeling that whoever this man was – and he was feeling more certain than ever it was Sam – he was far from being the Sam everyone remembered.

He read the brief report that came with the images. It said that Sam had not regained consciousness and hadn't returned alone. A few other images showed an animal that had "supposedly" appeared atop of him. Henry put his thumb and forefinger on the screen and widened the picture. Was that a saber-toothed tiger?

Henry looked up from the phone and stared out the window into the early afternoon simply because he wasn't sure where else to look. Then he gazed back down at the images and flicked through all of them again. He wasn't particularly into history. He paid attention in high school, and the military taught him about wars of historic and strategic importance, but as far as remembering about the ice age and the paleo-tonic period, or whatever it was called, that wasn't information he was ever interested in retaining. He ran his hand over his face again and exhaled a deep, slow breath just like he had witnessed Katherine doing on many occasions.

At GFO, they never spoke about abilities. Not openly at least. It was always done behind closed doors and with only certain people in attendance. Henry was one of them. It was in those meetings he learned that Rox was a healer and she controlled electricity, or energy to be more precise. He knew she had died more times than they had recorded and that her most gruesome death was being struck by lightning, though he had argued it was having her throat slit. The file noted that if she should become a threat to national security, they should initiate Failsafe Initiative, Phase II. Rox was to be shot in the head, followed immediately by two more in the heart. Her head should be removed and her limbs severed. Her body parts should be cremated, separately, nothing buried, and all of her remaining ashes were to be mixed in six separate containers of no less than ten-thousand milliliters of oil, each, and then burned.

However, Rox wasn't Katherine's biggest concern. That was Josh. Katherine struggled to control him, and she didn't always trust her mind when she left him. She took diligent notes before every meeting with him, and then afterwards, she compared her thinking to what she had recorded before their meeting. She listed him as the number one threat to national security. He remembered Katherine once saying that Josh could have them eating shit for breakfast, and they'd all be thinking it was corn flakes. Should he become a threat, there was Failsafe Initiative, Phase I: one shot to the head, two to the heart. His plan lacked the need for cremation. A burial sufficed.

The only ones who were known to successfully block Josh's mind influencing attempts were Rox and Meita. Katherine warned that if GFO was ever suspected to be involved in the death of Mr Mendez, they should immediately initiate FSI-PII as the loyalty between Josh and Rox was never to be underestimated. Josh and Rox were classified as allies, not friends.

If Henry told Walter there was a possibility Sam was alive, Walter would go looking for his son, taking Rox with him. Wherever Rox went, Josh followed. That would put Henry three team members down, and he needed all the help he could get at the moment.

Henry had under seventy hours before Mika would call in and find out his brother was alive. It was about a fifteen-hour flight from Singapore's Changi Airport to JFK, depending on the aircraft, plus one or two hours to make the arrangements, and another two hours to actually get to Halo. It would be faster to arrange a direct flight to Hartford.

He ran his fingers through his hair and sat down on the bed before lying on his back. Keenan presented an entirely different set of issues. There was no file on him, but Walter had called him a healer. Two healers? Why didn't Katherine have an FSI for Keenan? Was it because he was the "protocol"? Did that mean he could trust Keenan? Something about him made Henry hesitant. Maybe it was because of the threat at the airport. Maybe it was because there was no file on him. Or maybe it was because Henry had seen him lower his window and whisper Rox's name as they were driving up to the main house. He had never *seen* wind before. He had seen leaves fall or snow flurry because of the wind, but to actually *see* wind ...

His phone vibrated and he lifted it above his face so he could read it. Another message from someone in the office needing his approval for something as he was now running things.

He sat up. He would sleep later. Right now, he had an

incoming call to answer, an office to manage, a flight to arrange, and two operatives to bring back from yoga.

~

**Ally**

August 9th, 2:15pm EST

"And you're sure he's stable?"

"Yes, Rox!" said Kamal Sheppard.

"It's just that I can't connect with him," Rox explained.

Kamal chuckled. "That's because he's on some pretty heavy painkillers, love."

Rox cracked her knuckles as she paced in the kitchen. She walked between the wall and the long kitchen table. There was a bouquet of flowers in the center that would need replacing in a day or two. "You know, I can catch a flight there. I can take a helicopter to Hartford, and then get Meita to arrange a flight—"

"Meita hasn't checked in, Rox," Kamal said. "Calm down. I'm not a surgeon, but I've got him. Kevin's here, too. He's not left his side since they brought him out of surgery. I think the doctors are starting to think they're a couple. Stop worrying. Nothing's going to happen to him. I promise. Hang on a sec."

She took a deep breath and spun back around to pace in the other direction. She could trust Kamal. He knew about Josh's ability. He was one of them. She had told him they might all be in danger, so he would take the necessary precautions. Kevin was Josh's best friend from childhood. There was no one she trusted more with Josh's safety.

Someone was coming after them, and it was obviously connected to Katherine *and* Meita's disappearance. But how? Who could put both Katherine and Meita on the run?

Rox thought back to Uncle Ben and his teenage following. Those kids were too young to be wrapped up in this, but who's to say what was "too young"? Were she and Michael right because they wanted to give their children "normal" lives by keeping them as far away from the evolved struggle as possible? Or were they doing them a disservice? Whoever those teenagers' parents were, at least they had prepared them to do battle against the evolved, even if the evolved weren't the enemy the Fellowship believed them to be. Those parents would be grieving right now. Or at least they would be wracked with worry about where their children were. She had killed them. She'd hoped that taking a life would get easier, which was an odd thing to hope for, but with so many people coming after her who were willing to take her life, she'd hoped she'd develop a level of pragmatism that would make it easier.

"Back. What do you want me to do about Samantha?" Kamal asked.

"Wait. What happened?"

"Nothing. They were just telling me they're ready to move him."

"What? Why?"

"Calm down. They're moving him at *my* request. They're giving him an upgrade because I'm a medical student, Rox.

We look out for one another. You know how a cop will help another cop's family? That sort of thing."

She stopped pacing and balled her fist. She needed to calm down. But someone was coming after them, and after two years of Mika making inroads with Tusk's operations in Southeast Asia, she guessed she had gotten comfortable. She hadn't heard anything from Tusk since Singapore, and she was enjoying not having to look over her shoulder as much. Who was this new threat? And how had they managed to attack Josh? An orange filter threatened to slip over her vision, but she took a few deep breaths to calm herself.

"So, uh, what shall we do with Samantha?" Kamal whispered. "Did he tell you anything about her?"

She shook her head. "Just that he liked her. What's your take on her?"

Kamal exhaled into the phone. He must've been tired. He had taken the first flight from Dulles to Miami when he heard about Josh's attack.

Rox ran her finger down the crease between her brow. "Do you think we can trust her?"

"Uh-uh. Not going to even try to answer that," Kamal said. "I just met the woman. I mean, I know her like most of America knows her. She's a journalist, and a pretty good one at that, but that doesn't mean I *really* know her."

Rox was trying to pass the responsibility of making the decision whether they could bring Samantha into the fold, but Kamal wasn't falling for it, nor should he. It had to be her decision. If she were wrong, there could be catastrophic consequences. Samantha could go public with what they shared with her. The blame for that had to be hers alone.

"When are they going to release him?" she asked.

"I might have enough pull to upgrade his room, but they aren't just going to release him to me," Kamal said. "This is a situation where we could use a Meita."

They didn't have a Meita, but they did have a Henry. "Leave that with me. When they release him into your custody, tell Samantha you're bringing him home – no more – and that his family said she is welcome to come if she chooses. See how she reacts. If she says she's not going anywhere without knowing the location, then leave her. Josh can patch things up with her once I'm done healing him."

"Okay. I'll say something a bit less clandestine than that."

Rox liked Kamal. She hadn't seen a lot of him since he saved her, Walter and Sam at Watership Down, but she remembered his jovial personality during their escape. He was a nervous talker and always spoke his thoughts. That had its pluses as well as its minuses. But he was always good-intentioned, and that meant a lot to her. It meant she could trust him. Kamal was watching over the most precious person to her after her children.

The late afternoon light shone through the window overlooking the picnic area, and Rox absently stopped pacing to lift her hand up to the window. The pane was cooler than it would have been this time a month ago, but it was still warm.

She and Josh had a complicated past. He was like an

older brother – minus their past sexual relationship and the fact that he was quite a bit younger than her. He had taught her that true love didn't die, it just transformed with time. It wasn't that she loved Sam more than Josh, she just loved them differently.

"Ad lib. I trust you," she said. "Just get him here."

"You sure 'there' is the best place to be right now? Didn't you say your kinsman turned up last night?"

Keenan did arrive out of the blue and they still could not be sure he was not followed. But she felt more confident in their odds with him present. While they lacked numbers, they weren't hurting for strength. Sometimes – in fact most times – strength was the most important part of the equation.

"Listen, I'll call you back soon, so keep your phone on you," she said. She would get Henry working on Josh's release into Kamal's custody. Kamal might not be a doctor, but he was a paramedic, and a damn good one at that. He would keep Josh alive until she could heal him, of that she was certain.

"All right. I'll let you know what she says, and stay safe," Kamal said.

They hung up, but Rox didn't stop pacing. Henry was going to have to be a Meita as well as a Katherine. He had been hired from Watership Down when GFO shut it down. Rumor had it that Katherine said if she couldn't make him useful in three months, she was going to have him killed. A part of Rox knew there was some truth to that rumor. She was glad he made it.

But what was she going to have Henry do? Katherine was

resourceful. Always two steps ahead in terms of planning. She had contacts in the most obscure places. *Everyone you meet is a potential ally,* she had counseled. *So, treat them as one until they prove otherwise.* But then Katherine would use them, which made Rox feel uncomfortable. *A friend is not the same as an ally,* Katherine had once told her. *It's important you learn the difference.*

Rox liked Katherine. Perhaps "like" was a bit of an exaggeration, but Rox respected her a great deal. They often didn't agree on the best way to handle things. Katherine preferred the direct (and self-serving) approach, while Rox preferred a more fair and balanced one.

Rox was about to pour herself a cup of coffee and then find Henry when she heard footsteps running towards the kitchen. She grabbed another mug from the cupboard and was about to pour one for whoever was racing in when Henry slid through the door and grabbed the counter to stop from falling.

"I got lost," he said between breaths. "Here!" He passed her his mobile phone.

Rox gave him a sympathetic smile. It took a few days to successfully navigate Halo. "Hello?"

Whoever was on the other end was wheezing, like each inhalation was broken into smaller fragments. "Rox?"

"Meita?" Rox misjudged the height of the counter and put the mug down too hard and the base shattered.

No! She couldn't heal Meita.

A coughing fit broke out on the other end, and Rox heard someone instruct Meita to pass them the phone.

"Hello?" the voice said.

The bottom dropped from under her, and Rox closed her eyes to keep from toppling.

"Hello?" he said again.

That voice lived in her nightmares. That voice belonged to the man who had stolen her pride and her dignity. She had begged *that voice* to stop the pain, to stop the deaths and the rebirths. He had taken her children, and it was only because of the woman he was now holding captive that she had gotten them back. *That voice* would do horrible things to Meita, just as he had done to her. Rox could heal, but Meita? Whatever physical damage he did to Meita, there was no evolved cure to fix it.

"She's not like me." Rox's voice came out much softer than she wanted. "I mean, she's not evolved."

"Well, technically, yes, she is evolved, Tara," Tusk said. "But I'm not sure how that's germane at the moment."

Rox wanted to threaten him. She wanted to tell him if he hurt Meita she would kill him. But the truth was, Tusk was like Meita. She couldn't use her ability on him. But Rox had learned there were other ways to hurt someone. She was no longer the hopeless, confused woman with only four years of memories searching for her identity. Rox had found herself. She had *become* herself, and the softness in her voice dropped. "What do you want?"

"I've got a message. Meita says that Eagle Eyes' at yoga."

For a moment, Rox wasn't sure if this was some sort of trick, but then Henry snapped his fingers, and she looked up. He mouthed he was tracing the call.

"Is that supposed to mean something to me?" Rox asked.

Tusk sighed. "Look, I honestly don't know. But right

now, she's got *my* weapon pointed at me. The one who saved you, I might add!" Was he still talking to her or was he talking to Meita? "And that is what I'm instructed to tell you."

"Where are you?"

"We're at—" It sounded like a balloon had burst. "Will you stop shooting things!"

"Tusk? Meita?" Rox shouted. "Meita?" Did he drop the phone? "Hello?"

"Rox?" It was Meita.

"Where are you? I'm coming to get you."

"Yoga. Katherine ... she's—"

"I know, she's gone to yoga, too. We got the protocol from across the pond, so don't worry. We're tracing her steps now."

"Mary ... Mother ... God ..."

Rox spun around and yanked open the drawer nearest the refrigerator. She pulled out the pad and a pencil. It's tip was broken and she tossed it to the floor and grabbed a red pen. "Are you alright? What did he do to you?" she asked as she scribbled down what Meita had said and passed it to Henry who had come around to see what she was doing.

"Hello?" It was Tusk again.

"Put Meita back on the phone!" The orange tint that threatened to descend earlier now covered the kitchen with its glow. Rox felt the hum from the coffee maker and microwave make its way up the back of her neck, and she rolled her shoulders forward to relieve the discomfort, but it stayed wedged just at the top of her spine.

"I think she's got a punctured lung, but she won't let me take her to the hospital," Tusk said, but it seemed like he was talking to Meita again and not her. "Neither will she let me tend to her."

"Where are you?" This was probably some sort of trap, but Rox would have to take the chance. If it had not been for Meita, she would've never gotten to her kids in time.

"She won't let me tell you," Tusk said.

"What do you mean she won't let you tell me?" He was not making any sense.

Tusk must've passed the phone back to Meita because she heard Meita's low voice whisper the word "ally".

Ally? Tusk? An ally?

"Meita, listen to me. I don't know what he's told you, but you know him. You know he can't be trusted. Just tell me where you are, and I promise I'll come get you. I swear."

"Can't." She coughed again, and then she heard the phone pass back.

"She says the line isn't secure."

"Fuck you!" Rox would kill him before she ever let him anywhere near her family. "Put Meita back on now! Put me on speaker." She looked up when she felt Keenan drawing nearer. It was strange knowing where someone was simply by feeling their presence. It reminded her of Sam, and she had to ball her hands into a fist to contain the energy trying to fight its way out of her.

"I'm trying to help, you know," Tusk said. "A little gratitude would go a long way under the circumstances."

"Help? Help! You don't help. You take. You destroy, and I will kill you for what you did to her."

Of all the retorts Tusk could have given her, a snort was not one she was prepared for. "I saved her life, you know!"

"What game are you playing?" Maybe they were both high? Perhaps Tusk injected Meita with something and then accidentally injected himself as well.

"We're driving. She says give us six hours. Maybe more if I have to pull over and resuscitate you!" He shouted the last two words, but again, not into the phone. It was like he was having a two-way conversation.

Rox's breath caught. There was no way Meita would have volunteered their location. "How do you know where I am?"

"Listen, she's signaling that I need to hang up now and drive." Tusk said something that Rox couldn't make out. "But you've got the message about yoga – which is obviously some kind of code for help. One more thing, Dr Mallory Fined, AmLife, put that on your radar. She and Harry are trying to steal my work, and you don't want to know what'll happen if—"

"I don't give a shit about you or your work." A small part of her was trying to remember to remain calm, but she couldn't stop the memories of what he did to her from bubbling to the surface. She inhaled and looked down at her arm as if it were on fire again. Her hands started to shake as the power from the walls crept closer.

"She's right, you know," Tusk said.

"Who? About what?" Rox asked through clenched teeth.

"I am an ally."

"Over my dead body."

His laughter was the last thing she heard before the call ended.

"Rox?" She didn't look up because she felt the shift in the air. It was Keenan. He could tell she was struggling to control herself. She had grown stronger since being struck by lightning, but strength was not always a good thing.

"I want you to take a deep breath."

She didn't want to take a deep breath. She wanted to explode with rage. She wanted to suck the very life out of Tusk and watch as he died. Josh was usually nearby when she started having thoughts like this and he would always calm her down. But Josh wasn't there. In fact, Josh had almost died, and that just added to her frustrations. How was she supposed to heal everyone when they were so far away?

"Shall we go for a run?"

It was Danny. He was standing beside Keenan, both of them looking at her with concern.

"I don't wanna run," she said.

"A walk then." He slowly took a step towards her. He stopped just in front of her with a smile on his face and that same twinkle from last night in his eyes. "The whites of your eyes, they've gone orange. Think it's freaking Henry out."

She looked at Henry who was standing behind Keenan. He wasn't cowering. In fact, Henry looked just as capable as any of them. Katherine wouldn't have brought him onboard if she didn't think he could provide value. Rox smiled. One thing she could be certain of, and that was where Katherine placed her trust. If she trusted Henry, then so could she.

Rox placed Henry's phone on the counter and pushed it over to him. "I, um …"

Henry nodded and reached for his phone. "Will she call back?"

"Yes." Rox felt her heart rate slowing and the orange receding, but her pent up frustration was still there. Danny was right. She could probably use a run. "They're driving. Tusk thinks she's got a punctured lung, but she won't go to the hospital and she won't let him treat her."

"Do you think we can trust him?" Keenan asked.

She clenched her jaws again to hold back the electric charge her body was trying its damnest to discharge. "No. But Meita called him an ally."

"Do you think Meita is of sound mind?" Keenan asked.

Rox shook her head. "But, she referred to herself as Eagle Eyes and mentioned yoga. She wouldn't be able to do that if she was seriously out of it."

"Well, that is at least one of our missing cohorts located. Or partially located," Keenan said. "Why do you not go for that run with your trainer? If we hear anything in the meantime, I will send a call for you."

Rox followed Danny out the kitchen side door and down the steps leading to the picnic table. She didn't mean to, but she looked up at the planks still nailed into the thickest branches of the tree. "I think it'll be best if I take that run by myself."

He shook his head. "I can handle it."

She sighed. How did she explain that the confusion and frustration she was feeling wasn't about him? It was about the memories that still woke her up in the middle of the night. It was the imagined stories she created about what would have happened to her children if she hadn't gotten there in time. It was about the Mekong River and the towns that survived along its coast. How any of those places could've easily been the prison for her children if only one thing had gone wrong out of all the million things that had gone right?

"I know what he did to you," Danny said.

She turned to him. "No, you don't."

"I was there, remember?" Danny said as he came closer. "I was there when Sam—"

"Don't!" She squeezed her eyes shut. "Don't say his name."

Danny rocked back on his heels like she had taken a swing at him. He opened his mouth to say something, but instead crossed his arms over his chest and stared at her.

She didn't mean to hurt him. She liked Danny. In fact, he was the first man she had liked since Sam disappeared. But Sam's name on his lips didn't *feel* right. Not now. Not so soon after they had been intimate. Not when given the choice …

"You don't know what it's like …" She should turn around and go for that run, but she needed him to understand. "It's like … I can't get angry because when I do, I become this magnet for energy." She reached up and rubbed the back her neck. "And it coalesces here. And it wants out, but I have to contain it. But containing it hurts, Danny. It hurts and I feel this pressure in my jaw." She opened her mouth wide, trying to relieve the tension that she'd been carrying there. "But there's no release because how do you safely let lightning out of its bottle?" She looked up at Danny and gave him a sad smile. "He did that for me. He calmed the storm and he made it all disappear with a single touch."

"He's not here."

"You don't think I know that? You don't think I feel responsible for that?"

Danny dropped his arms and shook his head. "No. That's not what I'm saying. My point was, *Sam* isn't here. So how are you going to learn to calm your storm?"

She stretched her jaw from side to side to relieve the pressure. She asked him not to say his name. "That's what Keenan's helping me with."

"How long you been working with him?"

"Keenan? Two years."

"And this is as far as you got?"

Rox inhaled deeply. She wasn't sure what kind of game Danny was playing, but she wasn't in the mood to stick around and find out.

"Don't run away," he said.

She stopped, but didn't turn back to face him.

"From where I'm standing, Rox, *Sam*'s never coming back." She sensed him walking closer. "I'm not asking you to get rid of the feelings you have for him. I'm just asking you to find another way to calm your storm. Your team's down two members, two key members ..."

When she turned around, he was right there, too close for her to ignore.

"... and Henry – when that call came through – he didn't come looking for Keenan or me or Walter. He came looking for you."

She took a step back to gain some breathing space, but

he followed her.

"Give me three constructive things you could have done if you had better control of yourself."

"What?"

"If you hadn't lost your temper with Tusk, when the call was over, what were three things a *leader* would've done?"

She blinked like she had been struck. "You don't know what it's like."

"I don't need to know. They don't need to know," he said, pointing back towards the house. "They just need you to *lead*. Because if what I'm hearing is true, we're all going to be dead one day, and it'll be up to you whether Halo continues on."

She looked up at him, but instead of the anger she expected to see, there was curiosity, like he was genuinely interested in her response. "I should've stayed and asked Henry about that trace. If he found anything."

He didn't say anything more and just waited.

"Listen to the recording of the call for any sounds that could help us locate her." Rox took a few steps in the opposite direction from him before turning back around to face him. "I could've asked him what he thought! Henry works closer with Meita than any of us, he'd have some idea of what she'd do in this situation. Or maybe where she'd go."

The twinkle in his eye returned as he leaned forward. She wasn't sure what he was going to do, but then he kissed her. It wasn't rushed, but it was confident, like they'd been having sex a lot longer than just the one time.

She stepped back out of his embrace. "AmLife. Dr

M-something, Find or Finet or something. I need to go and have Henry find me everything he can on her."

Rox could tell he wanted to continue exploring their kiss, but instead he stepped back and slowly opened his eyes. The twinkle alive once again. "Go. Lead."

## A nun and a priest board a bus

August 9th, 4:20pm EST

Two Asian people on an intercity bus wasn't anything noteworthy, but a priest and a nun garnered a few extra glances. Katherine always paid special attention to her attire.

Katherine was part of an old and white fraternity that was slow to integrate, and inclusivity was not high on its list of short-term aspirations. Appearance was everything in her line of work. Appearance and gut feel, so she dressed in clothing that presented her as a capable professional. Never any suits. The jackets were too formal, not to mention the challenge of finding matching pants and skirts for someone as short as she was.

"You know it is sacrilegious to don the habit and not have taken the vows," Father Ong said to her.

"I shall pray for forgiveness," Katherine whispered.

"I was not always a priest, *Sister* Katherine." There was a smile on his face. "I was no different than you. Angry at the world, with no one to blame but myself."

"Let's not forget about that treason bit. I think that's a major distinction, don't you?"

"Well, I never said we were identical."

She reached for a phone that wasn't there. Screen withdrawal. Amazing how much one's life can change in just a day or two.

"But I was right about that anger," he said, and then smiled at a little girl a few rows ahead of them who turned around to stare.

He was right about her anger, but there were some things that therapy couldn't heal. Some tragedies stayed with a person. Sometimes, it was easier that way.

"Who'd you lose?" Father Ong asked.

Katherine looked out her window at the passing landscape. This wasn't a conversation she wanted to have with the good Father. Some wounds never healed.

Henry would've delivered Keenan to Halo by now, which meant that Rox and Walter would be helping him look for Meita. Meita was one of this country's greatest assets, and yet it had no idea she even existed. "Hmph." The irony of ignorance was a beautiful thing. But that's what made this country work.

Katherine dug a finger beneath the habit to scratch her forehead. She rolled her shoulders forward, trying to get accustomed to the outfit. The rosary she wore around her neck was not her normal choice for an accessory, but it served its purpose.

They were on their way to Halo, but they couldn't go by any method of transport that satellite or traffic cams or closed-circuit cameras could capture. In a perfect world, she wouldn't have brought Father Ong with her, but she couldn't be sure she hadn't been followed to the church.

Plus, she had a soft spot for the priest. He represented a part of her history she hadn't realized she didn't want to say goodbye to, and knowing he was evolved changed things. Did his handlers know? They had to have suspected something given his aging.

"Tell me, how many people know you're evolved?" she whispered.

A sad look slid across his face, erasing the earlier smile. "No one. Everybody I love is gone."

A baby started crying a few rows back, and Katherine's breath caught. It had been well over a decade since the sound of an infant impacted her in such a way. She focused on the dark blue fabric of the seat in front of her. It was well-worn, but still sturdy. There were light blue and tan dots woven into the fabric, no doubt to help mask the stains that it inevitably carried. There was a black plastic cupholder and tray attached to the seat. Someone had taken a permanent marker to it and drawn a picture of a broken heart. A sticker of an angel was beside it.

The tear fell before she had a chance to catch it. Damn babies. They were so loud. Always interrupting. Always so needy. No other species on the planet was born so utterly dependent. The bus was a bad idea. She could feel the tension from the mother as the woman tried to shush her baby silent. Katherine remembered nights of trying to rock a baby back to sleep. She had paced in her room, her eyes closed, her memory keeping track of each step so she would know when to stop, turn and head back in the other direction. She remembered praying, bartering, cursing, pleading with any god that would listen to help her child fall asleep. Sometimes prayers got answered, just not in the way intended.

"We are not designed to carry our burdens alone," Father Ong said as his hand covered hers.

She flinched, but she didn't pull away.

"When we are young, we are so selfish," he said.

Katherine would sell out every country on every planet in the known universe to pace with her daughter again. She would set the world to burn and walk away from it if it meant she could hold her just one more time.

"You know I've been married three times," Father Ong said.

She hadn't meant to look at him in surprise, but she would've remembered reading that.

"Not very priestly, is it." He chuckled. "We aren't born men of the cloth, Katherine. In most instances, life happens, and this is the path we are led to."

"How old are you?"

"One hundred and sixty-seven." He nodded as he said it. "Old enough to know better, but not old enough to know how to let it all go."

"Aren't you meant to be giving these things over to Christ? Or God, or some archangel?" Katherine said.

"Do you meditate?"

Katherine hadn't attended church regularly since she was in high school, then there were the few times she was guilted into attending during university, but she was certain the Church frowned upon meditation as it was seen as an Eastern philosophy, something to do with Buddhism or Hinduism.

"I used to. I spend a lot of time deep breathing. Does that count? Why?"

"Anyone who has practiced meditation long enough will tell you that there is no such thing as a perfectly sustained, meditative state. It's a myth. Our minds are meant to think. That is what they do. Meditating is simply about becoming aware and then *trying* to stay at equilibrium during life's ups and downs."

Katherine took one of those deep breaths. She was beginning to think that flying would have been worth the risk. How long was it to Hartford?

He chuckled at her. "All I'm saying is that giving your burdens to Christ or God, or some archangel as you put it, is about *trying* to let go. Learning to trust. No one ever has a perfectly sustained, burden-free life."

"Ong?"

"Hmm?"

"You're one hundred and sixty-seven?" She pointed to their outfits. "Do you really believe all of this?"

There was a long moment of silence as he looked ahead to the front of the bus. It was almost full, but Katherine expected it to empty out along the route.

"Some days I really do."

They both stared out of the same window and watched as the other cars passed them. They were on I-95, and from there, they would ride for about forty-five minutes or so before they stopped again to pick up and drop off more passengers.

Father Ong's mobile started ringing, and they both raised an eyebrow.

"The church?" she asked.

He lifted it out of his backpack and put on the reading glasses hanging on the outside of his cassock. "Unknown."

It stopped.

"If it's important, they'll call back," Katherine said, and she turned to look out the window again. A sixteen-wheeler was passing by as well as two SUVs, both with families. A burgundy-colored coupe that was packed with boxes like the owner was moving switched lanes. A black sedan with tinted windows slipped in the narrow space created by the coupe and immediately began to slow down. Another black sedan, its windows also tinted, pulled up just behind the first one and closed the distance between them to prevent another car from merging in.

Katherine took a deep breath just as Father Ong's phone began to ring again.

"Says 'Unknown' still," he said.

She nodded and reached for it. "Hello."

"Katherine?"

She recognized the voice. "Kelley."

"You are not an easy woman to find. I've been looking for you."

"I'm amazed you found me at all."

Kelley chuckled. "I had inside help."

"What do you mean 'inside help'?" Meita was missing, and even if she weren't, Meita would never divulge her location. Henry? No, after Meita, Henry was her next best hire. He was loyal. He was noble. No, not him. Katherine was glad she didn't have him killed after all.

"My mom. She told me a lot about you."

"Did she now?"

"Mmm. Like, I didn't know you used to be Catholic."

Katherine rolled her eyes. Religion, so predictable. Kelley must've reviewed footage from every church.

"So, what can I do you for?" Katherine asked.

"The President can't meet you."

Katherine swore under her breath. Without the President's support, things were going to get messy, and by messy, she meant bloody. Rox wouldn't back down if her family were threatened. Keenan wouldn't let anything happen to his protégé. If Rox was in trouble, that meant Josh was there ready to twist anyone's thoughts to his will, and even though Walter should've retired by now, the man was as fit as any of the men half his age, and his experience made him deadly.

"But she has arranged a meeting for you with the Secretary of Homeland Security."

Homeland Security? That was not where she thought Kelley was going, but an olive leaf was an olive leaf no matter the branch it was extended from. "And if I decline?"

"Then she, and I, wish you luck against one of the most well-connected senior senators in the United States Congress."

"You know he's the bad guy, right?" Katherine said.

"Yes, we do know that and that's why we're *helping* you meet with someone who can offer you the assistance you need. The President cannot, and will not, ever be seen to turn against her own party."

"Even if someone in her party is participating in human

trafficking and using his congressional power to advocate the illegal, unethical, and let's not forget *inhumane* experiments on evolved *human beings*?"

Kelley cleared her throat, which meant Katherine had struck a nerve.

"You have twenty seconds to decide whether this offer is to your liking," Kelley continued. "If not, the four cars that are currently surrounding the bus you're on will turn around, leaving you on your own. My meeting with you never happened. This call we're having never happened. And, quite likely, all the work you've been doing around the globe and within the United Nations will be as if it never happened."

Katherine was beginning to understand why the President chose Kelley as her Chief of Staff.

"Nineteen …"

"How does the President really feel about this? I mean, I know she can't get involved, but where does she fall on the issue of evolved ones needing protection?"

"Would we be having this conversation if she held opposing views on this issue? Sixteen …"

Artemis Ronald Fowler, more informally known as Artie, was a wildcard when it came to EOs. He had purposefully kept quiet on the topic, and so Katherine had no idea which side he would take. First rule of negotiations, never go in blind.

"Ten … Nine …"

Katherine would need some information on him if she was going to meet with him. She looked down at her watch. She was about forty-five minutes from downtown DC by special escort. Meita was missing and there was no one better at gathering fast intel than her.

"Five ..."

"Who else knows my whereabouts right now?" Katherine asked.

"The analyst who tracked you to Father Thomas Wáng, her immediate supervisor and the President of the United States. Two ..."

"How'd you locate me?" Katherine asked quickly.

"It wasn't easy. We followed the trail of two hundred and eighty-three Asian women in the downtown DC area, and even then we still couldn't locate you until I remembered something my mom said about you two attending catechism classes together. One ..."

"I'm in. But how did you connect me with Ong? I mean, Father Wáng?"

Sirens began to wail and everyone turned to look out the window. Everyone, but Katherine.

There was a lightness in Kelley's voice, like they were playing chess and she was moments away from declaring checkmate. "The United States is experiencing an unprecedented amount of cross-agency collaboration, especially when it comes to evolved humans. And who do you think we have to thank for that?"

The bus slowed and pulled over onto the roadside as four black sedans, each with flashing red and blue lights in their windows, surrounded it.

"Carter is stirring up trouble," Katherine said. "He's trying to create a divide."

"Then there's a lot riding on your meeting with the

Secretary, isn't there? We're counting on you, Katherine."

The phone disconnected.

"Shit!" Katherine banged the seat in front of her with the back of her hands. "Get up, Father. Our ride is here."

She stepped over Father Ong before he could grab his backpack out of her way.

"What's going on? Are they here for us?" he asked.

"Yep." Katherine marched down the aisle and stopped at the bus driver who was looking just as confused as the other passengers.

"Sister?" the driver said, when he looked up and saw her.

"Open the door. They're here for us."

The driver hesitated, but then pulled the handle that swung the door open.

"God bless you," Katherine said, as she marched down the stairs and out onto the side of the road where two agents were already approaching.

"Ms Cheung? Ms Katherine Cheung?"

She nodded as she walked towards them. "I need to borrow your phone."

They looked at her strangely for a moment, and she realized it was probably because she was still dressed in a nun's habit. She rolled her eyes. "May I?" She held out her hand to both of the agents.

It was the one who looked the youngest who passed his phone to her. "Ma'am, I mean, Sister, Father, please come with us."

The number she dialed rang twice before it was answered. "Henry?" she said as she followed the agents to their car.

"Katherine? Oh my god, where are you?"

A smile spread across her face. He was worried.

"We've located Meita! She's en route," he quickly added.

It felt like all the air had been sucked out of her. She lowered her head into her hands, and it looked like she was praying, so she offered up thanks to whichever of the gods who had saved her agent.

"Are you alright?" one of the agents asked as he opened the door for her.

She was now that they had located Meita.

Katherine cleared her throat and gave a short nod of her head. She slipped into the car and reached for her seatbelt, signaling she was not sliding over and that Father Ong was going to have to walk around to the other side.

"Where are you?" Henry asked.

"Interstate. How is she?"

The agent in the front passenger seat turned around to say something, but Katherine held up her hand for him to be quiet. Henry explained he was worried about Meita. It was obvious she was hurt and she was even claiming Tusk had helped her escape.

Katherine was silent as she listened to his update. Rox couldn't heal Meita, so whatever injuries she had, she would have to get over them the old-fashioned way. And Tusk helping her escape? Katherine didn't know what to think about that. He had always been in it for the science, so why help the very person who was responsible for the closure of so many of his facilities? Why turn on Harry?

"I need you to find me any news updates on Senator Henry Carter. Any new bills he's supporting or new initiatives. Maybe he's been put on a task force," Katherine said.

"Well, he's the chair for the Science, Space, and Technology Committee."

"Yes, Henry, I know that. I'm talking—"

"But they just awarded a grant to AmLife."

AmLife? The small genetics company? "Who runs it?"

"Dr Mallory Fined. Tusk thinks she's trying to steal his research."

Katherine stared out the window as they sped through traffic. The sirens were off, but the lights stilled announced they were on official business, so traffic continued to switch lanes out of their way.

Katherine started to laugh, and Father Ong and the agent in the front passenger seat turned to look at her. "This is good news, Henry," she said.

"Ma'am?" Henry said.

She pulled the seatbelt off of her neck where it was rubbing into her skin. "Your priorities are to get Meita back to Halo safely. Then once you have secured her safety, you are to extend protection to Tusk."

There was a moment of silence.

"Henry?"

"Yes, ma'am, I'm here, but Tusk was responsible for kidnapping Walter's daughter. I don't think he's just going to open Halo—"

"Yes. I assume not. Sadly, that makes your job harder, Henry, but I'm sure you'll rise to the challenge." Then she continued on as if there were nothing else that needed saying on the matter. "I need you to find me everything you can on Artemis Ronald Fowler, Secretary of Homeland Security. Send it to this number here."

"That's my phone," the agent in the front said.

Katherine smiled at him like he were a toddler who had just stated the obvious.

"Yes, ma'am. Anything in particular?" Henry asked.

"I need to ascertain his views on evolved ones," she said. "In particular, if anyone in his life is evolved?"

"You think he knows someone who is?"

The smile on Katherine's face stretched. "That's what I'm asking you to find out." But yes, she thought he did. Why else remain so quiet about a topic that everyone and their mother had an opinion on.

She ended the call and was about to pass the agent his phone back when it rang. She looked at the number and recognized it as one of the numbers GFO used. "Hello?"

"Ma'am?"

"Yes, Henry."

"One more thing. Sam is back."

Katherine wasn't sure what to say at first. She had pretty much counted him as dead. Meita was in touch with various agencies which monitored spikes in the atmospheric pressure as well as industrial-scaled electrical anomalies, but Meita was at yoga. Had she received a message but hadn't yet been able to pick it up?

"Ma'am?"

"Is he alive?"

She breathed a sigh of relief when he said yes. But then Henry dashed any hopes of a simple resolution when he explained that Dr Dotz had said she had to induce a coma.

"What's his status? Physical and mental?" she asked.

"Well, according to Dr Dotz, he was brought back by a huge, and I quote, 'large bolt of lightning' and that he was unconscious. He looked dehydrated and malnutritioned, and that he did not return alone."

A large bolt of lightning was not a big surprise to her. It was how he had left, and so it made sense that he should return in a similar fashion. But how had he managed that without Rox? And why now? Had it taken him this long to make his way back? And if so, from where did he come?

"I want that body," she said. Rox hadn't moved on and was still pining for him. Walter had refused to draw up the death certificate without a body, which was within his legal right.

"Good, ma'am, because I'm helping them to arrange transport of the body to Halo."

"Excellent. Who is accompanying him?"

"Mr Koh is sending the doctor and her husband …" he paused, and Katherine heard him flipping through papers. "Mal. Her husband, Mal."

Katherine nodded. She liked them. No nonsense, good people. They could become useful in the event things didn't go so well with *Artie*. "What's their ETA?"

"Within the next day or two. The doctor wants to stop off in Europe."

"Not soon enough. I need them here ASAP."

"Ugh, ma'am, they're already en route, but there's a reason why they want to stop off in Europe. They've a bit of an unprecedented problem."

Katherine reached up and scratched her forehead where the habit was beginning to really irritate her. "He's alive, Henry, right?"

"Oh, yes, but you see, he didn't come back alone."

She inhaled deeply and held it while she waited for him to continue.

"Ma'am, according to Dr Dotz, he's brought back a saber-toothed tiger with him."

Katherine's breath came out in a big exhale. She opened her mouth to say something, but couldn't think of anything to say. A saber-toothed tiger? Were they not extinct? Sam's ability … they had never been able to pinpoint it. Time travel? Could it be possible?

"Bring it with him," she said. "And find a scientist at the Smithsonian who can carbon date the thing." That would definitely tell them whether Sam was able to travel through time or not.

"Yeah, ma'am, that's the problem. Dr Dotz says she's scheduled a layover to make sure it doesn't wake up mid-flight, and well, you know, kill everyone."

Katherine laughed. She wasn't sure if she found the situation hilarious or that she needed to release some of her pent-up frustration. She had gone to yoga, which set in motion a series of protocols from which there was no return, and now GFO would need to re-establish itself. Meita was also at yoga, but was rescued by the very man she had been working to take down for more than five years. Katherine was dressed in a nun's outfit, seated next to an *evolved* priest who was no more a priest than she was a nun. Sam had slipped through a gap in time and space and literally disappeared two years ago, only to return on a bolt of lightning like he was some mythical god, and if that wasn't enough, he had brought a saber-toothed tiger along for the ride.

But Sam had a thing for wild animals. He had stormed the shores of the Dominican Republic with a wolf. What the hell was its name? Sheera? Something like that. It didn't matter.

"Henry, tell Dr Dotz to give it enough elephant tranquilizers to knock out a herd of wooly mammoths, and she is not to stop until the wheels of her plane touch down in Halo country! Hartford, to be exact. I want *it* and Sam at Halo yesterday."

"Alright, ma'am. And what should I tell Walter or Rox?"

"Not a goddamn thing."

She ended her call with Henry and passed the agent his phone. "You repeat anything you heard and I'll have you both tried for treason."

"You're not a nun, are you?"

"What gave it away?"

~

## Full disclosure

August 9th, 6:30pm EST

Katherine looked at her watch again. They had been sitting in the small waiting room outside Artie's office for fifteen minutes. Not long, but longer than she was accustomed to waiting.

"Father, may I get you a coffee, a latte or something to drink?"

There were a number of things that made Katherine instantly dislike the blonde woman who bent down with her knees firmly pressed together so she could speak to Father Ong at eye level, and none of them had to do with her age.

The first thing that Katherine did not like was the matching set of pearl earrings, necklace, and bracelet she wore. Pearls, while beautiful and innocent, represented a time and era when Katherine's kind and all the women like her were not welcomed. It reminded her of a period when women wore white gloves and typed for a living. Their attire was chosen not to reflect self-interest or personal taste, but to project an image of fastidiousness, propriety, and manners. A woman wearing all-pearl accessories evoked an emotional response in Katherine. It was one she readily admitted being void of logic, but nevertheless one she firmly chose to maintain.

The second thing she did not like was the stockings. They were the shimmery, sheer kind made of silk, and their cost was indirectly proportioned to their durability. Purchasing a quality pair was akin to throwing away money.

The third thing was the pale salmon-colored suit. It wasn't the color itself, but the fact that the outfit did not suit one so young. It was clearly made for someone older, and Katherine didn't trust anyone who *wanted* to be older. It showed extreme naiveté. And if the first three reasons weren't enough, the jacket had shoulder pads.

Katherine shuddered, and then sighed at the scarf

wrapped around the ill-dressed woman's neck. It matched the color of her stockings. The ends of the scarf were tucked inside the front of her jacket, and truth be told, Katherine thought it was a lovely scarf, but it was the huge ladybug pin rather unstylishly set in the middle and clearly too heavy for such delicate material, thus making it flop over to reveal the pin's underside that fermented Katherine's opinion about the girl. Katherine wasn't sure which annoyed her more, the hole that the young woman was creating in such a fine piece of accessory or that she was clearly too young to be wearing a pin in the first place. A woman *earned* the right to wear pins.

"Yes, please. Tea, do you have tea?" Father Ong asked.

"Um-hmm, what kind?"

"Black with milk if you have it," said Father Ong.

"Not a problem." Then she turned to Katherine. "And, Sister, what—"

"My name is Katherine, but you may call me Ms Cheung."

The woman blinked back in surprise, but recovered with the speed of someone accustomed to being verbally accosted.

"Yes, Ms Cheung, what can I get for you?"

"A coffee. Freshly brewed. Black."

"Yes, ma'am. Would you like sugar or milk with that?"

"Did I ask for sugar or milk with that?"

The woman's lips pressed into a thin line as she rose to her full height. She quietly turned around and left the room in silence.

"You know that was rude, right?" Father Ong said with a hint of humor in his voice.

"If she's ever going to be good enough to work for me, she's going to have to learn to deal with a lot worse." Katherine scratched her forehead where the habit still irritated the skin beneath it. "This is a man's world she operates in, and hiding herself in an old woman's suit with jewelry her dead grandmother left her isn't going to do her an ounce of good in making a name for herself."

"I don't think she's going to want to work for you."

"I don't think anyone cares what she wants. Not dressed like that."

A different, older woman rushed into the room and smiled at them. "Secretary Fowler will see you now." She led them down the hall and around a corner to a large office at the end.

Artemis was waiting by the door as they walked in. "Melissa, you can take off now."

The older woman nodded a thank you and closed the door as she left.

"Katherine, your name is being whispered in a lot of corners at the moment." He walked over to one of the leather chairs around a redwood coffee table and sat down.

His office wasn't what Katherine was expecting. Instead of glass and chrome accentuated with blacks and whites, his office reminded her of a cabin in the woods.

Artemis Ronald Fowler grew up on a farm for the first seven years of his life. He learned how to fish, trap, and, believe it or not, was an avid whittler. There were at least five different miniature statues situated around his office that, according to Henry, he or his son had made.

"Well, as long as they aren't Chinese whispers," she said. "You know how reliable they are."

Artemis pulled at the collar on his shirt, and Katherine smiled. "So how is it that you have one of this country's most talked-about groups working for you?" he asked, changing the subject.

"Secretary Fowler, listen, it's late, I'm dressed as a nun, and I've been forced into … corners, as you put it." Katherine leaned forward and rested her arms on her knees. "What Senator Harry Carter and Dr Mallory Fined are planning to do is reprehensible. I'm not asking you to do anything to stop it."

He raised an eyebrow. Negotiations at this level were rarely conducted so abruptly, but time was not on her side, GFO's or Halo's.

Artemis nodded. "I guess we disagree on that point."

"And what point would that be?" Katherine had hoped that Kelley sending her here meant Artemis was on their side, or at least willing to listen to her side. Objectively.

"I've read the report from Senator Carter and Dr Fined; they talk about a real threat to our national security, Katherine. And people are going missing; Halo's clearly involved. The question is, are they kidnapping them or are they setting them up with new identities?" He shrugged. "Both of which are federal offenses."

Salmon-colored suit rapped on the door and then opened it. She placed the tray with their drinks on the redwood table between her and the Secretary, and left.

"You make this?" Father Ong asked, pointing at the coffee table.

"Mr Wáng, apologies, we've not been formerly introduced," Artemis said.

Father Ong shook his head. "Don't worry about it. I was just admiring the craftsmanship."

Artemis reached for a wedge of lime and squeezed it into his glass of sparkling water. "Thank you. My father taught me everything I know about carpentry. My grandfather taught him."

Father Ong lifted the lid on his individual pot of tea and took out the strainer containing the tea leaves. He placed it on top of the tea holder and poured himself a cup before adding a drop of milk. "I knew a man – this was a long time ago – I'm talking at least eighty, ninety years ago, who was also a carpenter."

Katherine sat back and swallowed her smile.

"Like you," Ong continued. "His father had taught him, and his father before that."

"It's a dying art form," Artemis said. "Replaced by mass-manufactured furniture that lacks character." He leaned forward and ran his fingers over the top of the side of the table that wasn't covered by the tray. "Lacks soul."

"You know how old I am?" Father Ong asked.

Artemis blinked, and then sat back as he took a sip of his water. "I make it a point never to guess anyone's age."

"Yeah, that's probably good politics." Father Ong chuckled though he was the only one. "People fear what they don't know. What they don't understand. History's riddled with leaders who took advantage of that fear and created a hateful world for the things they feared."

Artemis nodded, and looked at Katherine, but she just

shrugged her shoulders. She had no idea where the priest was going, but she wanted to see where he took them.

"Well—" Artemis said.

"I think I heard somewhere that your son also has a knack for carpentry. Is that right?" Father Ong continued.

"Yes, like me, like my father, he likes to work with wood. Now, Katherine—"

"Did you know that most evolved abilities are benign?" Father Ong continued. "Well, I think the more technical term is 'passive'. You know, things like synesthesia, speed-reading, woodworking, or stand-up comedy." He laughed again. "I mean, anyone who can stand up in front of a group of strangers and tell jokes has got to be evolved."

"You know," Katherine said. "There are some evolved people whose only gift is to identify the evolved."

Artemis' breath caught.

"Halo isn't involved in their abduction." Katherine leaned forward again. "Halo is saving the lives of the very people you're supposed to be protecting." She let him think on that before she continued. "They want the same thing you want. For their children to grow up in a world where they can achieve the American dream."

"Hard to do that, though, if they have to hide themselves from the world," Father Ong added. "I still carry the memory of that man and his father who were from the village next to mine. Shame what they did to them. I mean, we didn't know anything about being evolved, but the world was a different place back then. People feared what they didn't know."

Katherine almost choked trying to keep from laughing.

"What are you proposing?" Artemis asked.

"I'll dissolve GFO as it currently exists and start a new division adjacent to you. My team and I will work together to further understand evolved abilities and to make sure any of those radical EOs Carter keeps going on about – yet no one has ever seen – are stopped before they cause a threat to society."

His eyebrows arching meant he hadn't been expecting that. She was offering him a silver platter that very few nations would be able to replicate. An entire trained team of evolved ones (albeit past their prime). Artemis hadn't realized it yet, but she was giving him access to the most powerful weapon the world had ever seen. Rox.

Keenan would be angry with her for that. Hell, he might even kill her, but sacrifices had to be made. It would get messy if she tried to take on Carter given his connections, especially now that he had Fined's financial and medical backing. Confronting him would put her allies in a difficult position, making them choose between loyalty to her and fear of the political repercussions from Carter. She wouldn't do that to them, mainly because she knew most people used fear to justify their acts of disloyalty.

"Not adjacent, but under," Artemis said.

Katherine's face remained calm, but inside she was seething. Oh, she was going to take his offer and he knew it; she had no other options, but she didn't *want* to work for him. He was a good-enough man; she was just clearly smarter than him.

"Budgetary oversight." She didn't want to give budgetary oversight for her personal wardrobe let alone

GFO to him, but she needed his protection. They all needed his protection.

"No." He sat back, signaling that was not up for negotiations. "I get budgetary oversight when you report directly into me."

"It's either you or the President," Katherine said.

Artemis chuckled. "You wouldn't be here if the President would take you."

He was right. People were always excited about electing the President. They were the supposed leader. The harsh truth was very different. Congress held the power, and men like Senator Harry Carter represented an institution that simply refused to make way for progress or change. Fear was their banner, and they would spread it like a disease before they allowed anything to come between them and the power they held.

"No dotted lines," Katherine said. "The Evolved Division always reports to the Secretary of Homeland Security. Always."

He stood and went over to his desk. It was also redwood and matched the coffee table. His chair was one of those modern, ergonomic ones with mesh fabric. Katherine wandered over to his window and considered the framed photographs on the ledge. Artemis Ronald Fowler was a family man. He had two sons and a wife who, according to the rumor mill, he had never cheated on. In a town where power was the most potent aphrodisiac, that was saying something.

She picked up the photos of his sons. They were in the woods, on a hike she presumed, and they were smiling at the camera. Perfectly straight, white teeth. Light brown eyes and matching hair. They looked authentically happy. The oldest one had his hand resting on the tree they were standing beside, and she wanted that to mean something. Did he have an ability like his father? There was an equal chance that neither of the Artemis boys would ever develop an ability.

"Alright, names," Artemis said as he sat back down at the coffee table. "I want the names of the men who'll be working to defend this nation."

Katherine snorted. *Men.* The most powerful person on the team was not a man at all. "You'll be happy to know that you have two decorated officers on your team. Major Sam Watts and Commander Daniel Cummings."

Artemis looked up in surprise. "You mean the military knows about them?"

Katherine smiled at his innocence. "No. Sam's hidden his ability for the very same reasons so many of your kind do." She held his stare until he looked down at his paper to write their names. "Danny is not evolved, though I've never met a man who could read a person or a situation as well as he can."

"Are they still enlisted?"

"No, retired and off the grid," she said. "You know that virtual reality social media platform, V-R?"

He nodded. "My boys are on it constantly."

"It's creator, Michael Leon Harding—"

He looked up sharply. "What, you're telling me that Harding is evolved?"

She shook her head. "No, I'm telling you he's part of

the team."

"But is he evolved?"

"Not to my knowledge. Just one hell of a smart techno whiz."

"Wasn't he living in Singapore up until a few years ago?"

Katherine nodded. "Yes, and now he's living with the rest of Halo. There's Kamal Sheppard, doctoral student in genetics. Henry Teasdale, former First Officer and currently GFO's lead project manager. Josh Mendez—"

Artemis snorted. "Of course he's involved in Halo. Should have known that. He's the most vocal public personality about EO rights." He shook his head. "He's too polarizing. We don't need him. Doesn't he have a family business he can retire to?"

"Yes, he does. But if you want Rox, then you'll have to take Josh."

"Rox?" He looked up from his paper. "Does Rox have a last name?"

That was a long story she wasn't about to get into at the moment. In fact, that was a story she'd leave to Rox to tell. "No."

"Alright, and who's Rox?"

"The one who's going to keep your team together, keep 'em honest, and the only one who'll lay down her life to make sure that each and every one of them comes back home safely."

"She's the leader?"

Katherine nodded. She was their leader. She still had a lot to learn, but given she was going to outlive all of them, she was the obvious choice for the job.

"Anyone else?"

Katherine took a deep breath and exhaled it slowly. "Dr Clifford Tusk."

"You say his name like I should know it. Should I?"

"No, but he'll need a few pardons, and a hell of a lot more forgiveness."

Artemis stood up and shook his head. "No. Everyone's got to be squeaky clean if they're going to be on my team."

"Then you've got yourself a problem, because Tusk is the closest scientist on the planet to understanding *and* replicating the evolved genome. His protégé is Kamal Sheppard." Though Kamal didn't know that yet.

Artemis looked back at Father Ong who just shrugged his shoulders as he refilled his cup of tea.

"Is the FBI after him?" Artemis asked.

"Doubt it. But there's a possibility that Carter's going to throw some major dirt his way."

"Possibility?" he asked.

"Yeah, it could go either way. Carter and Tusk were college roommates and have been working together building ... let's just call them 'questionable' facilities around the world where they 'studied' evolved subjects and received potentially 'controversial donations' from interested parties."

Artemis walked over to his desk and dropped his pad and pencil. He put his hand on his hip and stared out the window. "I'll need to meet him."

Katherine nodded. "Easily arranged. He's in Halo's custody right now."

"Custody?"

"Full disclosure?"

"Yes."

"He's responsible for the kidnapping and experimentation on Rox and Major Watt's younger sister."

"Holy shit! Katherine, we can't have a man with that kind of history working for this organization. If that gets out ..."

"I understand. My team is going to like it a lot less than you, but like I'll explain to them this isn't about them. Or their personal stories. This is about evolved ones everywhere. They'll understand that. It's what they've been fighting for."

Artemis massaged his forehead like he was trying to relieve a headache. "Now I understand why the President sent you to me. Is there anyone else I need to know about?"

"Meita bint Tariq al-Shaikh recently retired," Katherine said.

"When?"

"Three, four hours ago."

"What?"

"Carter and Fined had her followed, kidnapped, and tortured on a shipping container in the Patapsco."

"What the hell kind of organization have you been running, Katherine?" he snapped.

"The kind that has saved countless evolved human beings around the globe. My team puts themselves in danger to ensure that *everyone* gets a fair shot. The question is, where was *your* team when my team was doing *your* job?" She wasn't going to allow herself to be questioned by a bureaucrat. Not one who had kept his head in the sand while his own kind were being exploited.

"I was doing my job, which at the time, didn't include giving evolved humans special treatment."

"I don't think your kind's asking for special treatment," Father Ong said. "Just a chance to live in peace."

Artemis looked at the two of them. "And I guess you want the good Father Wáng on your team as well?"

She shook her head. "He's a priest. What use have I got for a priest?"

"I want to meet everyone."

"And then there's Shaira," Katherine said.

"And who is Shaira?" Artemis asked.

"A wolf."

"A wolf?" He didn't bother to look up from his paper where he continued to scribble down the names she gave him. "And is this wolf evolved?"

"That's a very good question. I don't know. I don't think Sam or Rox knows either."

Artemis opened his mouth like he was going to say something, but instead closed it.

"The wolf's pretty damn well-trained though, I must say," added Katherine. "She helped rescue two 'subjects' from WD-11, and has accompanied the team on several assignments involving the safe extraction of evolved humans under threat."

"You want me to authorize a wolf?"

"The police have dogs," Father Ong said. "Why can't you have a wolf?"

Katherine didn't mean to laugh, but the Father had a good point.

"And this is it?" Artemis asked. "You don't have any dinosaurs or unicorns that also need authorizing?"

"No, no dinosaurs, but I've just got word a saber-toothed tiger just joined our team. So ..." She shrugged. "There's that."

Father Ong choked on his tea, but Katherine continued. "Halo's gone international, of course. We work with various teams around the globe when needed."

Artemis sat back down in his chair and looked at her for a few moments. He shook his head in disbelief and stood up like he had forgotten the reason he sat down. "This meeting," he said, looking back and forth between Father Ong and Katherine, "stays here. Everyone and everything discussed remains in this office."

"I'm pretty sure it's going to be common knowledge within the next couple of hours that I've been here, Mr Secretary," Katherine said.

He came over and extended her his hand. "I extend the protection of the United States of America's Homeland Security to you and your team until the time we bring you onboard, when you will become *employees* and work under *my* direction. Screw me on this, Katherine, and I'll bury all of you."

"Betray us, Artie, and lightning will strike you down," Katherine said as she shook his hand.

~

## No trespassing

August 9th, 10:30pm EST

Rox enjoyed running the perimeter near the woods with Shaira. During the day, she would follow the wolf through the trees in a game of "catch me if you can". Sometimes, Shaira would race out of sight, only to circle back and try to ambush Rox. During the summer, the trees and bushes were full with leaves that created more hiding spaces, but as winter approached, the crackle of dried branches tended to give the wolf away.

Rox's watch vibrated when she reached her goal, and she slowed down to a brisk walk. The night sky lacked the light pollution that was common in and around cities. Here, the stars were bright, like nightlights in the sky. An occasional cloud would pass overhead, but that did nothing to diminish the peace that being out in the open provided.

Rox understood Sam's attraction to the countryside. She could hear her thoughts here. Nature calmed the mind in a way a city just couldn't accommodate. Is this why Sam chose to stay? The lack of gasoline and diesel smell that smothered the fresh air? Halo was free of the commotion that came with traffic and congestion. She thought back to the busy streets of Singapore. There was always a taxi whizzing by or someplace to hurry off to. Her thoughts were always planning, scheduling, and trying to fit in as many things as she could in a single day.

Halo was different. Here, she could explore her feelings for Danny. She smiled when she thought back to last night.

She glanced down at her watch. It was around the same time they shared their first kiss. She was a bit surprised it had taken her as long as it did to actually *see* him as anything more than one of her trainers, but then again, a "boyfriend" hadn't exactly been a top priority. For the past three years, the man she dreamed about was always just out of reach. Now, there was someone who existed outside of her mind.

Josh was in the main house resting. She had connected with him long before the ambulance pulled into the driveway just before dinner. He was strapped to a gurney, and Kamal was seated in the back with him. Kevin had driven behind them in a separate car with Samantha. She got out slowly, a bit apprehensive about what to do or where to go, but Kevin assured her she could make herself at home. Then Walter came out and introduced himself as a close family friend. He offered to take her in, but she said she was alright and waited until the two paramedics helped transfer Josh inside the house. There was a pile of paperwork Kamal had to read through and sign, but he seemed quite confident in what he was doing, so Rox left him to it. It took a lot of her energy to get Josh back to full health. His chest and shoulder were sore, and they would be for some time to come, but he was up and moving about in a manner that wouldn't be possible for anyone who suffered a stab wound mere centimeters from his heart.

Samantha reached to stop Rox when she released the buckles securing Josh to the gurney, but then he sat up as if he were simply waking from a nap.

"Took you long enough," he had said, to which she

replied, "Well, next time don't get yourself stabbed so far away from home."

Home. Two years ago, home was a small one-room annex off Michael's beautiful, six-bedroom bungalow in Singapore. Before that, home had been whatever derelict building she could find or women's shelter that had a bed for her. And before that there was her home with Josh, but that home hadn't been real. As easy as it would've been to pretend, she was glad she had the courage to leave him. People were multifaceted. They were capable of horrific actions that caused intense pain, but that same person could also carry the immense power to heal. No one ever truly fit in a box of good or evil. No one ever truly lived up to the stereotype. She loved him, perhaps in ways that would never make sense to anyone who hadn't shared a connection the way they had. Love, Rox had learned, came in so many different flavors. The love she had for Josh couldn't be compared to what she felt for her children or the love she still held for Sam.

Would she ever be able to let him go?

Shaira's eyes disappeared behind a tree into the woods, and for a moment, Rox almost didn't follow her, but she wasn't ready to go back inside. Henry had spoken to Meita, and Curtis, Danny, and Kamal had left to go meet them in Hartford. They were hoping to be back before midnight, but Kamal would make the decision whether to take Meita straight to the hospital or to secure her first at Halo. Danny asked her what she wanted to do about Tusk, and although she wanted nothing more than to make him pay for all the pain and suffering he had caused, she realized if he had truly helped Meita, they all needed to figure out why. She told Danny to restrain him and bring him back to Halo. There were jamming devices around the border of the property that would prevent anyone from tracing him if Tusk was wearing a tracking device.

Rox had also called Michael. He confirmed that the kids were safe and nothing seemed out of the ordinary. Emma and MJ were enjoying being so close to a college campus and were talking about which school they wanted to attend. Rox explained what was going on and asked Michael to keep his phone on so she could reach him if necessary. His voice gave away his frustration at being so close to danger once again, but this was his reality now. He would never be able to put his head back into the sand and believe that Emma's withdrawn personality was solely the result of losing her mother at such a tender age. Knowledge changed things. Emma needed Halo. Ruby needed Halo, too, even if she couldn't admit it.

How many years ago was it that Rox trespassed through these very woods looking for help? Now she walked through them in the dark of night with ease. It had been cold then. Snowing, if her memory was correct. Her feet were so cold and she had stubbed her toes on every root and branch that was sticking up that night. She laughed quietly at how astounded everyone was when that first tranquilizer dart didn't take her down. If she had known then all that she would have to go through to find her family, would she have done it? Almost always the answer was yes, but sometimes, at moments like this when she was alone and the stars lit up the night and there was no one around but Shaira, sometimes, she would give herself the freedom to wonder what her life would've been like if she had remained with Sam and never went to Singapore. Would he still be here or would fate have intervened to take him away regardless of the scenario?

Maybe the only way she was ever going to let go of Sam was to leave Halo. She was sure sleeping in his room wasn't helping her move forward. His bedsheets had long lost his scent, but every now and again, she would sit in front of the trunk at the end of his bed. She'd close her eyes, lift the lid, and breathe in the fragrance of him that still lingered on the summer clothes he kept inside. As much as she wanted to pull out one of his shirts and pull it over her head to use as a nightie, she resisted the temptation. His scent would fade if she wore it, and so she would close the lid a few minutes later and then climb into his bed to begin her fight with sleep.

Rox was about to whistle for Shaira so they could head back when she heard a low growl a few paces ahead. She crouched and looked up. Shaira's gums were bared and her body still. The wolf glanced over at Rox before she lifted one paw and then carefully placed it down like she wanted to keep their location a secret.

Rox reached for a weapon that wasn't there. She was out for a run. No phone. No batons. She peered out into the darkness in the direction Shaira was facing and waited. Nothing. She waited five seconds, then a twig cracked. Shaira held her position.

One of the many *no trespassing* signs was up ahead, and near that was a motion sensor about shoulder height that would switch on a security camera inside the main house. Rox looked over her shoulder at the nearest tree and tried to gauge if she would be able to make it there without making a sound.

Then Shaira charged, and Rox was following before she realized she was in motion. There was a brief cry from someone, but then it was silenced by Shaira's growls and the sounds of gurgling.

Rox arrived just as death's energy slammed into her, and an orange tint covered the darkened wood. She scanned the woods for more movement, but there was nothing. She continued forward, at a slow pace that was difficult to maintain with the excess adrenaline running through her. She went to the *no trespassing* sign and waved her hand to activate the security camera.

Shaira trotted over.

"Good girl," Rox whispered. She followed the wolf to where the man lay dead. Death seemed to follow her like a shadow at high noon. There was never any escaping it, just a bitter co-existence.

Rox crouched to check the man's pockets while Shaira stood watch. There was a handgun holstered to an equipment belt holding three additional magazines. There was also a rifle, but he obviously didn't have time to get a shot off before Shaira was on him. There was something hanging from his neck, and it took her a moment to realize it was an activated glow stick. It was covered in his blood so it was impossible to see its florescent light. He had a cell phone in one of his pockets, but that was it. No wallet and no identification.

Was he connected to the man who attacked Josh? Did he have something to do with Katherine and Meita's disappearance?

The man was dressed in jeans and a checkered shirt with buttons down the center. His jacket had fur around the collar, but some of it was missing. A baseball cap without a logo sat near his rifle, but it was too dark to distinguish the color and with the orange tint still covering her vision, she wasn't sure she could've determined it anyway. Whoever this man was, he wasn't fit. He had a belly. There was no way he was ever going to succeed getting past any of them.

Who would send him and to what purpose?

She opened up her mind and called out to Josh. *We've got an intruder on the southeast side of the property. Shaira took care of him.*

Then the wolf's ears perked up, and she gave a low growl in warning to Rox.

"Tommy?" It was no more than a whisper, but it didn't need to be any louder.

*We've got more.*

Rox left her mind open, but she took a few deep breaths to calm herself. With the extra energy from the dead guy, she was feeling confident. Instinct would have her run full tilt towards whoever it was calling for Tommy, but experience told her that wasn't a good plan.

She scanned the woods for the voice in the darkness and was surprised when she saw it. It wasn't the person she saw, but his energy. It was steady and strong, and glowed like a light source in the darkness. That had never happened before.

Rox shook her head and looked again. The entire forest was still covered in the soft hues of muted orange, but the one whispering for Tommy was a bright beacon, not quite pulsating, but circling, moving as the man moved.

She quietly checked the chamber and the magazine of Tommy's handgun. It was loaded, and so she slipped the safety off and made her way behind the nearest tree. With her back against the trunk, she squeezed her eyes tight and then opened them.

*What's wrong?*

*I might be seeing things.*

*No. I'm with Kevin looking at the security feed now. We've definitely got intruders. So far, we count seven. No, eight. Make that twelve.*

Twelve, plus the one Shaira took out and the one calling for Tommy. *They're armed. Tommy has a handgun with magazines for reloading and a rifle.*

*Any idea who they are?*

Rox shook her head. He couldn't see, but he would know she had done it.

Tommy's cell phone vibrated and the woods went silent. Rox looked for Shaira, but the wolf had disappeared. She was hunting. This was her woods, and no one wandered through without an invitation.

A gunshot broke the silence. Rox came from behind the tree looking for her orange beacon, and once she found it, she lifted her hand and sent the death's energy she held across the space that divided them. The man calling for Tommy didn't have a chance to move or to lift his weapon.

Instead, his body was pulled into a rigid pose before he collapsed to the ground.

The night returned to its normal shades of grays and blacks.

*Walter and Kevin are on their way,* Josh said. That was good, but she would've preferred to have Danny here. He was the only one who could rival Sam in the field.

Rox grabbed Tommy's phone as she ran off in the direction of the gunshot. *Okay. I'm looking for Shaira.*

*No, head back. Shaira can take care of herself.*

She didn't respond. She didn't need to. They both knew she wouldn't leave Shaira to battle eleven. Especially not if they were armed.

The thin wisps of clouds that were passing by slowed as she drew the kinetic energy from everywhere around her. She reached out to feel for anything else, but all she got was the rapid heartbeats of the rodents scurrying their way to safety.

She placed her back against a tree and listened. She had to slow down her own racing pulse if she was going to make out the sounds of someone approaching. But the woods were silent. Unnaturally so, and then there was a howl. A call to arms that rose goosepimples along her spine. It was due west, and so she headed in that direction just as rapid gunfire created temporary explosions of light.

Rox couldn't see far enough in front of her to justify running as fast as she was, but these were her woods now, too. This was her home, and these people were trespassing. Rox knew what Halo did to trespassers.

It started to rain. It wasn't in the forecast, but that didn't matter now. She yanked on the kinetic energy created by the colliding storm clouds overhead and allowed it to course through her body as it increased her speed.

A crackle of light lit up the forest and was immediately followed by a crash of thunder. Three men were clustered together about two hundred meters in front of her, and they were shooting at something. She knew it had to be Shaira. Danny would tell her to flank them so she could pick them off from behind. Her aim was still crap, but it would be good enough to take out three targets who hadn't seen her coming.

Rox had a better idea. She gave two short and sharp whistles just like Walter had taught her. Rox saw the glimpse of fur switch directions and race towards her, so she stopped and lifted her hands. When her fingers snapped, a jagged streak of orange lightning came crashing down on the intruders. The impact created a wave of energy that blew through the trees, picking up twigs and smaller branches and projecting them outwards in a circle like an explosion. Rox crouched and created a shield in front of her just as Shaira came bursting into the clearing. She pushed it out so that it protected the wolf as the force of the expulsion slammed into her shield. Rox ground her teeth as her feet slid backwards, but she didn't let go until the forest had resettled.

She lowered her shield as her legs buckled. That had taken more energy than she had planned on expending.

*Rox? Was that you?*

She answered him.

*I've got drones up. We've got five coming from the southwest side of the property and another four coming up the lane in the middle. But they're spread out.*

*My side?* she asked between breaths.

*Clear.*

*I'll make my way to the middle.*

*You sure you're alright?*

She was tired, but they were trespassing, and unlike her, they came bearing weapons. *Yeah.* She'd find the energy.

*I'll let Walter know you're heading towards him.*

*How far away are they from the house?*

*Under a mile maybe.*

*Is Walter alone?*

*No. He's got Keenan with him.*

Walter would never admit it, but he was getting too old for the physical aspect of Halo. He was still more fit than half the men she had come across, and definitely more fit than Tommy back there, but age was an irreversible fact of life. She had quietly sent him healing energy on a few occasions, and while he was far from dying, the reality was, he was aging. That, she couldn't heal.

"Go, find Walter," Rox said, and Shaira took off.

Rox raced through the woods after her, dodging low hanging branches and widening her stride to jump over unearthed roots. She knew there was a stump with jagged edges coming up on her right, so she ducked under a bough and skirted to the left.

The wind had picked up, meaning Keenan was nearby. She felt the tunnel of wind come and it gave her an idea. She whispered his name as she ran past a *no trespassing* sign. An explosion quieted the rain for a moment, and she knew someone on the other side of the property had stumbled across the thin piece of wire connected to a shock grenade. A muscle in her neck threatened to seize at the memory of flying through the air and landing on her backpack. She wanted to say that the grenades were a bit of an overkill, but now that Walter had added more signs, some of them explicitly warning of the presence of landmines, the intruders had been fairly warned.

Keenan answered her.

*Link me up with Keenan,* Rox instructed Josh.

Josh did, and she explained her idea to both of them. Keenan thought it was risky, but this was Rox's home. She signaled a few minutes later that she was in position, and Keenan released a torrent of wind down the middle of the drive. She pulled on the storm clouds and watched as lightning jumped from one cloud to the next before directing itself towards her. She snapped, and it landed in the middle of the tornado and the hairs on her arms lifted. Her ears popped and Shaira's fur lifted up as if she were being sucked up by an invisible vacuum.

They had never done this before, but now seemed like a good time to figure out what would happen if they combined abilities. Keenan pushed the wind in the direction of the four intruders coming up the lane.

An electric shock lanced up her jaw when the storm cloud went past her, and Shaira whimpered as she crept closer to Rox and rubbed her face against her legs.

Rox fought the desire to pull from the storm cloud swirling its way down the drive and kept her focus on the wind as it cut through the trees on the opposite side. Some of its energy dispersed, and for a moment, she thought it was going to go out altogether, but then she felt another burst of wind rush down the lane to join it, so she lifted her hand and fed it enough of her energy to keep its charge.

She knew when it found its intended target because there were brief, confused screams, followed by the sharp rap of thunder before everything fell quiet. The wind dispersed and the rain slowed.

Walter and Keenan came down the lane, their weapons raised and their attention on opposite sides as they searched through the woods. Shaira howled and Walter lowered his gun.

"What do you think?" Rox asked, when they found her leaning against a tree trunk trying to catch her breath.

"Sloppy," Keenan said with a genuine smile on his face. "But it was a good idea."

Walter had an earpiece in, and it looked like he was getting an update. "The other four are down."

"Four? Josh said five," Rox said. *Josh? What happened to the last one?*

*Drones aren't picking him up any more. Neither are the surveillance cameras.*

That meant one had escaped. She wasn't sure whether to worry about that or to celebrate the fact that it looked like everything was over. "Any idea who these guys were?"

"Dead is what they are now," Walter said.

"It's a little too coincidental that Tusk 'rescues' Meita," Rox said, using air quotes, "and then all of a sudden, we're attacked. We haven't been attacked since …"

"Ever," Walter said. "Well, you. When you came." He pointed to Rox.

"I didn't attack you guys. I was looking for help!"

"That's not what Curtis said." There was a smile on Walter's face.

Rox was tired. It'd been a long couple of days and they had almost lost Josh. Now they had been attacked, and she wasn't sure she could handle losing anyone. She walked over to Walter and wrapped him into a hug before she could stop herself.

He stood rigid at first, but it didn't take long for him to return the affection and plant a kiss on her forehead.

When she stepped back, they looked at one another like neither of them were comfortable with showing that much affection to the other. But she loved him, and she knew he loved her back.

"Josh says the drones are not picking up anyone else," Keenan said. "But we did lose one drone with the storm cloud we just unleashed."

Rox reached out with her energy and sent it as far as she could. She could feel Keenan doing the same. He was faster and his reach farther, but neither of them felt anything else.

"What are you going to do with the bodies?" Keenan asked.

Walter shrugged. "Bury 'em, I guess."

Rox shook her head. "Henry'll handle it. I don't want any evidence they were here."

"Do you have a hypothesis on who could have sent them?" Keenan asked.

Rox could only think about Tusk, so it surprised her when Walter said the Fellowship.

"But how?" she asked as they walked back towards the house. "They wouldn't know where we live."

"Agreed." But Walter said he had a hunch that Josh's attack, his arrival at Halo, and then these guys showing up had to be more than a coincidence.

"That means he would've been followed," Rox said.

Both Walter and Keenan nodded.

"I'm sure Kevin and Kamal had other things on their minds," Walter said. "Besides, is there anybody else who knows about this place that we don't trust?"

Rox considered that for a moment. This was Henry's first time at Halo. He had access to both Katherine and Meita's schedule and he always knew their whereabouts. He, at one time, had worked for Tusk. Could he still be working for him?

*Nope. I checked him out as soon as you healed me. He's clean.*

"What're you doing out here?" Walter said, and Rox looked up to see Samantha.

She was holding a phone in her hand in the horizontal position like she had been videoing. "Josh is Halo. You're all Halo."

*Have you read your girlfriend yet?* Rox asked Josh. *Is she on the level?*

*Yeah, why?*

Then Rox opened her mind so he could see what she saw.

*Shit. She promised me she was going to stay in her room.*

*Well, obviously, she lied.*

# CHAPTER SEVEN

## Bigger evil

August 10th, 4:30am EST

The flowers from the center of the table had been placed on the ledge in front of the bay windows overlooking the picnic table. It was odd having the kitchen filled with so much tension. It was the place where everyone unwound, where they laughed, ate, and came together to share stories.

Leave it to Tusk to take that away from them, too.

Danny pulled out the soles to Tusk's shoes and tossed them on the floor before running his fingers along the insides. He was about to hand them back to Tusk when Rox stopped him. She remembered running in the woods surrounding Wonderland and the cold ground gnawing at her feet. The dry pine needles stabbed at the soft skin between her toes and fallen branches scraped her ankles as she ran for her life.

"May I have my shoes back now, please?" Tusk said.

Rox took them from Danny and stepped on the lever that lifted the lid to the trash bin. "It's amazing what one can do with the proper motivation."

Tusk looked at Danny, but Danny didn't move, didn't flinch, didn't have an itch to scratch or a shiver to make him shudder.

"Sit," Rox said.

Tusk hesitated, but then sat down, and Danny and Kevin pulled out the chairs on either side of him. Walter was there, too, at the head. He turned his chair around so he was straddling it. She had warned him that they wouldn't be killing Tusk right away, and Walter had shrugged like killing Tusk later would work just as well.

Meita made Rox promise she would protect Tusk, and if Rox didn't owe Meita for rescuing her children, Rox would've never agreed. So now, she had to make sure no one killed the only man in the world they all wanted dead.

*Breathe.*

"I am breathing," Rox said.

Tusk looked at her in confusion, and it took every ounce of self-control not to launch across the table and put into practice everything she had learned over the past three years. She was stronger. She was fitter; she could kill him. But Meita had called him an ally and Henry had seconded that by saying he had spoken with Katherine. Of course, Katherine would strike a deal with the man who had tortured just about everyone in the room, one way or another.

Rox let the silence linger and continued to pace. She didn't feel the need to say anything, and it seemed like no one else did either. Shaira paced alongside her. Most of the blood had been washed off by the rain, but there was still enough around the wolf's snout to draw Tusk's attention.

Good. Rox hoped he was petrified. She reached for his energy again, but again, she couldn't grab hold. It was like trying to capture water. She just couldn't get a grip. He was like Meita. Like Ruby.

Thinking of Ruby made the orange tint slip over her vision again, and Shaira sensed the change in her mood and growled.

*Ruby and Jay are safe at university. I hung up with Michael not too long ago. MJ and Emma are with him. No one's going near them.*

So much for them having a "normal" college experience. But then they were never going to have a normal anything. Jay's ability had finally developed, and with it came side effects neither Rox nor Josh were prepared for. And Ruby? "Normal" had died for her along with her mother. She was a teenager with anger-management issues that even two years of therapy with Bethany hadn't resolved. Rox wanted to blame Tusk for that.

Samantha was also at the table, but that was only because their "conversation" had gotten interrupted when Danny, Kamal, and Curtis pulled up with Tusk and a very pale Meita in the backseat. Rox asked Samantha about the video she had recorded during the attack. She said it was not live, but it was uploaded and if anything happened to her, her producer would post it.

Rox laughed at that. "You think a video will stop me from killing you if you betray Josh?" she said. "Sweetheart, death herself couldn't stop me if you hurt him."

This wasn't about the video. It was also about letting another person into their circle who hadn't been through any of what they had been through together. Meita and Josh had rescued her, Kamal, Sam, and Walter from WD-11. Kevin had been there when she traded her life for her now-adopted son, Jay. Danny had been there when they rescued her and Miles from Wonderland. Keenan had been there when she returned from saving her kids in Laos. Everyone at that table had paid the price to sit there. But her?

*That's not fair.*

"Fuck fair," Rox said.

"Does she do this often?" Tusk looked at Danny. "I mean, speak her thoughts aloud like that?"

Rox stopped pacing and turned to face him. Tusk should be more afraid than he was because the only thing keeping her from killing him was a promise she was rapidly talking herself out of. *Why are you protecting him?* Rox asked Josh. *He kidnapped Jay!*

Josh got up from his chair and faced her. *You don't think I know that? He's my son.*

*He's my son, too!*

Josh turned his back to the table and went to the refrigerator. *When was the last time you ate? You're acting like you're hangry.*

*Oh, I guess having the man who locked me in a facility for who knows how long, tortured me, then kidnapped my children has nothing to do with it.*

"Astounding!" Tusk said and pushed back like he was going to stand, but Danny put a hand on Tusk's shoulder to keep him seated. "Leona floated this idea that one of you could read thoughts, but I explained how absurdly difficult that would be. But now …" Tusk stared between the two of them. "Is that what you two are doing?"

It was Samantha who inhaled sharply.

"Oh, hello, dear," Tusk said, turning his attention to her like he hadn't noticed her before. "My name is Dr Clifford Tusk. I don't think I've had the pleasure of meeting you."

Josh slammed the jar of mayonnaise on the counter. "Don't talk to her."

*We need to get him out of here,* Rox said. *Isolate him or he's going to tear us apart at the seams if he stays.*

*I want him gone as well. In fact, I want to be the one to kill him for what he's done to you and to Jay, but right now, he's worth more to us alive than dead.*

She knew they were doing that awkward thing where they just looked at one another without actually saying anything. But she didn't care. She wasn't sure what short-term plans Katherine and Meita had for Tusk, but she was going to kill him once they were done. There was no way she was going to let him live, not after what he had done to all of them.

Rox looked over at Walter, who just sat there, his face as placid as a lake on a humid day. He hadn't said anything since he sat down, and that worried her. Tusk had taken his daughter, and whatever he had done had changed her. Val was better than when Rox first arrived to stay at Halo two years ago, but Val complained of headaches and body pain in places she couldn't readily identify.

Walter would want him dead just as badly. Everyone at that table had earned the right to kill him, except Samantha. Was it fair bringing her into this? She was a journalist. Would she choose the story or Josh?

Rox swallowed her yawn. There was no point in stalling. They were tired. No one had gotten much sleep the night before when Keenan arrived. Then someone followed Josh and attacked them. Henry made a call and shortly afterwards, agents claiming they were from Homeland Security arrived and took over the case. It was the exact opposite of what Rox was hoping for, but Henry said to trust him, so everyone gave statements to the agents who took photos of the bodies and the positions they were in when found. Then they left three hours later, taking the bodies with them.

"What do you know about the Fellowship?" she asked Tusk.

"Fellowship?" he repeated, and then shook his head. "Never heard of it."

Rox pulled back the chair Josh had been sitting in before he got up to make sandwiches. This was Walter's house, but it was her house too, and Tusk was not a guest in it. He was a prisoner, and it was time they started to treat him like one. *Grab your girlfriend a pen and paper.*

*Why?*

Rox shrugged. Because she wanted Samantha to have some skin in the game. Rox didn't like the idea of her just sitting there and listening without participating. Plus, the woman was a journalist and interviewed people for a living. Maybe she could help them get some answers.

"Start from the beginning," Rox said. She didn't believe Tusk when he said he didn't know anything about Fellowship, but she didn't want to start off at an impasse. "I want to know where you found me."

Tusk sat back and looked around the table. He was outnumbered and he knew it. He didn't look like he necessarily feared death, but he had taught her there were a lot of things you could do to a person that would make death feel like a gift.

Josh returned to the table and placed a sandwich in front of Rox and a pen and notebook in front of Samantha. She looked up at him confused.

"I need you to take notes," Rox said as she took a bite. "And jot down any questions you think I should ask."

Samantha looked back up to Josh, and then at Tusk before turning her attention back to Rox. "Why me?"

"Because everyone else is preoccupied with either restraining me and Walter or making sure he doesn't try anything."

"Who is this guy?" Samantha asked.

Rox understood Josh's attraction to her. It was the eyes. They were large and a honey mustard-brown framed by eyelashes women paid a fortune for. But Rox knew Josh well enough to know it wasn't just about her looks. She was an intelligent woman who exuded confidence. That was what he saw in her, and that was why he was with her.

"This man experimented on evolved humans without their consent. He kidnapped them, tortured them, and in some cases murdered them. He took children – my children – and has been hunting our kind for I don't know how long."

Samantha sucked in her breath.

"Tad dramatic, don't you think, Tara?" Tusk said. But no one laughed. No one said a thing. Everyone's attention was on Samantha. Rox was offering her an opportunity to earn a seat at the table, but it would be up to her if she took it. No one was going to force her into it. So they waited, and Rox watched Josh hold his breath as the woman he cared about decided their future.

"Why does he call you Tara?" Samantha asked.

Rox sighed. That was a long and convoluted story. "It's a name I used to go by."

Samantha wasn't an idiot. The rise of her eyebrow said she knew there was more to it than that, but she held her tongue and looked back down at the pen before picking it up and nodding that she was in.

"Where did you find me?" Rox asked Tusk.

He nodded his head like he approved of the question, and then he crossed his arms. "I just so happened to be in Costa Rica looking for subjects. There was a rumor that there was a woman living in a little town called Quepos who could control water with her mind, or her hands, I never did find her because the locals weren't very trusting, and then the earthquake happened."

"Earthquake?" Samantha asked. "In Costa Rica?"

"No, dear," Tusk said. "Peru."

Rox remembered the story from Michael. He had gone to the remote town where she was on assignment to find it decimated. Tara Alexandra Harding was listed as one of the many who were missing and presumed dead.

Tusk looked around the table like he wasn't sure he wanted to continue. Rox was tempted to say something, but instinct held her quiet. He hadn't been afraid of anything since arriving at Halo. Why show hesitation now? But then he shrugged like he had changed his mind.

"Nancy and I got there as soon as we could, and we were able to claim about ten bodies before anyone got suspicious."

Samantha wrote down the name Nancy on her pad.

"Was I … dead?" Rox asked.

He smiled at her. "When it comes to you, Tara, I think it's best to say you weren't showing any vital signs."

He had taken her as one of the dead bodies he was going to experiment with. There were so many directions in which their conversation could go. But Rox was curious about something. "Who's Nancy?"

For the first time, Tusk looked like his confident demeanor wasn't infallible. Was Nancy someone he had been trying to cure? A lover? A wife? His daughter or sister? Was this what got him into experimentation? Was he trying to save the life of someone he cared about?

Tusk turned his head sharply to the side, and the crack of his neck filled the silence. "Nancy *was* my assistant before you killed her."

Nancy? She killed a woman named Nancy? Rox remembered everyone she had ever killed. "I'd remember if I killed her." Wouldn't she?

Tusk leaned forward across the table towards her. "When you escaped my facility in Colorado, Wonderland, you did so by incapacitating my assistant, Nancy. You stole her access card and not only did you escape, you took one of my subjects with you!"

*Cotton candy lipstick.*

*Who?* Josh asked.

Rox ignored him as she tried to remember the specifics of her escape. She had been so hungry. So tired. She felt weak and even though her body had physically healed, she had been wracked with pain. "When I left her, she still had a heartbeat." Rox was sure of it. If she had drained all of Nancy's energy, she would have known it.

Tusk sat back and waved his hand, dismissing her statement. "Well, you might as well have killed her. She got arrested and ... protocols had to be followed."

Rox laughed. She hadn't meant to, but what kind of world must Tusk inhabit to think she could be at fault for the death of a woman who had been holding her captive? Who had been assisting in her torture? *I stole Nancy's access cards? Nancy stole me!*

She leaned forward, but Samantha interrupted her. "Continue. When you first took Tara, you thought she was dead ..."

"I took what I could from you in terms of tissue samples and organs," Tusk said. "Then I put you on ice and forgot about you."

Rox fought the urge to vomit. He had harvested her organs like her life held no meaning and her only value was in death.

Tusk wagged a finger at her. "But then a few days later, you came stumbling out of the storage unit with lips as blue as the sky." He was wearing a smile on his face that told her he regretted nothing of his actions. "Do you remember that?"

Rox ran her hand over her stomach in an attempt to ease the nausea and to make sure everything was still there.

She shook her head. She didn't remember waking up in a freezer. She didn't remember anything about her life before or after the earthquake. Her first memories were of Josh. He was her beginning.

"Do you see now?" Tusk finally drew her stare, and even though she wanted to look away, she couldn't. "Imagine what it would mean if we could understand *how* your body regenerates?"

The coffeemaker beeped and broke the stretch of silence that hung as everyone contemplated what her ability meant for humanity.

Rox cleared her throat. "That didn't give you the right to—"

"It gives me every right, Tara. I do what I do to further our understanding of humanity. To develop cures not treatments. To create a clearer, more accurate roadmap for the human genome. It's not pretty," Tusk said. "But it is necessary."

"And my children? Was it necessary to take them?"

Tusk sighed like he were explaining a complicated story to someone lacking the intellect to keep up.

"What did you do when you discovered that she … wasn't dead?" Samantha asked.

Tusk smiled at them both. "Everything and more."

"That's vague," Samantha said as she lowered her hand under the table and gave Rox's leg a squeeze. It wasn't particularly discreet, and Rox wasn't sure what she was trying to communicate, but she took it as a sign to remain quiet. "Specifically, what did you do with the organs you took? Sell them on the black market? I don't imagine the kind of research you conduct can be cheap. Or legal. You'd have to have some kind of revenue source to continue your work."

Tusk went to stand up again, and again Danny pushed him back in his seat. He cut Danny a side look that said he was annoyed, but Danny's face remained as void of emotion as before, and Rox was surprised how that saddened her. She wanted to see that twinkle again. He *deserved* to twinkle.

"Her samples were useless," Tusk said and turned his attention to Rox. "They always are. That's what I was trying to explain. The only way to do any type of experiment on you is to literally experiment *on* you. When you're alive."

Josh brought the pot of coffee and a tray of cups. He dropped it on the center of the table like he had lost his patience.

*Don't forget to breathe,* Rox said.

"What does that mean?" Samantha asked Tusk.

"Tara's organs, her tissue samples, her blood samples, every sample you take from her degrades at a fantastical rate. She is the perfect living specimen this world has ever seen. A woman who can literally drown, whose heart will stop and blood will cease to flow for well over ten minutes." Tusk placed his elbows on the table and leaned forward completely ignoring the coffee. "And the miracle isn't that your heart restarts. It's that there's no brain damage."

The box. Rox wasn't able to look at him anymore. She tried her damnest to forget the water rushing in at her feet. It was so cold, and her body trembled from its memory. She curled her toes in her boots and tried to breathe through the images replaying in her mind. She had tried to latch on to Tusk's energy, but it wasn't the box preventing her from pulling from him, it was because he was like Meita. Like Ruby.

"You see me as evil," Tusk said. "But I didn't *want* to burn you, Tara—"

"I reckon we've heard enough?" Walter said as he stood. "We can go ahead and kill him now."

"But the way your tissue rehydrates itself after—"

Rox caught Danny's eyes, and he got to his feet so he could block Walter.

"C'mon, Pops. Not like this. Not now," Danny said. "You'll get your chance."

*Samantha just asked me to have Danny take Walter out for a walk,* Josh told Rox.

Rox sat back in her chair. *It's his home, Josh. I can't kick him out of his own kitchen.*

*She's been watching him, and she says he's going to blow.*

*I'm not asking him to leave. He's got as much right to beat the shit out of him as anyone else.*

*We won't get anything if he loses his temper, and Tusk stops talking.*

*Then you have a word with him!*

"Continue," Samantha said to Tusk.

Rox looked back at Tusk, but he was already staring at her. Studying her. "I won't apologize to make you feel better," he finally. "I'm not here looking for absolution."

"Then why are you here?" Rox asked.

"Because I'm not about to let my life's work go to someone with more money than vision simply because she's savvy enough to seduce away *my* steady funding stream."

"Maybe she's more interested in an ethical type of research?"

Tusk laughed a genuine laugh. He reached for a cup and poured himself some coffee. He inhaled it first before sipping. His nod afterwards was more subconscious, like it was a habit he performed when tasting something to his liking. "That boy, Miles, the one who could literally feel the emotions of others? He could be the answer to helping psychopaths integrate into society as normal human beings."

"And 203?" Rox asked. "What about her?"

Tusk looked confused, and Rox realized she hadn't used her real name. "Su Chen? The woman at WD-11 who escaped with us?"

Tusk still looked like he had no idea who she was talking about, but then he snapped his fingers. "The woman with the trans dimensional hearing? Her? Well, she was a bit of an anomaly. Her abilities weren't really anything that could benefit mankind."

"Says who? You? That's the problem with *your* kind of research. You pass judgment like you're some kind of god, and you ruin lives. You hurt people in unimaginable ways and in the end, where's the medicine or the roadmap' that will help psychopaths reintegrate into society?"

It was his turn to slam his hands down on the table. "You took him, twice, I might add, before I could make any breakthroughs." He pushed back like he was going to stand, but Kevin grabbed him and pulled him back to sitting.

"You talk about God? We created God! In the absence of knowledge, what has mankind done since the beginning of time? We create stories, Tara. But I'm not looking for some bedtime tale, I'm searching for the truth."

"At the cost of your humanity?" Samantha asked.

He stared at her in silence like he wasn't sure how to respond.

"How many people are worth the sacrifice, and to what end?" Samantha said.

Tusk shook his head like she didn't understand. "I'm trying to make people's lives better, to make them worth living. You think the current medical system gives a shit about cures? C'mon, don't be so naive. There's no money in curing people. There's no profit margin when the patient doesn't need physical therapy because their muscles sew themselves back together or their tissue regrows and their organs regenerate. Do you know how many people die each year because of adverse effects to anesthesia administered during routine surgeries?"

"Last estimate I read was about two thousand, five hundred," Kamal said as he came into the kitchen. "Not a lot given the number of people that undergo surgery."

"Tell that to the loved ones of the two thousand, five hundred," Tusk said. "I was able to create a sedative that mimics anesthesia with zero side effects."

The room fell silent again.

"It's not my responsibility to save humanity," Rox said.

"No, it isn't," Tusk agreed. "It's mine."

"Alright," Samantha interjected. "Tell us about the Fellowship."

Tusk kept his eyes on Rox when he shook his head. "Like I said, I've never heard of them."

"They kidnapped me," Rox said. "Two nights ago."

Tusk sat back in his chair and crossed his arms over his chest. He let his head fall back before he lifted it a few seconds later. "There are a lot of organizations interested in evolved abilities." He explained that small groups of scientists had formed cooperatives with side projects to study EOs. He had joined a few in his early days, but they were just as interested in making a profit as they were in helping people.

"Don't pretend like you're so noble," Rox said.

"Oh, I'm not. I don't pretend to be anything. But at least I'm trying, Tara, and that's a hell of a lot more than you and your merry band of evolved ones here." He looked around the table. "You guys help evolved people run away and start over. Ever ask how many evolved ones' you've helped escape from law enforcement? How many of them had committed a crime and just needed a get-out-of-jail free card?"

"None," Walter said. It was the first time he had spoken since Tusk arrived, and she had almost forgotten he was there.

"How can you be so sure?" Tusk asked.

"Because no evolved one gets saved without my approval."

"And you are?"

"The man who's gonna kill you."

Tusk smirked. "Many have tried."

"Who's Leona?" Rox asked. Walter wanted a piece of Tusk. They all did.

Tusk's lips thinned as he tapped his foot a few times before stopping. "My *former* assistant."

"Like Nancy?" Rox asked.

"She was nothing like Nancy!" Tusk was either tired or they had struck a nerve again because he was letting his frustrations show.

"So, tell us about her," Samantha said. "Why such animosity?"

"Leona is Dr Mallory Fined's niece. She lied to get access to my research and then tried to steal it. In fact, she stole the sedative I created, gave it to her aunt, and then used it to kidnap Meita in there."

"What?" Rox said.

"Dr Mallory Fined?" Samantha interjected. "The head of AmLife? One of the world's most influential female scientists and business leaders?"

"Mallory's only interest in science is how it can line her pockets," Tusk said. "We went to medical school together. She was a half-rate then and nothing's changed."

"Why?" Samantha asked. "Why you? Why your work?"

A smile that belied the situation spread across Tusk's face to reach the wrinkle of his eyes. "I'll let you in on a little secret. I'm the closest anyone has come to unlocking the evolved genome." Tusk took another drink of his coffee. "My fellow scientists may not like my methods, but they sure as hell appreciate my results. I am the one who discovered that men have only one opportunity to become evolved." He looked back and forth between Rox and Samantha. "But females, your hormone levels go through two major shifts in your lifetime, giving you two opportunities for evolution."

"Yeah. I remember you explaining that to us in the conference room," Kamal said.

Tusk sat back and looked at him like he was trying to place him. "What are you talking about?"

"Oh, sorry, I'm Kamal Sheppard. I worked for you at WD-11." Kamal leaned back against the counter with his cup of coffee. "I mean, I was *Doctor* Kamal Sheppard to you. I was what you'd probably call a double agent in that I 'worked' for you, but I was really spying on you so I could figure out what happened to my roommate."

"You're the doctor that went unaccounted for!" Tusk nodded like he understood. "Yes, we assumed you were either murdered or you were the traitor. How'd you get access to my facility in the first place?"

Kamal looked at Rox, and she nodded for him to continue. "That's a long story, but the shorter version is two guys showed up in suits with a slip disk and told me either I could go undercover and find out what you were working on or I might just disappear like my roommate."

"Your roommate?" Tusk asked.

"That's the long part of the story," Kamal said.

Tusk scratched the stubble that was growing on his cheek. "You ever met a woman?"

"Uh, in the facility? You mean at WD-11?"

"No, I mean, whoever put you up to this, got you inside?"

Kamal shook his head. "But I was meant to do a hand-off with a woman. She was going to meet me in Santo Domingo and help me get back to the US afterwards."

Tusk sat back like he was thinking. "You have any clue what the woman looked like?"

Kamal shook his head no.

"Why?" Rox asked.

"You think it's Leona?" Samantha asked.

Tusk stared off into space like he was weighing up the odds. There were dark circles under his eyes. It had been a long day for him as well. Rox looked up at the clock and it read ten past five. This was her second night of little to no sleep.

"Possible. If it was, then it means that Mallory's been after my research for longer than I suspected."

Henry came into the kitchen with his phone in his hand. "Walter, Rox, can I speak with you for a moment?"

Rox stood and reached for the back of her chair as an energy pulse swept through her.

Shaira jumped up from where she was lying by the kitchen door. Her ears pointed forward and her tail stilled as her nose sniffed the air. Then she howled. It was deep and long. She was calling out, and a hope Rox couldn't deny sprouted inside.

*¿Amor?*

*It can't be.* Rox shook her head. *Josh?*

*I read Henry's thoughts. I didn't want to tell you because we don't know what state he's—*

She came around the table as another one hit her, but it didn't slow her down. She grabbed the handle of the door and Shaira was out before it was fully open.

"Rox?" Walter said.

She looked at him and said the one word that would make him whole again. "Sam."

## Reunited

August 10th, 5:10am EST

"Restrain him," Rox shouted to Kevin, as she tore out of the door with Walter right behind her. They both leapt down the stairs of the porch and followed after Shaira's disappearing body into the fading darkness.

She wasn't aware that she was pulling the kinetic energy from the clouds and reversing their direction. Thunder slapped above, but she didn't hear it.

It couldn't be true, a small voice warned her. She had to manage her expectations. Two years had passed. That was a long time for someone to be missing *and* still be alive. She could heal a lot of things, but death wasn't one of them.

"Where is he?" Walter shouted as the rain started.

The next wave of energy that passed through her was so strong, she slowed as her head lifted up and the familiar tint of orange colored her vision. She was getting closer.

They lost sight of Shaira in the rain, so Walter whistled for her, but when they rounded the bend, there she was, standing in the middle of the narrow lane leading to the house, bathed in the headlights of a van.

Walter grabbed Rox and pulled her back into the trees. They had no way of knowing if whoever was with Sam was friendly or if this was another wave of attack. Shaira ran straight towards the van and then vaulted onto the hood. She howled once again like she was calling, waiting for a response, and then bared her teeth.

Rox was parallel with the van when she noticed a second one behind the first. The waves of Sam's energy were hitting her hard and fast now, and she fought against her better judgment to approach the two vehicles.

*Josh?*

*I see.* He responded, and then he chuckled. *You'll never guess who it is!*

*Now's not the time for guessing games!*

His laughter continued for a second longer, and then he said it was her favorite doctor.

*Dotz?*

*And her zen-master husband, Mal.*

"Dotz?" she shouted, finally taking a step from the woods. "Dr Dotz?"

The window of the first van with Shaira on top lowered just a bit and she heard a woman shouting something to her over the heavy rain.

Rox ran up to the window. Dotz pointed to the hood, and Rox whistled for Shaira to get down. The wolf jumped down, and Dotz lowered the window a little lower.

"Hello!" she said with a bright smile on her face. "We've got a special delivery for you. Hop in!"

Rox slid the door on the side open and a wave of Sam's energy slammed into her.

"Is it him?" Walter said as he ran up behind her. He climbed into the van and looked down at his son. "Oh god." He reached down to undo the straps, but Dr Dotz stopped him.

"Let's get him inside first," she cautioned.

Walter was about to disagree, but Rox put her hand on his arm. Shaira jumped into the van and squeezed between them. She circled, looking for a place where she could lay or maybe sit and watch, but in the end whined and then rested her head on Sam's legs.

The door slammed closed behind them, but Rox didn't hear it. Rain and tears mixed as her brain tried to discredit all the reasons that this wasn't Sam lying here. It made no sense. It was impossible.

Just as quickly as the rain started, it ended. Keenan was on the porch. Beside him was Henry, Kevin, and Kamal. Tusk was kneeling beside Danny, who had his hand on the doctor's neck and a gun at his head.

"Can you ..." Walter's voice caught as the door slid open behind him.

"I've had to induce a coma," Dr Dotz said.

Rox remembered that Dr Dotz wasn't a medical doctor. In fact, she was some kind of anthropologist psychiatrist or something like that, but did it matter? She brought Sam back to them.

A sob escaped as Rox scooted closer to Sam. She pushed every ounce of energy she had into him. The pulses stopped immediately when her hands touched the sides of his face, and the orange glow weakened the more she gave to him.

Keenan was there. He would revive her if she gave too much, but Sam looked so different. His face, it was pale and covered in an unkempt beard. His cheeks were sunken, like he had been ill and hadn't yet recovered. Dark circles painted the skin under his eyes. In fact, Sam looked … emaciated. When was the last time he had eaten?

"Son?"

Rox almost didn't recognize Walter's voice.

"Can you hear me, Son?"

There was just so much less of him. What must he have gone through to return looking like this.

"Let's get him inside," Dr Dotz said.

Dr Dotz was right, but Rox was afraid that any sudden movement could disrupt the energy she was feeding him. Or worse, wake her from this wonderful dream that threatened to be nothing more than a cruel nightmare.

But then she felt his pull. He was waking up.

"Son?" Walter leaned over him and moved the hair out of his face.

"Uh, guys," Kamal said as he stuck his head into the van.

Rox's vision was fuzzy. She was tired before and healing Sam was taking a lot out of her. She wasn't a doctor, so she didn't know what was wrong with him, but she knew he had been very ill. The sound of a bone popping back in place made her jump, but then her light-headedness made her giddy, and so she laughed.

"What?" Walter said, turning around to Kamal.

Kamal paused like he had forgotten what he was about to say, or he wasn't sure how to say it. He pointed to the other van behind them.

"What!" Walter said. "Speak!"

"Saber-toothed tiger. Well, technically, it's a saber-toothed cat."

"What?" Walter said.

"No, he's right," Dr Dotz said with a smile on her face. "That's the reason it took us so long to get here."

Rox started to laugh. A saber-toothed tiger! She was clearly losing too much energy to make sense of what was being said. She looked at Shaira, who had not moved and still laid on the lower half of Sam's body. Rox smiled at the wolf and laid her head down on Sam's chest. His heart was beating. It was a strong beat. A loud one, too. He would wake up. In fact, she thought she saw his eyes flicker, but she couldn't be sure because her eyes were starting to flicker themselves.

In between blinks, she studied the lines on his face. His lips were cracked, his eyes were sunken, and his beard was a fire red that covered him from the cheekbones down. It was long and it reminded her of a cartoon Viking. His hair was equally unkempt and curled at the tips. Its color reminded her of the orange tint that covered her eyes.

She brushed his hair off his forehead and then ran her fingers down the side of his face. She slid them down to his chest and felt the rise and fall of his breath through his shirt. It was threadbare, like he had not taken it off in years.

Her fingertips tingled as she felt the energy transferring. A smile settled on her face as her eyes closed. When she opened them next, he was staring down his chest at her.

"I've missed you so much," she said. Then she let the unconsciousness sweep her away knowing that the man she loved had made it home.

~

## Bad feelings

August 10th, 5:25am EST

The nightmare woke Leona first. She was at an outdoor market in Laos. Brightly colored fabrics hung from the top of each tent, and fruits and spices she had never seen before filled the first section of stalls. Ornate dresses, kids' clothing and toys, followed by luggage and handbags were on offer. Everyone was shouting and calling out their prices in both Lao and English, yet she heard nothing but the crunch of her shoes.

The farther into the market she went, the darker it became. Heavy woolen canopies reached from one stall over to the next one in front of it, blocking out the sun and trapping the smoke from the incense. Joss sticks burned on the floor in metal urns. There were more hanging above each stall, the smoke blocking their faces from view.

Leona waved her hand in front of her as she walked through the grey clouds. The air was heavy with fragrances she couldn't identify, and she coughed. She rubbed her thumbs over the tips of her fingers and it told her to keep moving; what she was searching for was at the next stall. The next one. The one after that.

Leona finally stopped at a table filled with different shades of purple, green, and white glass baubles. Some were set in large pendants meant to be worn around the neck while others were so tiny they kept rolling off the table and disappearing into the ash-filled urns on the ground. She leaned closer when she saw a pendant the shape and size of a dagger. It took her a few tries before she could grasp it, but then she lifted it up to the sliver of light sneaking through the heavy fabric of the canopies. A red, viscous liquid ran down its handle to drip on her hand.

She called for the merchant, and a woman appeared, her face hidden behind the haze of smoke. Leona squinted and told her something was wrong with the pendant.

"It's a dagger," the woman said.

"I know, but it's—"

The market erupted as merchants touting their wares became audible.

Leona lifted her hands to cover her ears, and the liquid ran down her elbow. She dropped the dagger back on the table, and the woman spun to face Leona. Her face was still indecipherable, but sunlight had finally penetrated the canopy at the stall's back, and it bathed the merchant's table in bright oranges and yellows that bounced off the glass objects the woman was selling.

Leona lifted her hand to shield her eyes against the rainbow of colors exploding in front of her when she noticed that the dagger was once again in her hand. But she didn't remember picking it up.

The woman backed away, like she was trying to get away as the market silenced like someone had pressed mute.

Everyone was staring at Leona and the dagger she couldn't put down. They were pointing, their faces a blur of smoke as their lips moved soundlessly.

A sliver of pain started in Leona's stomach and then spread up to encompass her entire chest. She looked down, and the knife she had been holding was sticking out of her abdomen. Blood as free as water ran down its handle once again to create perfect drops of blood on the toes of her shoes.

Leona sat up and grabbed her stomach. The dark, smoky market had been replaced by the dresser at the end of her bed. The ceiling fan was on and with each rotation, the two chains hanging down clicked together. She breathed a sigh of relief. Then one of her phones on the bedside table vibrated, and she screamed. She cast a worried look around her bedroom before she answered it.

The clock beside her bed read 5:25. "Hello?"

It was Dean. They had conducted the raid early despite her instructions to wait. It had not gone well. He was going to have to lie low for a bit because the cops were looking for him, and his contact at the sheriff's office said the Feds were involved as well.

Leona laid back against the headboard and pulled her knees up to her chest. She stared into the darkness of the closet's open door and tried to figure out if she was still in the nightmare.

Dean was going to get caught. He couldn't lead them back to her because she never used her real name or any contact details that could be traced to her true identity. It didn't matter though because she realized he was going to die before he was taken into custody.

"I just need you to help me get some papers," he said. "You know, maybe a new passport or something so I can get out of the country for a little while. I got a cousin up in Canada I can go pay a surprise visit to."

That wouldn't be necessary if they had followed her orders.

Her ability was one of precision. She needed to ask a precise question, unopened to misinterpretation, where the answer – or feeling she derived from the answer – was binary. There were no accompanying explanations.

Leona had rubbed her thumbs over her fingers about an attack on the location that Josh had arrived at for later *tonight*, not last night. She had no idea how last night was going to turn out. She only knew they were going to be successful if they attacked on the night she had asked about.

"You there?" Dean asked.

"Yeah, I'm still here," she said. There was nothing she could do to help him. Not that she wanted to. If he couldn't follow simple orders, then he deserved whatever he got. She had provided them with the funding to get the weapons and equipment they needed. She had given them the location, and even told them the best time to raid. "Why didn't you wait?"

"I don't know, man. Tommy said there was no need to wait. Tonight, tomorrow, it didn't matter." He sniffled. "You think they used their abilities on us."

She ran her thumb over her fingers and nodded without answering him. But what kind of abilities gave them an advantage over fourteen armed men? Nothing so banal as empathy or what Dream Weaver had. No, they had something better than that. Some kind of active ability she hadn't considered yet.

"So how you gonna get me those papers I need?"

"It won't matter," she said.

"What?"

"You'll be dead before you can use 'em."

Leona ended the call and switched on her bedside lamp. The phone rang again, but she ignored it as she flipped it over and removed the SIM card. She broke it in half and flopped back down on her pillows.

That had been her best chance at getting someone like Josh Mendez. She was convinced he had an active ability, and probably something like hers for him to be able to survive the other night at the restaurant.

However, all was not lost. Her aunt still had the woman who destroyed Alchemy. Leona would wait a couple of hours before calling. She needed the time to think.

There was a question she needed to ask, but for the life of her, she couldn't get the words right in her head.

Leona ran her thumb over the tips of her fingers. A bad feeling settled over her.

~

## Protection

August 10th, 5:45am EST

Mistake one: he should've arranged the bed before he brought her up.

Mistake two: he should've turned the bedside lamp off because he was sure the light was going to wake her.

Mistake three: he should've just accepted Marissa's offer to help him, but Sam was back, and she was just as excited to see him as everyone else.

Henry walked through the door sideways so as not to bang Meita's head on the frame as he carried her into the room. He used his foot to push the door close behind him and realized too late that it was going to slam. Luckily, Meita didn't move.

He carried her to the side of the bed and thought about lying her down while he arranged the pillows, but then remembered she said lying down made it more difficult to breathe.

Her head rolled to the side, and he looked down at her. She favored her left side, and when Kamal had lifted up her shirt to have a look, Henry looked away. Someone had deliberately struck her repeatedly in the same spot. The neat bruising around her wrists and ankles meant she had been tied down, unable to move or twist away from the blows. They would have been delivered systematically and without pause until either she talked, something broke, or her torturer grew tired.

He sat on the side of her bed with her cradled in his arms and wondered just how long she held out. Most people watched movies and thought the hero could hold out for days, but the truth was pain broke everyone. There were techniques to help withstand it for a little while, like a mental place you escaped to which helped block what was happening, but in the end, it was all fantasy, nothing more than an unrealistic fairy tale meant to give you hope in a hopeless situation.

Pain served a purpose, and that purpose was to help focus all of one's senses into stopping whatever was inflicting the agony. That focus was hardwired into one's survival. There was no training that could undo that.

Henry pulled her tight against his chest as he scooted further onto the bed and then swiveled until his legs were up and his back was against the headboard. Despite the cut on her lip and her swollen eye, it was hard to ignore her beauty. She was at least ten years his senior, though she didn't look it. Her skin was smooth and rich like honey, and her lashes were thick and long. He picked up a strand of her hair and pulled it up to its full length so he could see it better. Auburn highlights that matched her lashes.

He slipped his arm from under her legs and stacked the pillows so they were under the arm he was using to hold up her torso. There weren't enough pillows to keep her propped up *and* to prevent her from rolling over to lie flat, so he kicked his shoes off and got as comfortable as he could with her lying on his lap.

Meita whimpered, and Henry froze, debating whether to lower her back onto the pillows. But he liked holding her. It probably comforted her as well, knowing that someone was looking after her. He lowered his head and whispered in her ear that she was safe now. Her brow unfurled and her breathing eased as she settled back into his embrace.

Meita was sophisticated and worldly, and spoke more languages than he could name. She was the smartest woman he knew. How many ideas had Meita gotten approved by making Katherine think the ideas were hers? She was also seriously out of his league, but knowing that didn't diminish his feelings. As she laid there in clothes entirely too large for her, held together by a cut power cord, he couldn't help but see what had been staring at him all along. No way his grandparents would have gone for a woman like her, but Meita was a woman you fought for. She was worthy of new traditions.

He laid his head back and closed his eyes for a moment. It had been a long day. Sam was finally back and from the looks of it, he was going to be okay. He was quite a bit thinner than Henry remembered, and his eyes ... they had a glazed sort of expression that said he wasn't sure where he was or if he could trust what was right in front of him.

Henry guessed that made sense given Sam had been missing for two years. Was he alone for all that time? What kind of men lived during the age of saber-toothed tigers? Neanderthals? They would not have spoken English, not the one Sam spoke. Would they even have such robust communication systems?

He needed Katherine to return his call because with Sam back, he doubted Walter or Rox would be interested in what Tusk could offer them. Kevin had taken Tusk to one of the medical rooms and secured him to a chair. A camera was on him and the room had a motion detector in it, but Henry didn't like leaving Tusk in there for long without physical supervision.

Henry overheard some of the conversation that Rox and Samantha were having with him. Were all the people at WD-11 there against their will? Henry had been told they were mentally unstable, but the question was did they arrive that way? Was it even true or was it just a convenient lie to keep him and the other guards from asking questions?

He wasn't sure how long he drifted off for, but chirping

from outside the window woke him. When he looked down, Meita's dark brown eyes were staring up at him. He wasn't sure if she was awake or if she was caught in the middle of some dream, so he smiled. Her eyes drifted close, but her hand slid across his stomach and up his chest. She gathered his shirt in her fist, and then she sighed herself back to sleep.

He looked at her legs as they spread out across the bed. Her feet were bare and the trousers she wore were cut off above the knees. The collar on her shirt was too big to hide her cleavage at this angle. He wanted to ask how she had wound up dressed like this, but it didn't matter. He slowly slipped one of the pillows from under his arm where he still cradled her and pushed it behind his lower back. His muscles relaxed and his eyes felt heavy again.

"I've got you," he whispered as he drifted back off to sleep.

~

## Now

August 10th, 8:10am EST

Rox unwrapped the sandwich Josh had left on the counter for her and took a massive bite. She poured herself a glass of orange juice and drank it empty before pouring another. She took her sandwich and her drink over to the bay windows in the kitchen and sat down on one of the cushions in the sunshine. She ate in silence with her back against the cool window, staring out at the blue sky. She was tired, but the need for sustenance was stronger.

She could feel Sam's energy pulses, but she didn't know exactly where he was in the house. Could he still feel her? Was he interested in *feeling* her? Did he blame her for his disappearance? Would he ask her to leave Halo?

He was probably with Walter. Those two had a lot to catch up on. They were probably sitting in Sam's office with a bottle of whiskey. She smiled at the joy she knew Walter would be experiencing because his son was alive and back home. For the last two years, Walter had walked the impossible line between hope and acceptance. He deserved this moment of joy. He was a good man. A good father.

Rox looked at the sun above the treetops and wondered if Mika knew Sam was alive. She kept in touch with him whenever their schedule permitted, but where the West saw the rise of fear-based and anti-EO groups, the East saw opportunity. He was busy trying to locate and shut down medical facilities that were making hundreds of millions of dollars on false claims of being able to give ordinary humans abilities. He was always working, which meant their catch-ups were brief, but they shared a common grief that bound them together and was sealed by guilt. Both blamed themselves for Sam's disappearance.

But none of that mattered anymore. He was back. She would speak with Katherine about how best to move forward. Rox could move into an apartment in DC near Meita. The nation's capital had a unique charm. Besides, she had never lived on her own, well, not counting the years she spent homeless. She would hate saying goodbye to Shaira. The two of them had bonded, but now that Sam was back, she was sure the wolf would be fine.

Then there was Danny. She sighed, laid her head against the window and closed her eyes. She balled her fist and held it against her abdomen until Sam's pulse dissipated. Two nights ago, she was sure they were both expecting a very different outcome from their intimacy than the one presented to them now. She liked him. She didn't want to hurt him. But how could she move forward with him now that Sam was back? Even if Sam rejected her, did she really want Danny? Did she ever *really* want Danny?

Rox looked down at her watch. It was just after eight, but the house was still quiet. They had a long night, and everyone was sleeping in. A guard walked past the window and waved at her. She nodded in return, and the pulse that hit her was stronger than the ones prior. She looked over her shoulder.

Sam was standing in the doorway.

She froze, unsure of what to do or what to say. He looked so different. He had lost a lot of weight, and not in a good way. He had showered, and the clothes he was wearing hung a little too loosely on him. He kept the beard, but had thankfully trimmed it short, and his hair was pulled back in a ponytail. "I, uh … I was …" just heading upstairs? About to get another glass of orange juice? Thinking about you?

"Rox?"

It was the way he said her name that gave her the confidence to make eye contact. There were nights when she laid in his bed and dreamed about him saying her name as they made love. They had never gotten to see that horror movie. So much had happened. So much continued to happen. Maybe there was never going to be a perfect moment. Maybe now was all anyone ever had, and it was up to them to make the most of it. The universe was not bothered with individual desires. It had to keep the order. Maintain the balance. What significance was one person's desires if they weren't willing to fight for them?

She put her glass on the table and took a deep breath before looking up at him. "I didn't wait." She wanted to explain that she *had* "technically" waited, but just not long enough. If he had come just two nights earlier … but what did it matter? He was here now.

Sam slipped his hands into his pockets and nodded.

She opened her mouth to say more, but there was nothing more to say. She studied his face, hoping for a clue about what he was feeling, what he was thinking. But he just stared at her.

"I thought about you," he finally said.

She nodded like she understood, but mostly she just needed to move, to release some anxiety.

"Every day," he continued. "Some days I made love to you in my mind and others I hated you for not being there, and for the part you played in … everything."

The Rox of two years ago would've cried. The woman she was now coped. Adjusted. Survived.

"I mean, I know it's not your fault." He leaned back against the counter and looked up at the ceiling. "For a while there, I just needed someone to blame."

It made sense. After all, if she hadn't been struck by lightning, he wouldn't have been sent to wherever it was he went.

"But seeing you last night," he said, and her heart started to beat faster. She looked down at the bits of orange pulp sticking to the sides of her glass. "You gave me everything you had."

She wasn't sure where to look next.

"I love you," he said softly. "I *still* love you."

Joy mixed with guilt. Always the guilt. Two more days. How could she have given up on what they had? On him?

"I'm so sorry," she said.

He crossed the room and cupped the side of her face. "I don't want to waste any more time being sorry," he said as he leaned in and kissed her.

Their mouths aligned like it was a script they had rehearsed a thousand times. The energy pulses between them ceased, and a calmness took its place.

His tongue slipped in her mouth and her insides became liquid. This was the man she wanted to be with. It was his hands she wanted holding her hips and his thighs she wanted pressed against hers. She pushed up on her toes and gave him everything she had once more. She pushed her energy, her passion, and her love into their kiss.

She reached up and released his ponytail. His hair fell around his face and brushed against her cheek.

He broke their kiss and licked his lips. "I waited two years to do that."

"I love you." She said it with urgency. "I don't want another second to go by without you knowing just how much I love you."

His hands slipped around to her lower back as they hugged. "Two years ago, I would have carried you up to my bedroom." He laughed. "But I'm feeling a bit sore after traveling twelve thousand years on the tail of a lightning strike."

Rox chuckled and laid her head against his chest. She felt the steady beat of his heart and it was like coming home. "I've been working out while you've been gone. Maybe I can carry you up to *my* bedroom."

He threw his head back and laughed. "Alright," he said and grabbed onto her shoulder like he was about to hop into her arms.

She tickled his sides and almost stopped when she felt his ribs, but he jumped back with a silly smile on his face, the smile where the left side went up.

"Are you ticklish, Sam?"

He backed up into the counter. "No."

She was going to store that away for later.

"I saw that someone has been sleeping in my bed. And when I checked my drawers to get a fresh shirt, imagine my surprise when I pulled out a red sports bra."

She laughed as they left the kitchen and passed Walter sitting in a chair in the living room, his head tilted to the side, the paper across his lap, pretending to be asleep.

They went past the library down the hall to the stairs at the end. Most of the house was still in bed, and Rox yawned at the mere thought of lying down.

"Tired?"

She nodded.

"Dad told me about the attack."

Shaira was lying in front of the door to Sam's room like she always did. She lifted her head, but did not move, so they stepped over her and closed it behind them.

"He also told me that you became field lead."

Rox nodded, but her mind was on a shower. The rain had washed away most of the dirt and grime from her clothes, but it did nothing for her smell. "Danny's training me," she said, and then stopped. She looked over her shoulder at him and his hands were in his pockets again.

"Dad told me about him as well."

"I—"

"You don't need to explain," he said. "I was gone, and no one knew if I was coming back."

There was pain on his face, but not like she had expected.

"There were times," he said, "when I thought I was never going to get back here."

It took more will power than she thought not to hug him, but it wasn't pity he was looking for.

"I got struck by lightning," he said as he looked up at her.

"Hurts, doesn't it?"

"Like a motherfucker."

They both laughed until they fell silent.

"I'm not the same," he said softly.

"Neither am I."

"Sitting down there, talking to Dad, I'm not sure I heard everything he said because I kept asking myself if this was real, you know?"

She nodded, because she did know. Sometimes, experiences were so traumatic that reality was hard to accept for fear it was nothing more than a fantasy world created to escape the pain.

"When I found my family, it took me a while to accept they were real and I wasn't making up some hallucination while stuck in one of Tusk's boxes again."

"Rox?"

She waited.

"I wanna make love to you."

Her mouth fell open into a smile, and then a laugh. Her entire face felt hot, and all of a sudden she didn't know what to do with her hands. "I, uh, I'd like to make love to you, too."

He lifted his shirt and pulled it over his head. Three parallel lines of scar tissue ran from just above where his left nipple should have been and down past his belly button to disappear beneath the waistband of his trousers.

The smile on her face slipped, and she pushed out with her energy only to realize there was nothing for her to heal. He had healed himself.

"Bear," he said.

She blinked back tears and nodded. "Bear."

They just stared at one another and allowed the energy pulses to sweep through them. Then she grabbed the hem of her shirt and lifted it over her head. "I need to shower."

"Then let's shower."

She walked backwards into the bathroom without taking her eyes off him, and he followed. She felt both self-conscious and empowered as he watched her unbuckle her trousers and slip them down her legs. For a moment, she thought about apologizing because she was wearing a black sports bra and white cotton panties, but she kept quiet.

She stepped out of the trousers and took a deep breath. There was no sexy way to remove a sports bra, so she shimmied her way free until she was standing in front of him in just her underwear. His chest started to rise and fall in faster succession, and when he released the button on his jeans, she couldn't help but look. She didn't mean to, but there was the proof he wanted her just as much as she wanted him. When her eyes met his again, he was wearing that lopsided grin she loved.

She slipped her hands inside the waist of her panties and slid them down. He followed her movements and she could hear them both breathing.

"Sam?"

"Turn on the water."

His lips brushed her shoulder when she turned to start the shower, and her eyes slid closed. Goosepimples erupted everywhere he touched. She leaned back into him as he guided her into the cascade. It was warm as it slid down her chest and legs.

His fingertips tickled the skin at her belly, and her legs weakened.

"I've dreamed about a moment just like this for years," he whispered in her ear.

"Me, too."

He stepped back, taking the warmth from his body with him, and she looked over her shoulder. He was rubbing the bar of soap in his hands.

"Turn around," he said.

Sam slowly lowered himself to his knees and started with her feet. He covered them with soap as the warm water from the shower beat against his back. Then he moved up over her calf muscles, massaging as he worked his way up. She remembered the beach at Watership Down and how he knelt in front of her to secure her weapon around her thigh.

His hands kneaded her hamstring before rising. He didn't miss a spot as his fingers traveled up her body, around her waist up to her breast. She held her breath as his thumbs soaped her nipples. She grabbed his shoulders to keep from falling, and he stood up to capture her mouth. He swallowed her cries as he lifted her up and spun her around so that the water rinsed her clean. Then he slowly lowered her down.

Sam had lost a lot of weight, but he was still strong. She felt the control in his arms as he took his time, making sure he settled her in the right position.

The shower became too hot and there wasn't enough air to breathe, and she cried out when their bodies finally joined. Nothing in her life prepared her for this feeling of such *rightness.* She slowly allowed gravity to pull her the rest of the way as her eyelids fluttered open. Sam was staring at her with a look of concentrated joy.

"Nothing else matters," he said softly.

She nodded.

"Not yesterday, not two days ago, not two years ago." He reached out and turned off the shower and then pressed her back against the wall. "Now. That's what matters."

She captured his face in both her hands and brought his lips down to hers as she wrapped her legs around his hips, opening to him completely. He was right. For all their abilities, neither of them could change the past. Their choice was either to hold on to it or to let it go so they could make way for a future together. The kind of future they both wanted.

He carried her out of the bathroom and lowered her down onto the dresser. His mouth left a trail of small bites along her neck that caused her to contract around him. He slipped out of her and told her to turn around. She slowly turned around until the back of her thighs were pressed into the front of his. He lowered his head over her shoulder and captured her lips in a kiss that spoke of his need. Sam wrapped one hand around her waist, and when he dove back into her, she felt him all the way to her core. She broke off their kiss to inhale deeply and grabbed hold of his hand. Their fingers intertwined and she noticed the difference in their skin tones.

*Nothing else mattered.*

She pressed her palm onto the wood of the dresser as every part of her felt electrified, like the energy pulses that usually slipped between them were coalescing in the pit of her stomach.

The orange tint slipped over her, and when she lifted her gaze to the mirror, her eyes looked different. Instead of rounded pupils, there were horizontal slits that pulsated with lightning.

She lowered her head, not sure how much longer she was going to last, but then Sam's free hand tangled in the length of her hair and lifted it up until their eyes met again. That was her undoing. She hadn't meant to cry out, but she arched her back and lifted up from the dresser until her back was pressed into his chest. The lights flickered, and then went out as ripples of pleasure coursed through her, sending out tiny pulses of electrified waves around the room.

***

They laid on the bed with her head resting on his abdomen. She traced the scars running across his chest while he twirled one of her curls around his finger. They had just finished making love again, and neither of them had the energy to move. Her stomach growled, and she felt his chest rumble with laughter.

"We could spend the entire day in bed, you know," he said.

"I'd love to, but I need to check on Meita, see if Henry heard anything else from Katherine, and then see whether Tusk is in the mood to cooperate."

"You've become quite the busy woman."

"Yeah." She sighed. "I also need to check in with Michael. He's got the kids at a hotel near Ruby and Jay's university, so I just want to make sure no one's gone after them."

He untwirled his finger from her curl. "Your hair's beautiful."

She rested her arm across his lap so that she could prop up her head on her hand. "Yours isn't so bad either."

He laughed, obviously having forgotten that his was long now, too. "I'll get it cut at some point."

She reached up and pulled a few strands down over his left eye. "No, this suits you."

He shook his head. "Not sure I'm the long-haired kinda guy."

Her stomach rumbled again and he reached down to pull her up against his chest. They had slept until early evening. She wanted nothing more than to stay hidden in his room ... their room ... and pretend there were no other responsibilities that needed her attention.

His kiss almost made her rethink her list of priorities, but he broke it off. "C'mon, let's get you fed."

She stretched and grabbed fresh clothes from the dresser.

"Rox?"

"Hmm?" she asked, as she grabbed a new sports bra from one of the drawers.

"I love it that you've made my room yours while I was gone."

She stopped and turned to stare at him. "I didn't move much. Most of your clothes I left where they were."

"I know." He smiled. "I like seeing your lace panties in my underwear drawer."

"I always hoped you would find a way back." She wanted to keep it light; she didn't want to think about him being gone or the feelings she'd been forced to experience in his absence. Moving on was hard when one didn't want to.

He came over to her and wrapped her in his arms as he spun her around. "Now," he said, as he kissed her face over and over again. "Nothing else matters but now."

He was right.

# EPILOGUE

## One year later

Small Town, USA

Blood oranges were Meita's favorite fruit. She held up three of them so the merchant could calculate the price before she put them in her canvas bag. He thanked her for her business, and she made her way down the path to the next section of stalls selling herbs and spices.

Meita had recently started exploring farmer markets as a way to get into her new hobby of cooking. She was going through her mother's recipe book and learning how to make some of her culture's more traditional meals. Finding the ingredients wasn't as difficult as she thought it would be, but the time each dish consumed in preparation was the most challenging aspect for her. Sometimes, she would have to prep a day in advance to ensure the meat was sufficiently marinated before she cooked a dish. It seemed like a woeful waste of time, but time was a luxury that had finally arrived, and there was no reason to rush anymore.

She asked an old man for half a pound of dry sumac and passed him the small plastic bag in which he could put the dark powder. She grabbed a few bunches of dried oregano that were still on their stalks and a small, pre-wrapped bag of dried mint leaves she would have to crush when she got home.

Meita looked up at the bright blue sky and let the sun warm her skin.

"Beautiful day, isn't it?" the old man said, and Meita nodded.

She had grown accustomed to people commenting on the weather whenever she was dressed in a sweatshirt or something else far too warm for the summer months.

The mind, it played its tricks.

Meita looked down at her watch. She would have to leave soon if she was going to make it back to DC in time for her lunch date with Henry. Her feelings for him took her by surprise almost as much as his feelings for her. He was attractive in the sporty, jocky sort of way, but those types rarely looked at her for a variety of reasons, and so she had never allowed herself to contemplate what being in a relationship with someone like him would be like.

She slipped her oversized sunglasses off her head and lowered them over her eyes. She kept her wallet out as she made her way to the end of the pathway and walked over to the other section of stalls which did not sell food.

Meita had come to really enjoy her farmer market excursions. Farmer markets, she'd come to learn, sold much more than fruits and vegetables. There was hemp clothing, books, candles, honey, oils and all sorts of things that were artisan-made. There was even a man at one stall who sold kids' furniture he fashioned out of redwood.

There were a few evolved people here, the honey producer and the candle maker, and the carpenter and the old man selling spices. There was also a woman with long dark hair styled in a braid hanging over her shoulder. Every now and again, she would reach for its end and twirl its straight edges around her finger as she slowly made her way down the path in front of Meita.

It had taken Meita longer than she had preferred to find her, but that was mostly because it took Meita over six months to recover, and she was still not back in top form. In fact, Meita would never be as she was. Tusk's unethical, but effective research in the area of stem cells had led to a few experiments that worked to repair her injuries, though bright days like today always made her eye water. At first, she had refused to allow him to help her, but then Henry had reasoned if she didn't, it would mean that all his subjects had suffered for nothing.

In the end, she would never have twenty-twenty vision again, and she'd never be able to engage in excessive aerobics because of the scar tissue on her lungs. But she was alive, and that's what mattered.

It had been an odd transition, no longer working at GFO, but then GFO had morphed into ED, the Evolved Division, a special branch of Homeland Security.

Meita missed the difference she had been making and the adrenaline rush of knowing that lives depended on her ability to resolve, negotiate, and influence. The days she woke up with nothing to do and nowhere to go were the hardest. Walter advised her it usually took a year or more to settle into retirement, and that developing a hobby would help. Hence the cooking, which led to the farmers' markets.

The aroma was the first thing that drew her attention as she continued down the path. She couldn't work out if the next section of stalls belonged to one proprietor or if they had simply coordinated. Their stalls were pushed closer together, and they had erected poles to drape brightly colored fabrics from one to the next so that it extended over the pathway to create a tunnel of fragrances and multicolored sights.

The first stall sold all-natural perfumes, the next few offered organic essential oils, and the last one at the end had scented candles and incense sticks for the home.

Meita moved in beside the woman with the black hair and smiled at her, then turned her attention to the different items on display. The woman ran her thumb over the pads of her fingers, and for a moment, Meita wondered if she had been recognized. According to Tusk, Leona had seen a picture of her, but a lot had changed about Meita since then. For one, her hair was shorter and dyed a lighter shade of auburn; Meita was also dressed in jeans and a sweatshirt, an outfit she would never have been caught dead in before the shipping container.

"I wish I could get my home to smell like this," Meita said to Leona.

"Me, too. I recommend the room sprays at the stall just behind us for bathrooms. They have this one fragrance that's peppermint and lemongrass."

Meita reached for a box of incense at the back and feigned like she dropped her wallet from under her arm.

"Oh, you dropped his," Leona said as she bent to pick it up.

The tube no larger than a refillable, travel-sized perfume spray was already in Meita's hand. She pushed the top button when Leona tried to stand and stuck the retractable needle into her arm muscle.

"Ow!" Leona said. "What was that?"

Meita took her wallet and dropped the box of incense back on the table. "Say hello to your aunt for me."

Dr Mallory Fined was the first person Meita had tracked down and killed after her retirement. Meita expected someone with such wealth to have more security. Perhaps it was her public relationship with Senator Carter that gave Mallory a false sense of safety, but it didn't matter. Meita didn't need to be in top physical condition to execute a mission. She never did. Her skills lay in her ability to blend, to be everything anyone needed her to be, and then be none of them all at once.

The toxin she injected Leona with would cause cardiac arrest and would take sixteen hours to completely disappear from her system, but that was okay given the county's only coroner was out sick due to food poisoning.

Small towns had their benefits.

Meita pulled a phone from her back pocket and dialed the only number programmed in it as she squeezed between two stalls and made her way back to the produce area. Bottles breaking drew everyone's attention, followed by shouts to dial 9-1-1.

Meita walked down the pedestrian arcade and exited the farmer market. She circled the block where she had parked to make sure she wasn't followed and then kneeled down like she was tying her shoelace in front of the car she had "appropriated" almost an hour ago. She took the SIM card out and wedged the phone as far underneath the front tire as she could before climbing in.

A few minutes later, she pulled over to let an ambulance rushing in the opposite direction pass, and then she lowered her window just a little to toss out the SIM card.

Meita reached over and grabbed her phone from her bag when she came to a red light.

*Farmer market was a success,* she texted Walter.

*Told you all you needed was a hobby.*

Walter was right. Retirement wasn't so bad.

***

## London

*All I'm saying is that it's August, and it's cold.*

*It's not cold.*

*What's your definition of cold?*

*I mean, yes, it's not as warm as we're used to back home, but you know, seventeen degrees isn't exactly cold.*

*It is when it's pissing down with rain.*

*Keenan says that August is the hottest month.*

*Yeah? I don't see him around here anywhere.*

Rox laughed as she stepped out of the van into the back of the parking garage.

"He in your head again?" Danny asked.

She nodded.

"Oi, PB, stay focused," Danny said to Josh through his earpiece.

*I thought his entire raison d'exister was to train you. Didn't Katherine send him the memo that your training was over?* Josh asked Rox.

Rox rolled her eyes. Katherine's "memo" was not what any of them expected. After Katherine had returned from "yoga", things had changed in a way none of them were prepared for. But they adjusted. That's what made them survivors.

"Einstein?" Danny said.

"What?" Michael was not exactly excited about his change of career, especially since he had very little interest in working for the government to begin with, but he had eventually come around. Of course, he hired an attorney who had negotiated the terms of his contract, and by extension theirs, so he was "okay" with the new arrangement even if he didn't like it. He was, however, the highest paid government employee.

"We got visual?" Danny asked.

"Check your screen," Michael said. His strength was with systems, infrastructure, and AI, but he had also developed a knack for tinkering, as he liked to call it, and was always learning how to tweak their equipment to increase performance.

"Thanks," Danny said as he turned the screen so that Rox could see the cafe broadcasting from the drone's camera. "Our target is the one sitting here." He pointed at a young boy seventeen years of age and evolved. He was sitting outside at one of the tables with his back towards the cafe window. A canopy extended from the side of the building out over the tables to cover him and the other diners from the rain. "He made the call," Danny continued. "Saber and PB are in position there, but you'll make the approach. The locals are on standby in case things start heading south. If that happens, grab the target and make your way back here."

Rox nodded. She had read the brief on their drive over. They were in the UK to discuss the possibility of a joint taskforce with the UK's Department of Evolved Affairs when the call came in. A young man belonging to the Fellowship in the UK had contacted them because he wanted out. But the Fellowship was a lifetime membership club.

"Doc, you able to find out anything about his ability?" Rox asked Tusk.

It was Michael who had actually released his physical frustrations on Tusk. When they were introduced to one another, Michael threw a right hook that not even Josh had seen coming. Michael would never forgive Tusk for having their two children kidnapped, but he and Tusk eventually built a somewhat dysfunctional working relationship where they only interacted when necessary.

Rox didn't like working with Tusk either, but Katherine had been right. This wasn't about her or what he had done to any of them. This was about Ruby, Emma, Jay, and even MJ who still hadn't shown any signs of evolving. As much as she hated Tusk, working with him helped to create a future where her children were safer, where all evolved humans were safer.

"Doc?"

"I'm here," Tusk said. "I'm just looking over my notes and comparing them to what I'm seeing on my screen. Give me a sec."

Rox took her backpack with her batons in it and slung it over her shoulder. She was dressed in a pair of gray cargo pants and a white, long-sleeved T-shirt made for performance. She was wearing a black jacket to protect her from the chill and the rain.

They all heard Tusk sigh. "I can't even form a hypothesis. His body temperature is high, but that could be because he's nervous. It also could be because he's wearing a lot of layers underneath. His ability could have something to do with thermoregulation. But then again, your body temperature runs high, R— uh, Paladin, so, it could be anything."

"Noted," Rox said.

It took her seven minutes to walk from the garage where she had left Danny to the cafe where Sam and Josh were seated. She walked inside and stood in the queue to order a coffee. When they asked her if she was eating in or taking away, she pointed to the table with the teenaged boy and said she would be joining him.

Rox didn't look at either Sam or Josh when she stopped in front of the boy's table and cleared her throat. He looked up from the book he was reading.

"Can I sit here?"

He looked around. "Nah, I'm waiting for someone." Then he lifted his thumb to his mouth and nibbled on its cuticle as he went back to his book.

Rox pulled out the chair and sat down.

He looked like he was about to say something potentially offensive, but then stopped himself. "Wait. You who I think you are?"

Rox wasn't sure what she was expecting. She had come into contact with enough teenagers now to know that each of them was different despite their universal similarities. But this one had an attitude and an edge about him that said he had no peer group.

"My name is Paladin, and it's my job to make sure you get out of here safely."

He ran his eyes over her in obvious appraisal.

"Are you alright?" Rox asked, uncomfortable with his scrutiny.

He leaned forward and lowered his voice when he spoke. "I got some people following me."

Josh had already listened in on the teenager's thoughts and knew he suspected he was being followed. Josh told her that the boy had been living with an incredible amount of pressure and chose to escape in books. His entire family was Fellowship, and so there was no easy way out for him.

Rox could feel the fitful waves of energy emanating off him, making his calm exterior nothing more than a façade. "I want you to picture the people following you. No need to move your head or do anything but think about them and where they're located. Can you do that for me?"

He said okay and closed his eyes, and then reopened them. "What? You can see my thoughts and all?"

Rox laughed. "No. I can't see your thoughts."

He closed his eyes again and they both fell silent.

*Got 'em. I'll link up with them as well.*

"Shall we get out of here?" Rox asked.

"So, what's the deal?" he said, as he reached for his pot of tea and filled his cup like he wasn't in a rush. "You got an American accent. You taking me to America?"

"No. I'm taking you to a team of people who assist others like you."

He put two squares of sugar in his cup and stirred it around. "What if I wanna go with you instead?"

It took her a moment to realize he was flirting with her. "What's your name?"

"Callum," he said as he lifted his cup to his lips with a smile.

"Callum, I am a *lot* older than I look."

He sat back in his chair and crossed his legs. "'At's alright. You can teach me a thing or two."

Rox could hear Josh laughing in her head. "C'mon, Callum. Finish your tea and let's go."

"You like to be in control, eh?"

*You gonna tell him you're married?*

*No, I'm not telling this* kid *anything about me.*

*Sam can hear and he's unimpressed with the British youth of today.*

Rox smiled, but didn't look over at him. *And you just love that.*

*Oh, you're not my problem anymore.*

*Excuse me? When did I become a problem?*

*The moment I went into that room and rescued you. The biggest mistake of my life, I tell you. If I could do things all over again—*

*You wouldn't change a thing.* Her smile grew wider, and

Callum thought she was smiling at him.

"Yeah, let's get out of here." Callum winked.

Rox jumped to her feet when Josh gave her the warning that one of the men following Callum was making his move. "Stay with me." She grabbed his hand and pulled him after her.

"You ain't gotta tell me twice, love."

Some of the tables were arranged to create narrow walkways for customers, but she squeezed them between two tables that were pushed too closely together for them to pass without touching.

The guests scoffed at her, but Rox held tight onto Callum as they stepped out onto the side of the road.

"Oi, Callum?" One of the men shouted and raised his hand.

Callum stopped to turn, but Rox yanked him after her. "I said to stick with me." *You got 'em?* she asked Josh.

*Uh, yeah, about that. I think there's more here than Callum thought.*

*What? How many?*

*Six.*

"Lead, we've got followers," Rox said to Danny.

"On it. We're coming to you."

Rox glanced over her shoulder as two of the men started running after them.

"Run," she said, and thankfully Callum had the sense to follow her instruction.

They ran to the end of the block where she pulled him into traffic to cross the street.

"Where's the police?" Rox said into her earpiece.

Callum pulled his hand free from hers. "No. No fucking cops."

She spun around to see the two men chasing them cut across the road. "Trust me, Callum. We've got to go." She reached for his hand, but immediately let go. Rox felt the pull of his energy and looked down at his hand. It was turning red, and it sizzled when the rain touched it.

"Extraordinary," Tusk said into their earpieces. "Can we zoom in on his hand, Michael?"

Whatever Callum's ability, it involved a heat so intense it made the skin of his hand bubble.

"Okay, no cops," Rox said. "But can we go because I really don't want to have to do the paperwork if we have a confrontation."

"Hey, lad." One of the two men had caught up with them. "Where you headed?"

Rox positioned herself in front of Callum.

"Nowhere, bruv. Just going with my new girl back to hers."

The man looked her over much the same way Callum had. "Nah, man, come with us. We're heading back home. We've been looking for you."

*Josh?*

*Bit busy ...*

"Callum, let's go." Rox grabbed his wrist as she healed his hand.

Callum's jovial expression from earlier was gone. "Sorry, love. It's safer for you this way."

Rox groaned. "You're going to make me do paperwork, aren't you?"

Danny pulled up and parked the van so that it was

blocking the street. He got out and walked over to her and Callum, but spoke to the two men who had given chase. "The lady here hates paperwork, so why don't you do us a favor and just turn around and go back to wherever it was you came from. Callum's coming with us."

The two men stepped forward like they were ready for a fight. Rox pushed Callum out of the way and pulled on the energy of the first one. His legs buckled and he fell sideways, crashing into a car parked on the side of the road. The other one stopped advancing and looked at them like he wasn't sure whether to attack or see to his partner.

"You do that?" Callum asked Danny.

Danny crossed his arms over his chest and shook his head. "I'm just here to keep her in line."

"Callum," said the other one, his voice a lot less confident. "You coming? Dad's well mad at you."

Sam appeared next to her and everyone jumped back.

"You alright?" Sam asked, his attention on the one who was still standing.

"I'll have to do paperwork now," she said.

"Bruv, you just came outta nowhere!" Callum said, his eyes large and his free hand covering his open mouth. "Holy … man, you guys are part of that evolved team outta America. That's why you sent Legs here to entice me, innit? What, you guys want me to join your team or something?"

Sam turned to the teen. "That's my wife you're calling Legs."

Callum shook his head in disbelief. "You lucky bastard."

Danny started to laugh and Rox couldn't help but join in. "C'mon, Callum. My *husband* will see to these two," she nodded at the two men, one still down on the hood of the car. "Josh got the others under control?" she asked Sam.

He raised an eyebrow like it wasn't a question worth answering.

"Danny, shall we take Callum here to the safe house?" Rox asked.

"Wait, hey," Callum said to Sam. "You be careful with that one. He's always got something up his sleeve."

Rox gave a long sigh. "Since I'm doing paperwork anyway." She held up her free hand and released some of her excess energy. A thin line of electricity slipped across the space between her and the second man. She didn't send all of it to him, but just enough to knock him onto his back.

Callum's eyes widened even more. "Yes! I wanna learn to do that. Can you show me how you did that?"

Sam leaned forward and kissed her on the lips. "Thank you."

"Any time," Rox said.

"You keep her safe until I get back," Sam said to Callum.

"Bruv, I don't think you need to worry about her safety. It's everybody else's you need to worry about."

"Let's go," Danny chuckled as he led them to the van.

"You gonna teach me how to do that?" Callum asked as she buckled her seatbelt beside him.

"No. But I'll make a deal with you. You show me yours, and I'll show you mine."

Callum winked at her. "You dirty girl."

~

## Sixty-five years later

Tanjong Rhu, Singapore

As much as Singapore had grown and changed, raising land from the depths of the ocean and becoming the East's first safe haven for those with evolved abilities, life on the little red dot largely remained the same. It had always been home to Ruby and MJ. MJ returned for university and stayed, while Ruby came later.

Rox was starting her thirty-five-year sabbatical from the Evolved Division. By the time she returned, a new administration would be in office and she would largely have been forgotten. There were only a few key government designations who knew she existed: every new Secretary of Homeland Security received a briefing and took an oath of secrecy, as did every Singapore Prime Minister. The two nations formed an evolved alliance, thanks to Mika and Katherine. East and West united to ensure that Article 31 was upheld and enforced.

Rox sat on the bench next to Ruby, looking at the Flower Domes across Marina Bay. Their rooftops were closed during the day and only opened at night when the scorching heat of the sun was gone. That's when the glass and steel dome would retract much like the National Stadium to fill the night sky with images of nature made out of light.

"Do you know where you're going?" asked Ruby.

Rox looked out over the water as the morning sun continued its ascent to midday. No. She didn't know where she was going. She didn't think there was anywhere to go that would make it easier.

"He wants to keep it a surprise," Rox said.

Ruby nodded like that made sense. Rox wasn't sure if anything made sense anymore. Maybe that was one of life's great lessons. Nothing ever made sense, and so you just had to roll with it.

Ruby reached into the small bag she carried with her and rummaged through until she pulled out a green roll of mints. Her hands shook slightly as she put one on the tip of her tongue and pulled it back into the safety of her mouth. Then she offered one to Rox.

Rox didn't like mints, but she took one and sucked on it anyway.

"They help me with my cough," Ruby explained.

For all of Rox's abilities, for all the lives she had saved and the control over death she exerted, not everything was in her power to control.

"Do you have more?" Rox asked.

Ruby nodded and pointed over her shoulder without turning her head to the medium-sized Filipina dressed in uniform. Theresa was sitting on another bench about fifty meters away reading something on her mobile glasses. She was the live-in nurse who cared for Ruby after her stroke.

"You're going to be alright," Ruby said and reached over to put her hand on top of Rox's.

Hope was a complex emotion. It kept people moving forward when evidence pointed to the contrary. It comforted in times of uncertainty, but it had its share of problems, too – when it was all you had, it became nigh on impossible to let it go.

Rox pushed a little bit of her energy towards Ruby, but it washed over and around her like it always did.

The back of Ruby's hand was drawn with lines and veins that had raised to the surface as her skin continued to lose its battle with gravity. This was what aging looked like. Rox had witnessed it with Sam, and her breath caught at the thought of having to bear yet another heartache. She looked out at the Bay and the calm ripples that slipped across its surface.

Ruby was right. As much as Rox hated to admit it, she was going to be okay. The guilt was simply part of the process.

Rox cleared her throat. "You heard from your brother?"

Ruby bit down on the mint, cracking it into smaller pieces before she answered. "He and I are going to the Esplanade tomorrow."

"The floating one?"

Ruby nodded. Then she looked over at Rox and winked. "I ain't dead yet."

Rox squeezed her hand as tight as she dared.

"You know, MJ and I tell Theresa you're my daughter." Ruby laughed.

Rox thought about smiling, but couldn't bring herself to do it. "Makes sense."

They settled back into their comfortable silence, a habit they never broke since Rox returned to Ruby's life some sixty-eight years ago.

It was quiet this time of the morning with just a few joggers and dog walkers out. A raft of otters climbed out of the Bay and ran across the path to disappear into the hedge near Theresa. The live-in nurse squealed with delight and recorded them with her glasses.

"I can stay if you want," Rox said, although she knew the answer. It was something they had fought over, a position that Ruby was not compromising on.

"I know," she said softly.

Ruby lifted Rox's hand and kissed its back. Rox was so surprised by the gesture she didn't know what to say.

"Listen, I'm going to tell you something my mom used to always tell me," Ruby said. "She would say, 'My love lives in your heart.' It used to fill me with such joy and sadness at the same time. But, truth be told, I don't think I ever knew what it meant until Emma died."

*Emma.* Roz cleared her throat. "You never told me that before."

"You never needed to hear it before now," said Ruby. "You know, your own demise puts you on a fast-track to maturity. You get real introspective real quick." Ruby chuckled. "Knowing that you don't have forever only becomes real when you can make an educated guess about how many more years you actually have left."

"You can always come with me," Rox said, even though she knew the answer to that as well. Ruby was happy right where she was. She had found peace with her limited time left, and she wanted to live her days out on her terms.

Ruby took a deep breath and let it out as if she were in the middle of meditating. "I could never bring myself to call you mom because I guess I felt like I needed to keep the love my mother left in my heart alive. Calling you mom would've erased that somehow."

Rox scooted closer and wrapped her arm around Ruby's shoulders.

"I wished I realized earlier just how lucky I was to not only have one mother, but to have two," Ruby said.

Rox leaned closer to give Ruby a kiss on her cheek. "I'm the lucky one."

It was the oddest thing having Ruby cup her face and stare straight into her eyes with tears of sadness and joy. "You are special, Rox. And you have a heart filled with love and goodness. Let that be your compass."

Their relationship had improved over the years, but neither of them were ones for intimacy, so Rox wasn't sure how to respond.

"Now, I need to get back before this sun gets any hotter. I'm melting out here as it is," Ruby said.

"I'll come with you," Rox said. "I can help Theresa."

Ruby cut her eyes at her mother. "I am fine. Theresa takes wonderful care of me. MJ checks on me every day and so I don't need another person fussing over me. Besides," she said, looking out at the Bay. "Your ride's here."

Rox looked at the approaching boat. There were a series of small piers along each side of the bank for taxis to drop off and pick up passengers as well as for other boats to dock for short periods of time. Keenan cut the engine and eased the boat to a pier. He nodded his hello, but didn't get out or signal for her to come. He knew what their moment was about.

"You go on," Ruby said.

Rox didn't want to leave her daughter. Ruby and MJ

were the last living relatives she had. But according to the contract she signed, while she was on sabbatical, she was not allowed to live in the USA or Singapore. Instead, to ensure the secrecy of her identity as well as her ability, she would have to set up residency elsewhere. Both governments required her to check in with them because they didn't want to lose track of her, but today was the last day on her visa to stay in either of the two countries.

"Last chance to escape the heat and humidity of this place," Rox said. "The Amalfi coast is nice this time of year."

Ruby waved her away. "I don't like boats. They bring back bad memories."

Rox embraced Ruby for the last time. "Tell MJ I love him. That I will always love him." She had said her goodbyes to her son yesterday, but still, there was no such thing as too many I love you's.

"He knows."

Rox wasn't sure what it meant that she wasn't crying. She stood up and waved Theresa over, and the nurse came, but kept a respectful distance.

"You know how to get in touch with me, right?" Rox asked.

Ruby chuckled. "Yes, but I won't need to call you. I think if anyone wants to come at me now, I ain't getting away."

Rox laughed, too; this time genuinely. "I love you, Ruby."

"And I love you."

Rox turned and started down the embankment towards the pier.

Keenan lifted his sunglasses to his head and helped her aboard. He didn't say anything, but he did wave to Ruby as he eased the boat out into the Bay.

Rox turned back and looked at her eldest daughter, but Theresa was already helping her into the wheelchair.

Rox went to sit beside Keenan at the helm. He slipped his arm around her, and she laid her head on his shoulder. He placed a kiss on the top of her head and the tears she had held back came slipping down her cheeks.

They cruised like that for a while. The sun was high now, but the breeze off the Strait helped keep them cool.

"That was the hard part," he said.

"I know." She tucked her feet into the seat and gave her legs a hug. A wolf pup climbed up the steps leading from the boat's cabin below. It jumped up on Rox's lap, and Rox buried her face into its fur and inhaled her scent.

Neo slowly walked up the steps a few minutes later, pausing so that he could stretch out his back. He looked around for the wolf pup and then sniffed at the sea air. Satisfied that the pup was safe in Rox's care, Neo sat down on the bow and lifted his nose to the air before resting his head on his front paws. He looked out at the waves with a sense of calmness that always struck Rox as odd for an animal its size. But then again, hadn't he been teleported forward in time on the tail of a lightning strike? Was it the same lightning strike that allowed him to stay alive so many years later?

Rox doubted she'd ever know why Neo could cheat death but not Sam.

"Have you thought of a name for her yet?" Keenan asked.

Rox lifted the pup and turned her around so she could get a good look at the little ball of fur. "I guess I could name her after her grandmother, Shaira."

Keenan nodded. "You could."

"But you don't think I should?"

He took his time before responding. "Will Shaira not always remind you of Sam?"

Keenan had been through everything she was going through, and she wondered who had helped him with his first transition. "What name would you choose?"

"A name is too personal a thing to take a recommendation from another," he said. "Take your time. It will come to you."

The sky over the ocean at night was breathtaking. More stars than she could count created a tapestry of stories that Keenan shared with her. He told her that Westerners were not the only ones to name the constellations.

"When I look upon them, sometimes I am melancholy for a time that shall never return," he said. "But mostly, I am filled with wonder about all the possibilities that exist on the other side of them."

Neo sighed and scratched the back of his ear, making the tuff of hair at the tip dance in the wind.

"When you look up at the stars, Rox, what is it you see?"

Rox stared up at the tiny white lights until they were visible even when she closed her eyes. She reached out and ran her hand over Neo where he lay tucked beside her and the wolf pup.

"Asha," Rox said. "I will name her Asha."

Keenan nodded his approval. "Hope. I like it."

* * *

The End

## Author's Note

Well, there we have it, Rox heads off into an unknown future. Life can be bittersweet, can't it? I want to thank you for taking this journey with me.

I have lived on three separate continents while writing this series. Rox has been through my highs as well as my lows. Sometimes, on the days when life seemed so large I thought I'd never be able to contain it, she was my anchor. Rox was my savior.

**Other books in The Evolved Ones trilogy**

***The Evolved Ones: Awakening* (Book 1)**
*Shortlisted for the Singapore Book Awards 2020 for Best Literary Work*

In a world where humans are evolving, people are more curious than afraid. They look for answers from a handful of scientists who try to uncover why some develop abilities while the vast majority do not. For most humans, it's an exciting time, but for Evolved Ones – EOs – it's a game of hide and seek that ends with far too many of their kind disappearing, permanently.

Four years ago, Rox awoke without a single memory and the involuntary ability to heal. Speech and most of her higher level cognitive functions were working, but everything about herself felt unfamiliar. Plagued by insecurity and confusion, she leaves the only home she can remember in search of her true identity.

**Reviews:**

*Awakening is a wonderfully wild, action-packed story for those who like X-Men and/or military-type thrillers.*

*I find it has a great storyline and the EOs' abilities are fascinating and complex which kept me interested. Engaging with action from one event to the next. The ending left you wanting to follow Rox to the next book.*

*This exciting thrill ride of a novel kept me riveted to the end. The lead character is a charismatic and strong female who defends herself in the beautifully detailed world created by the author.*

*This book is a must read! A true page turner! The author left nothing on the table! I'd rate 5 stars for sure!!*

***The Evolved Ones: Sacrifice*** **(Book 2)**

Home. In tropical Southeast Asia, Rox has finally reunited with her family. No more dumpster diving, shelter hand-me-downs, and rules about living on the run. This is her chance to start over and to finally figure out who she's meant to be.

But even the orderly streets of Singapore can't keep Rox safe. The scientist who experimented on her ten months ago discovers her new location and threatens to tear apart all she has fought and died for. With her loved ones under attack, the fragile relationships she has worked so hard on repairing fracture. She's tempted to disappear, but she's tired of running. Rox is finally ready to fight back, and she is willing to sacrifice everything to do so.

**Reviews:**

*Exciting and fast-paced fantasy! I've found myself racing through this second book, on a roller coaster of emotions. Wondering what decisions or choices I would make, if I were in the character's shoes … It's a good balance of real life and fantasy. I'm super impatient and excited for the last book in the series!*

*Amazing book with well-written characters. It makes me happy to be able to read about super heroes who are not teens! The problems the main character is going through are easy to relate to and because of that the book is very interesting … impossible to put it down. Can't wait for Book 3!*

*Beautifully written, full of suspense … and full of adventure. Can't wait for the third instalment!*

# Acknowledgements

I want to thank my husband and two daughters who are so proud I'm a writer. They tell everyone about my books, and that gives me the courage to spread the word, too.

My village is scattered across the globe now, but I am so grateful for the technology that defies distance. Thank you for your love and support, but most of all, thank you for your belief. You know who you are.

I want to thank my kind and gentle editor, Anita Teo – may our paths continue to merge.

This wouldn't be complete if I didn't thank you, my dear reader, for taking this journey with me. Although Rox's story comes to an end, I've still got more stories to tell. I am busy working on my next series, so let's stay in touch.

Follow my blog, NatashaOliver.com to get the latest updates about my general musings on life. Sign up to my newsletter (http://eepurl.com/hvorNP) to get the latest about book launches as well as what I'm working on next. (Hint: epic fantasy.)

If you liked *Acceptance*, leave a 5-star review from wherever you purchased this book. Bookstore purchases can be reviewed on GoodReads.com. Your positive reviews make it possible to reach more readers.

Until our next adventure.

## About the Author

Natasha Oliver writes urban fantasy with strong and diverse characters who reflect the contemporary female journey. She has an MFA in Creative Writing and teaches at Full Sail University. Natasha has lived and worked in New York, Washington DC, Tokyo, Singapore, and England.

natashaoliver.com | Insta *natasha_oliver_author*
FB *natashaoliverauthor* | natashaoliverauthor@gmail.com